THE WINDOW

SANTITA D'ANJOU

Disclaimer:
This is a work of fiction. All characters, locations, and businesses are purely products of the author's imagination and are entirely fictitious. Any resemblance to actual people, living or dead, or to businesses, places, or events is completely coincidental.

For my Aunt Christine. It brings me peace and joy knowing you are in Heaven cheering us on. We miss you.

ONE

As I leap back into consciousness, the room spins. Sweat trickles down my brow. My heart beats on the outside of my chest. When I gain full capacity of my sight and awareness, there is a lingering fear that it wasn't just a dream. The lucid dream has made it all seem so real. A few moments pass, my heart stops racing and my breathing becomes normal again. Right across my room, on my cherry-oak amour, lie my red leather bound journal. I stare at it for a while, contemplating if I should leave the safety and comfort of my bed. There is still a fear of danger, even though I am awake and what I just saw isn't real. I muster up the courage to retrieve my journal and run quickly over to get it. I dive back into bed and catch a glimpse of the time, it is 3:15am and nearly time to wake up for school. I decide to go ahead and make my entry now, while the dream is still fresh in my memory. I was once told writing your dreams down as soon as you wake up will ensure you don't miss any important pieces. This journal is filled with every dream I've had since I was ten years old. I remember the day my aunt Destine bought it for me, it was seven years ago.

My aunt Destine was my favorite person. My best friend. She was four-feet ten inches, but wisdom as tall as the eye could see. She had wide hips, so she rarely ever wore pants. She said they made her look fat, or "as big as a house," she would sometimes say. One thing everyone knew about my aunt Destine is she loved food, family, and the Lord. As a child, I remember going over to aunt Destine's house every Saturday to pick her up. She loved my mom's cooking, so she made it a point to visit every weekend just to get a taste of her famous tuna casserole and homemade sweet tea. She enjoyed spending time with us, and we loved having her company. She was my mom's older sister. After their mother passed away she had to assume the role of raising her siblings. There were only three of them: Aunt Destine, who was eighteen at the time, my uncle Ale, and my mom, who was only five when their mom passed. My mom never knew her dad, which was a huge part of why Uncle Ale turned out the way he did. Uncle Ale was the middle child and as the stereotype goes, a little unusual. He was very "troubled" Aunt Destine used to say. He stayed in trouble. Uncle Ale never got over his mom passing and eventually became an alcoholic. I don't think I can remember him ever being sober. The night he died was horrible for all of us. I remember one cold November night Aunt Destine, my mom, and I going into town to look for him. Aunt Destine had gotten a call from a close family friend, telling us that he was standing on the corner, harassing passersby for money, so we went out looking for him. We spotted him sitting on the corner of H.L. Greens, which was our neighborhood shopping center. On the sidewalk, he swayed back and forth mouthing obscenities to everyone passing.

"There's that fool," Momma said.

Aunt Destine didn't say a word. Her silence always revealed how disappointed she was in him. She couldn't bring herself to say one negative word about him, but I knew she despised how he had turned out just as much as Momma did. As we sat at the red traffic light waiting to rescue Uncle Ale, I watched him intently. I watched as his head swirled in a circle, as if he had just been spun around. Then, all of the sudden, he collapsed, hitting his head on the curb in the process. When the light finally turned green, Aunt Destined sped to the sidewalk. In panic she yelled, "Ale!"

My mom was hysterical. All she could do was walk back and forth praying to God he would at least open his eyes. Aunt Destine demanded, "Call 911!"

I sat on the cold hard concrete watching Uncle Ale twitch with what little life he had left in him, until finally the ambulance came. He was in a coma for three days and on the fourth day, since he wasn't making any improvement, they decided to take him off life support. After Uncle Ale's death, Aunt Destine and mom were inseparable, they were all each other had left. They both proved to be strong women because they didn't let Uncle Ale's tragic death tear them down.

I would often sit with Aunt Destine just to listen to her talk. She had a peculiar voice, which some might think strange, but her voice was far from strange. Her voice was precious. There was something about when she spoke; when she opened her mouth to speak, everyone listened. She had a meek and low tone that flowed with nothing but love. It was easy to be around her and listen to her. She always had some words of wisdom to light your path or encouragement to get you through the toughest of times.

The day she purchased my journal was a day like no other. On this day I would share something with Aunt Destine that would change my life. I had woken up from a familiar dream. A dream that never seems to end. A dream that always seems to torment me no matter how many times I have dreamt it.

There's a girl trapped in an old rickety house, but she makes no attempt to leave. It's as if she knows her efforts would be a waste of time. The girl seems to be me, but I can never get a glimpse of her face. It's as if I'm hovering over her, watching her, which is the case most of the time. She's in a house with nothing but windows encompassing it. The worst thing about these windows is there are no curtains. This frightens the girl all the more because there's nowhere to hide. The view from the house is a large expanse of trees and bushes. The sounds of nature coming from every direction brings on another level of fear for the girl. Sporadic lightning flashes across the ominous gray sky. As the girl studies the landscape, she is startled by an old man circling the house. He wears a long black trench coat and a black bowler hat. His long silvery hair hangs to his shoulders, so thin you can see right through it. The old man walks slowly around the house, never making eye contact with the girl. She watches his every move, for hours it seems, but he never says a word or looks in her direction. Eventually, he climbs the steps to the house, slowly. The girl begins to scream and as soon as she does I shake myself awake.

"Naomi! My mom yelled. "Breakfast is ready."

I glanced at the clock and it was 8am. It was Saturday, so I knew we were headed over to pick up Aunt Destine for the weekend. She would spend the whole weekend with us, which was fine by me, and since my dad had just walked out on us, it was fine with my mom too. She needed her company.

Aunt Destine didn't have any children so she spent most of her time with us, shopping at H.L. Greens, listening to music, going to church, and my favorite—drinking coffee. Boy could my mom and Aunt Destine drink some coffee, whether it was winter or summer. Aunt Destine loved sharing her coffee with me. Her coffee was always the best. My momma liked hers black and bitter, but Aunt Destine made hers with three creams and several packets of sugar (too many to count). These ingredients made Aunt Destine's coffee rich and creamy. At first, she would scold my mom for giving me coffee. She would say, "Johanna! You shouldn't give that girl that stuff. It can stunt her growth!" Eventually, I talked her into letting me try hers and eventually we became secret coffee buddies. "Just a little, Nai, with some ice won't hurt you," she always said just before giving me a tiny bit to taste.

Our weekends were filled with laughter and good conversations. Mostly, I told her about my dreams. I dreamt almost every night and they were always so vivid and what frightened me the most, the significant dreams would come true. When I told her my dad was going to leave, she asked how I knew. When I told her I dreamt it and then it actually happened, she never thought twice about believing my dreams. Aunt Destine told me I reminded her of Joseph. She said he was a boy in the Bible who dreamt a lot—like me. She would say… *dreams are windows to our spirit, and if you look out that window long enough—there is always an answer, a warning, or a piece to life's puzzle.*

That day, I decided to share my ever present dream with Aunt Destine. Of course I shared every dream with her, but this one I had never told her before. I was too afraid to tell her, or maybe too ashamed. I was ashamed of how simple and non-threatening it was when I was awake versus when I was asleep. I mean it was just an old man coming into the house, I would think to myself. What is there to be afraid of? I needed to tell her, I needed guidance, and an understanding of why this dream just wouldn't go stop coming.

The courage to tell her had finally come. I waited until my mom had started dinner that Saturday evening and decided to tell her outside on our back porch. It was our favorite place to sit when the sun was setting. There under the patio hung a rickety, bright green, iron swing my mom inherited from her mom. It was so old the paint had begun to crack and peel, revealing bright-orange rain rusted iron. Even though it creaked as you swung, it was a sound Aunt Destine and I had developed an immunity. We would sit to have our chats and sometimes swing until we were both rocked to sleep. The humidity in Georgia whether spring, summer, or fall was always frightful, twenty minutes outside and your clothes were sticking to you. A cool breeze was very rare in the early fall, but on this particular day, the breeze was cool and the open sky gave off a beautiful coral and gold hue. We could sit on the porch bare foot, drinking ice cold sweet tea for hours until my mom called us for dinner. I looked over at her and finally said what I knew she was waiting for, "Auntie, I had a dream."

Once I finished telling Aunt Destine the dream, she just stared at the sky, which is something she always did when I shared a dream with her. She would sit and think before saying anything. Once I asked her why she always did that, she simply said, "It's better to be quick to hear and slow to speak."

I learned to wait patiently until she spoke. It seemed an hour had gone by and still there was no response; I didn't know what to think. Was she just as confused as I was? Finally she rose to her feet. She looked down at me.

"You want to take a little drive?"

"Sure," I said, standing to my feet.

Then, looking up at the sky with her big hazel eyes, she said, "Well, go and get your jacket. The temperature is gonna drop soon. We need to make a stop at H.L. Greens."

I waited in the car while she went in the store. When she returned, I wasn't sure what to expect. She pulled out a brown box, about the size of a greeting card, but it was too deep to be a card.

"What is it?" I asked.

"It's something to help you begin figuring out these dreams on your own. I won't be around forever, ya know."

Then she pulled off the lid and there it was: a shiny ruby-red, leather bound book. At least that's what I thought. She told me it was a journal. She said to use it to write every detail down as soon as I wake from a dream. "This will help you interpret the meaning," she said.

Grateful to have guidance on how to figure out my ever present dream, I hugged the journal close to my heart.

She was right, from that day forward, interpreting the dreams were a piece of cake, but it did take time. Writing the dreams down wasn't all I needed for interpreting them, but it was a very important step. Aunt Destine would sometimes take days to get back to me about a dream. She taught me that quiet time alone, and meditation about the dream was just as important as writing it down. Even though I admired Aunt Destine and usually did exactly as she instructed, I never had written down the dream about the old man, the girl and the house with nothing but windows. I was too afraid to even write the words down on paper—afraid it might make the vision more real.

Thinking back on how I had come to possess this journal of dreams sends several emotions through me; my late Aunt Destine, Uncle Ale, and the absence of my father. It's now 4:32am and only twenty-eight minutes before my alarm goes off for school. I decide to take the time to finally make the entry that is seven years overdue.

TWO

Once I finish my entry, I trudge across the hall to my bathroom. I examine my face shuddering at what I see—rubbing my fingers over a few discolorations left from break-outs. I look just like my dad, unfortunately. My hair thicker and my complexion darker, but by and large, I'm just a girl version of him. Born and raised in the Dominican Republic, my dad was practically famous in our small town. When I was younger I considered this a good thing. Now that I'm older, I realize it wasn't. His dark and chiseled features made him irresistible to all. Although I was his world, so he said, other women and alcohol became his safe haven after getting fired from his job. Never ending nights and living it up with his buddies wasn't enough for my mom to leave. She loved him, so she remained faithful, until one phone call. A phone call that would change her life—forever.

Johanna Peterson Funtez. My beautiful mother. Her mom was white and her dad black. Her dad was as 'dark as the nights' sky,' she would say with so much adoration. "His genes out did my mother's and gave me this beautiful melanated skin."

So here I am. A mix of three cultures and races. My hair is a solid metaphor of me. Some days I can be *straight* forward and clear headed, some I am all tangled up and don't know who I am, and others I can be wavy and cool. I am three different girls stuck in one body, desperately trying to be tethered to one identity.

I towel dry my face and move on to my untamed coils of hair. I decide on putting it in my usual style—a high ponytail with a few stray coils hanging down in the front and in the back. When I walk out of the bathroom to get dressed, I hear my mom stirring in her bedroom, so I tiptoe around my room stumbling here and there, trying very hard not to wake her. I make it out the door with my plan in tact.

In fifth period, the exhaustion from the night before creeps up on me like an armed robber. My head sags back then snaps forward, when Mrs. Rayburn shouts my name from across the Chemistry lab.

"Naomi!"

Chemistry is one of those subjects I could have definitely done without, but in order to graduate I need to take Mrs. Rayburn seriously. This alone is daunting, seeing as though she dresses like a circus performer. She's a walking rainbow with no idea of how ridiculous she looks. In some strange, very unorthodox way, Mrs. Rayburn seems to enjoy the laughs coming up the hallway when she passes. She holds her head high and glancing in the direction of the whispers and laughs, then within seconds the laughter is silenced.

Recently she dyed her hair a rusty orange color, so as she walks toward me it takes little to no effort to snap out of my sleepy daze and give her my undivided attention.

"Miss. Peterson," she says in her thick Jamaican accent, "would you like to address the class on how ionic bonds are different from covalent bonds?"

"Uh…no ma'am. I am sorry Mrs. Rayburn," I apologize right away, in hopes she will stop with the questions, "I'm awake now and it won't happen again."

I learned a long time ago, it's always better to be polite and not talk back. Most times teachers will lay off if you admit you're wrong and apologize which always works in my favor.

"Sure, Miss. Peterson, I expect your full attention for the remainder of this period. Is that understood?"

I straighten up on my stool, realizing that while I was watching my eyelids, I missed several notes. I hustle to jot as many as I can before she changes the slide.

"Yes Ma'am, I understand."

And off she trots with no more strange inquiries about ink bombs and cover bombs.

When chemistry is over, my day starts to get a little better seeing Daniel, waiting by my locker. He usually takes my attention off my failing Chemistry grade, not in a good way. We met when I was fifteen at a youth ski trip. My best friend Emmy invited me. At first, I didn't like him and thought he was kind of weird, considering how he stared at me the entire trip with a geekish grin on his face. He showered me with stuffed animals, chocolates and love letters every week before I gave him the time of day. Even after all of the gifts, I still didn't like him. He just wasn't my type. I had an image of what my first boyfriend would look and be like and he wasn't it. But, eventually, he wore me down. It took a year before I actually developed feelings for him.

Daniel is only an inch taller than me, with sharp gray eyes and golden straw-like hair. He thinks he's the strongest in the school because he lifts weights just as much as he eats—and that's twenty-four-seven. Honestly, I can list off at least ten boys bigger and stronger than Daniel, but his ego is as deep as the Grand Canyon. He aspires to make the US Olympic wrestling team. Telling him to have a plan B is like telling a pig mud is nasty. Yeah. He doesn't to plan. Thinking before he acts is not his forte.

Another difference we have is his minimalistic views. I mean, my mom and I don't have much, but she always taught me to make sure I am presentable in public. Daniel clearly couldn't care less about how he presents himself. It doesn't matter the occasion, he looks as if he threw on clothes straight from the laundry basket—the dirty laundry basket. At first this was hard to get used to, but as I said before, he grew on me. I love him, but at times I feel as though I am not *in* love with him. Truthfully, I actually feel sorry for him sometimes. Sorry for not loving him they way he loves me.

Daniel loves me with all of his heart, but when he shows it by shoving his hand up my shirt and kissing me into submission of his will, I can't deal. We broke up for two weeks the last time he did that. His wandering hands has become too much for me. Time and time again, I have told him sex isn't something I'm ready for.

A few years before we started high school, Emmy and I made a vow to each other. We promised we wouldn't have sex until we married the guy we fell in love with. Emmy swears I will be the first to brake the vow. We still haven't come up with what the consequences would be if I am, but I have no intentions of losing to her. Besides, with how my mom and dad's marriage ended up, I want a husband who is committed, God fearing—as Aunt Destine used to say—and honest.

When we broke up, I told him I needed some time apart to sort through my feelings without any outside influences. This sent him into a rage—a rage which brought out a side of him I had never seen before. This conversation ended in him punching a hole in his bedroom wall and me running from the house scared to look back. I broke it off completely over the phone.

The way I felt during our time apart was something like relief. This could be a clean getaway; my way out of something I felt was truly a mistake to begin with. Then, when the second week began I started to miss him. It must have had something to do with him calling everyday. But, I stood my ground and never answered the phone. When passing in the hallway, I tried my best not to make eye contact with him. Intentionally he walked by me just to graze my hand with his and each time something happened in my stomach. I wondered if the feeling I felt was a warning to stay away or butterflies confirming my feelings for him.

To this day, I still don't know, but the day I decided to take him back was the day I saw him with another girl. Up against the lockers they laughed all in each other's faces. I hated the sight of him with with another girl, especially with the look he gave her; the look I thought only we had shared. Although the jealousy almost made me walk over to slap him, I ignored him as usual and continued talking to Emmy, acting as if I didn't notice. Just as I walked past them he pulled me by my arm into his body. Trying to pull always he continued to pull me in close, enough to his face that I could feel his steamy breath on my ear as he whispered, "I need you."

That afternoon I went home and cried my self to sleep. I couldn't eat. I couldn't think about anything but him. Daniel was a part of my normal. Watching T.V. while my mom prepared dinner, finishing homework, going to see the latest movies together, and most of all, sharing my dreams with him were all things I enjoyed having him there for.

By the end of the second week, his calls stopped. This scared me, so I decided to call him. He picked up on the second ring.

"Hey, Baby," he said, as if two weeks hadn't passed and we had never broken up.

Confused, I replied, "Hey. What are you doing?"

"Just sitting here thinking about you."

Minutes pass. I don't say a word.

Then he blurted out what he really wanted to say. "I miss you so much and I'm so sorry I…"

I stopped him before he could say anything else. All I wanted was for the pain in my heart to end. I wanted him to come over right then and hold me so that all of this could go away and my heart could feel whole again. So that was exactly what I told him. After twenty minutes of mushy talk and apologies, that is exactly what he did. Since the breakup, we fight as usual but he has managed to keep his hands from wandering and respects my wishes—most of the time.

When I reach the locker, Daniel seems to be preoccupied with another one of those cheesy tabloids.

"Hey, babe," I say as I give him a peck on the cheek.

He doesn't look up from the magazine. "What's up."

I steal a glance at the headline, "Prophets of the Now!" I roll my eyes. The magazines Daniel reads exploits fake news and people from all over are flocking to these types of magazines— searching for answers. It's 2035 and everyone's on edge. Inflation hasn't slowed since mid 2022 and currently, our economy is sure to crash. News reporters are talking about World War III being just around the corner, and the last pandemic wiped out millions.

The Spark is the magazine he reads the most. Once they published an article about a woman who claimed she knew when the world was going to end. She described the vision in detail. One line had everyone shook.

The date was painted in red, on houses, on the ground, in the sky, and even on peoples' foreheads. The day of the end is coming, March 30, 2030!

Well, that day came. People were so frightened they boarded up their homes and went underground. Some were so scared they took out their families and then themselves. Thousands died that day, including Aunt Destine. She was in her hospital bed watching the news. Her eyes strained with pain and thrist as she turned to look at me. She couldn't speak because the tube going down her throat to help her breathe prevented her. She looked right in my eyes and shook her head. To me, those were her last words. So from that horrific moment on, I have discounted every story they publish.

Just as I'm closing my locker, Emmy walks up.

"What's up girl?" She says.

"Oh hey, Emmy." I roll my eyes, gesturing over at Daniel.

She gives me a knowing nod and continues down the hall. They don't too much care for each other which is tough sometimes. Thank God Daniel never notices her or else I would have to deal with their hatred for each other all the way to class. He eyes are still glued to that stupid magazine. Sometimes I regret ever sharing my dreams with him. He never found an interest in prophecies until then.

I open my locker to get my jacket. "Any earth shattering prophecies I should be aware of?" I finally ask.

"Well, none as convincing as yours," he says without looking up. "You know I think you should publish some of your dreams, Naomi. People need to know there are some real premonitions out there.

"Okay. For what?"

"So we can prepare."

"Oh like those people did five years ago? Wow, you're hilarious, Daniel."

He closes the magazine, and leans up against the locker, "Well, we can't just wait around doing nothing, Naomi. We need to have a plan."

"I *need* to get to class."

He waves my comment away and repeats what he just said like I didn't hear him the first time. "We need to have a plan, Naomi."

"Here's my plan— to live my life as a good God fearing

person and steer clear of as many false prophecies as I can. This,"
I grab one of his cheeks, "my cute boyfriend is the only way to
prepare for the end." I close my locker and begin walking in the
direction of my next class.

He doesn't say anything, but I know he's right on my heels.

"Daniel, you cannot prepare for something like this, but
what you can do is hope you are not left behind when all hell
breaks loose, literally."

"What do you mean left behind, you going somewhere?" he
chuckles.

When it comes to spiritual things Daniel is like a polar bear
on a beach. He is a pantheist, he believes nature is God. He talks
about the Universe as if it is a person. This drives me crazy
sometimes, but I ignore it because I love him. It's hard to
communicate with him when it comes to my deepest feelings and
what I value most in my life. My Aunt Destine called it
something in particular. She told me once that my mom and dad
were "unequally yoked," and that's why their marriage didn't
work. When I inquired about what the phrase meant she said,
*"When two people are in a relationship together and they have two
separate beliefs they are like night and day… oil and vinegar…they
cannot coexist together."*

Looking at Daniel and for the thousandth time since we have
been together, I think, *what am I doing?* Emmy also thinks we are
a mixed-matched couple going a hundred miles to nowhere. I hardly
ever spend as much time with her because he demands all of my
time. If by some chance I plan to do something with her, he always
manages to talk me out of it. He's controlling and she knows it.

Daniel comes home with me after school to have dinner and get
some homework done. When the sun goes down mom makes her
exit to the living room.

"I'm not feeling myself today, kiddos. Naomi be sure to put the food away before you go to bed."

"Yes, Ma'am."

Daniel sits and watches television for two hours while I purposely ignored him, still annoyed about our conversation earlier. I look over at him.

"You know we have school tomorrow, right?"

He exhales, leaning his head back on the couch. Then he gets up to leave, but before he does, he pitches his genius idea once more as he walks toward the door.

"Come on, Naomi. Think about what I told you. You can't have been given this gift for nothing. Don't you think *God* gave it to you for a reason?" He smiles as the last sentence comes out.

"Look, Daniel, what you think is a joke is very serious to me. These aren't just dreams. They can really affect the people I share them with."

"Who said it was a joke, he is a *good* God, right? Why would he give you something that will hurt people?"

I open the door for him, ready for him to exit. He walks out the door, then turns around. I poke my head across the threshold to kiss his cheek.

"Sure Daniel, see you tomorrow."

I close the door.

After I put the food away I go to my room and fall straight onto to my bed. How did I get myself so deep into something I know is going nowhere? Then thoughts of my day rush through my head: the journal entry I made this morning and how I still don't understand the meaning, my lackluster day at school, my mom once again not feeling well and then back where these thrusts started—my dead end relationship.

Eventually I drift off to sleep. I float down into a deep sleep and I find myself in a mist of soft pink and lavender clouds. My body hovers over a girl who is looking out into a morning horizon from a balcony overlooking the entire world. The sky matches the pink and lavender clouds with sharp traces of orange. Suddenly the clouds drift to the west, revealing a huge clock in the middle of the sky. Just as I notice the time the long hand strikes twelve a loud toll shakes the foundation of the earth. Cascading lines of people appear at the base of the clock and go on and on throughout the earth and sky.

What are they waiting on?

I notice some people are clothed in bright white robes that practically glow, but others covering their faces in shame are wearing black robes. I peer down at the girl watching all of this, then realize its me. Once I do I glide into her body and immediately become a part of the line of people. Anxious, I look down at my robe to see what color I have on, but I can't see it. I rub my eyes trying to clear them. Everything else is clear, but the color of my robe is not.

The line moves closer and closer to the front of the line—the base of the clock—and I then notice seven large beings. Each being is in charge of taking a person from the line behind a veil that drapes down from the sky. Their large arm lifts the veil sheer veil and each time one person walks through. My curiosity plagues me again and I try to see beyond the veil, but again, I come up short. My attention is then drawn to the beauty of the robes the beings are wearing. The glow is that of a diamond reflecting the brightest light, so bright you have to look away at times.

Time flies by and before I know it, I am the first in line. One of the beings take me by the hand. In a gentle voice he says, "This way." Right before I reach the veil, I am overwhelmed with what is behind me, or who I am leaving behind. All I can think about is— Daniel— and wanting to say goodbye. My chest begins to pump up and down and I can't catch my breath. My legs give out, then I collapse. My large escort turns to me and scoops me up like I'm a baby.

Knowing my thoughts, he says, "Now, now….no more tears. I will make sure you get to say goodbye."

Each syllable out of his mouth brings me a peace I can't comprehend.

His voice is so familiar.

"Here."

He hands me something that looks like a phone, so I hold it up to my ear and I hear Daniel's voice.

"Hello."

"Hello, Daniel?" I say with tears in my eyes.

"Hey babe, what's up?"

"I just wanted to tell you," I pause for a moment, trying to get the words out, "to tell you…I love you."

"Oh. Okay. I love you too."

"Okay. I—I have to go now."

"Alright. Talk to you soon."

"Goodbye."

As soon as I hang up the phone, I feel a rejuvenation. I stand up straight and feel as though someone has lifted a weight from my back. Looking at my familiar companion, I see a smile painted across his face. This time I hold my hand out to him and say, "I'm ready now."

THREE

My body flies up into a sitting position the next morning. Immediately, I am ready to recall every detail of the dream in my journal. I grab for my journal and begin to write. What does this dream mean? Panic sets in. Does it mean Daniel and I are going to break up, again? Does it mean I'm going to heaven sooner than I expect? Having the gift of being able to see the future is not always fun. In the past, I have had dreams that didn't actually happen exactly how I dreamt it or maybe the dream was just meant to warn me or prepare me for something.

Once I dreamt I locked Daniel out of my house while it was pouring down raining. I turn back to that page of my journal and read it.

He beat and beat on the door yelling viciously at me, but I would never let him in because for some reason I was angry with him.

After writing it down, I took one of those long pauses Aunt Destine used to always take and an interpretation came to me. I wrote it down.

The rain signified trouble and despair, which is what I have been going through since I decided to commit to a relationship with him. Locking him out of the house is a metaphor of how I am really keeping him out of my heart. I love him, but I cannot fully trust and give my whole heart to him. His beating on the door was a sign of the anger that is built up inside of him. Daniel has had a rough life and sometimes he allows the frustration to spill over on other people.

After rereading the interpretation my nerves are calmed. This dream just needs some time to marinate. I stop writing and decide to go ahead and get ready for school.

My first few classes go pretty well, but when I enter Mrs. Rayburn's class everything goes glum. Just when I thought she couldn't get any worse, she does. The minute I cross the threshold of the classroom, I notice her neon orange army boots, the red and green flannel skirt draped to the middle of her shins and the powder blue lace blouse hugging her round belly. She looks at me with "What are you looking at" expression written all over her face. Still in shook, I have to force my legs to move. We break eye contact and she trots away to the board undaunted by the laughs and whispers behind her back.

"Okay, class, settle down. Today, we will discuss..."

Before I know it, I am no longer in her class, I am back in my dream from last night trying to decipher the meaning. When class is finally over, I scrabble for my things and head for the door.

As I am nearing the door, Ms. Rayburn yells from the back of the classroom, "Miss. Peterson, can you stick around for a little while?"

I stop in my tracks, frustrated that I didn't move fast enough. "Sure! Why not," I mumble.

I throw my book bag on top of a lab table a good enough distance away from her desk. Ms. Rayburn sits at her desk and I take a seat on a nearby stool.

"Miss. Peterson, I wanted to inform you that I am fully aware of your distractions in my class. You are missing key information for the final exam and I need you to focus if you want to pass."

"Yes, I know Ms. Rayburn, I do apologize for being distracted in your class. It's just…never mind."

She leans forward. "No, please continue Miss. Peterson."

Making no eye contact, I continue, because honesty is the best policy, right? "I have a lot going on right now and it's kind of hard to explain."

"No need." She leans back in her chair and stares up at the ceiling. "I understand."

At this point, I look at her. What does she understand? I didn't really tell her anything.

"Just stay on alert. Watch." She says the last word as a demand.

"Watch? Watch what?"

"Things are about to start happening suddenly. Don't be distracted. If you just stay on alert—and watch—nothing will come as a surprise to you."

I stare at her. *What is she talking about? Is she trying to tell me my future or something?* She does give me carnival palm reader vibes. I try to hold back a smirk.

"No disrespect Miss. Rayburn, but can I ask what you are talking about?"

She gets up from her chair, then walks around to the front of her desk. The distance she closes between us makes the room grow smaller.

"You are a dreamer, right?" She asks.

I'm taken a back. "Uh. Yes."

My thoughts race.

"And I can imagine that your distraction in my class is the dream you had the night before. Am I right?"

I cock my head, completely caught off guard, "Right."

She walks towards me, sending all of my senses into chaos. I don't know where to look, or how to sit on the stool anymore, so I stand up and focus my attention on getting my book bag on.

Ms. Rayburn holds out her hands towards me. "I know this sounds strange, but you remind me a lot of myself when I was your age."

The comment is so off putting, I blink several times, trying to disguise any expression that may have snuck up to my face. She notices.

"Well, not with looks," she laughs. "I mean, I am a dreamer too. Some call it a 'seers anointing,' but let's not get too weird, right?"

She gives another uncomfortable laugh then edges closer.

"You can call it so many things, but the fact is, you have a gift."

I interrupt her. "And how do you know this?

Folding her arms she says, "I know a dreamer when I see one—always daydreaming, doodling in a notebook, falling asleep in class, and the most obvious—you have a very small circle of friends. People don't get you. Or, you don't trust people knowing your secret."

I try to hold back my irritation with her, but I just can't. "You are right, Ms. Rayburn, I daydream, I sleep in class, and I have a small group of friends, really only two, but these things aren't uncommon to any high schoolers. Your observation is stereotypical."

"You may be right Miss. Peterson, but nobody daydreams for an entire class period without flinching, which is what you did today. And, I have seen that journal you sometimes pull out to look in. You're trying to get the interpretation during my chemistry class."

Who am I kidding. She's 100% accurate. I'm exhausted in

trying to hide how correct she is. My head falls. Then, I feel her hand on my back. Startled, I flinch, her bright orange afro only a few inches from my face.

"I'm sorry, Miss. Peterson. I had to tell you these things today no matter how weirded out you became. I dreamt of you and from what I have seen you have a rough road ahead."

When I hear she has had a dream about me, my attention is all hers because for some reason I believe her.

"What was it about?" I ask.

"All I can tell you is the gift you have is so important. Don't allow fear to silence you."

"Wait, what?"

Ms. Rayburn holds up her hand, "I'm not finished. I must warn you. 1. Look for more out of life, don't settle. 2. Stay away from the tower. And finally 3. Watch."

My head is spinning. I look at her waiting for her to say more, but she doesn't. She stares at me with the most empty expression and at this point I throw all of the respect out the window.

I throw my hands into the air. "What are you talking about!?"

She looks at me with sharp eyes. "Good day Miss. Peterson."

"Good day? That's all you have to say. That isn't an explanation. We barely know each other and you tell me something like this and expect me to have a good day?"

"This was my assignment, Naomi, to share nothing more, nothing less."

Even more freaked out by her than I was before, I leave without a single word.

FOUR

When I leave Ms. Rayburn's class I walk right to the front of the school and out the front door, like I'm in charge. I don't have single reservation of being caught or stopped. What Ms. Rayburn told me is so disturbing and with everything else I've been going through lately, I just want to go home. Without a car and with it being two hours before the buses arrive this, I have to walk. While I walk, I think about Daniel, how I love him, but also how this relationship is going nowhere. When we graduate, there's really nothing keeping us together. I'll move to Atlanta with Emmy and he will probably head to Maryland to live with his Dad—at least that's what he plans. While he pursues his Olympic dreams, he believes we will get married and I will move to Maryland with him. Honestly, I just can't see it. We're just too different.

Aunt Destine. Oh how I miss her—her smile, her sweet melodic voice, her smell. I could really use her advice right about now. Maybe she could help me with my mom. She sinks deeper and deeper into depression everyday. Talking to her about my problems would be selfish.

Not wanting my mom to ask me why I'm home so early, I take a detour. Ms. Rayburn's voice begins to ring in my head, *don't let fear silence you...don't settle, stay away from the tower...watch.*

"What does that even mean!" I shout up to the sky.

I turn the corner of Broad Street and my place of peace and tranquility is within a few yards. The library on 39th and Broad has been my escape since Aunt Destine's death. Once I started spending so much time here, Daniel started tagging along. While I search for a good book he reads wrestling magazines or *The Spark: Chronicles of Supernatural Findings*.

Usually the streets are gridlocked after 4pm, but since it's an hour past the lunch rush, the streets are bare. Even still, the fear of being caught resonates in my stomach. I stealthily look around hoping no one will notice me. Ducking my head, I skim past a mom scrolling her baby and a few business men in suits. When I finally walk into the two story marble building, I'm relieved that the usual evening and weekend clerks aren't working today. Mrs. Irene would no doubt snitch. A sigh of relief sweeps over me and I feel at ease. I don't recognize any workers, so the coast is clear to settle here until school ends.

I walk to the back of the library to my favorite plush blue coach. Relaxing my legs on the short burgundy stool that always accompanies it, I lean my head back, and gaze up at the ceiling. Ms. Rayburn's so called warning still runs rampant through my head and I just can't shake it.

Closing my eyes, I try to drown it out with a prayer:

Lord, please help me. I am so confused. I have no idea what is going on anymore. I need you. You tell me what to do and I will do it.

I run out of words at this point, which is often the case. When I open my eyes and lift my head, a boy is staring down at me.

Smiling, he says, "Well that was short."

I straighten up in my seat.

"Why were you listening? That is kind of rude don't you think?"

His skin is just about the same color as mine and his eyes—what ever color they are—are hypnotizing. Even with the butterflies dancing in my chest, I look away from him, irritated at his rudeness.

"Oh. Sorry. I was just looking for a book and over heard you. It's not often I hear people pray out loud anymore," he smiles.

"Well, I don't appreciate you listening and would like for you to stop staring at me, please. "

"Oh," he drops his eyes to the floor. "it's just that, you have…" he pauses and looks back up at me.

"What?"

Then, I notice the color of his eyes—green with bursts of hazel.

"Your eyes are amazing," he says without blinking.

He's one to talk. I can barely focus on anything else. "Oh. Thank you." I look away.

"Are you okay?" He changes the subject.

"Yeah, I'm fine."

Without an invitation, he sits down right beside me.

"So, tell me what's bothering you, maybe I can help?"

I scoot away from him, feeling uncomfortably close.

"I don't even know you. Why would I tell you anything? I don't talk to strangers."

He gives me the most gorgeous smile.

"What are you smiling at?"

"The fact that I must not be a stranger," he checks his watch, "because you have been talking to me for the past two minutes."

Involuntarily, a smile rises on my face.

"First of all, what's your name?" I ask.

"Joseph. What's yours?"

"Naomi."

No last names until I discover he's not a serial killer.

"Wow." He stares off into space.

"What?"

He doesn't hesitate. "My Grandmother loved to tell me the story of Naomi when I was a kid. It's an old name. Never in a million years did I think I would meet someone with that name." He smirks, completely unaware of his insult.

"So what are you trying to say?"

Realization strikes and his eyes grow big. "Oh no! I didn't mean it that way! I've always loved the name."

I try to force myself to look away from him, but his presence is magnetizing. I blush when his eyes soften and defenses drop.

"Your name reminds me of a story too."

"Really?" He folds his arms across his chest. "What story?"

"A story my auntie used to tell me."

"I have time." He scoots closer to me. "Tell me."

"It's a story from the Bible. My auntie loved to tell the story in Sunday school."

Joseph leans forward, "I think I might know it."

"Good, then I don't have to tell you the story."

"No. No. I don't know it."

He rests his elbows on his knees and gives me a wide smile. Inside, my heart pounds against my chest, nerves, maybe. Or, maybe I am enjoying his company too much, but I can't let him in on it. He may well be a psycho.

"Well, my auntie told me I reminded her of Joseph, so whenever she taught the lesson on him in Sunday School, I listened."

Joseph was the son of Jacob, who was the son of Issac. Jacob tricked his father into blessing him instead of his brother Esau.

"Do I need to go into the whole thing of how he tricked him?"

"Nope." His smile grows even bigger. "I think I have read about them a time or two."

"Okay."

So Jacob had several sons, and Joseph was one of his favorites because he was born from his wife Rachel. Jacob loved her dearly, but he had another wife.

"I can't remember her name."

"I think her name was Leah."

"Right! Wow, I'm starting to think I am wasting my time telling you this story."

"Go on, you're doing great."

Well, Jacob had two wives, Rachel and Leah. He was basically forced to marry Leah, but she bore him several sons and Rachel only bore him two sons. One of those sons was Joseph. Jacob so admired him that he made him a cloak of many colors, which made his other brothers very jealous. They didn't like Joseph because he was favored by Jacob. Their dislike became even stronger when Joseph decided to reveal a dream he had about them. Joseph told them of a dream he had where their stalks of grain bowed to his stalks of grain. They took this as haughtiness and plotted to kill Joseph. They put Joseph in a pit but Reuben, one of his older brothers, convinced them not to kill him.

"Wasn't there another brother who helped to save his life too?" Joseph asked.

"I'm not sure. I'm giving you the short, short version so pay attention."

He nods, then shifts in the couch, propping one of his legs underneath him. Feeling a little more relaxed myself, I feel my shoulders ease down into the normal position.

So, they sold him into slavery instead. Joseph prospered wherever he went and was favored by God. He was a dreamer and could also interpret dreams. He was eventually put in jail because his master's wife threw herself at him. Being the honorable young man he was, he refused her, so she lied on him, saying he tried to sleep with her.

Once in jail, he still rose to the top and became the chief overseer's personal attendant. Soon he was summoned by the pharaoh to interpret a dream, which no one else in all the land could interpret. The dream was a warning of a coming famine. The instructions were for the people to store their grains for the days to come. The pharaoh believed Joseph and placed him in charge of all the land and food.

Soon, everything Joseph said came to pass and the people looked up to him. Joseph eventually married and had some children but missed his father, Jacob, and his brother Benjamin. Being the chief overseer of all the crops of Egypt, Joseph's brothers had to come to see him to attain food during the famine. When Joseph realized who they were, he tricked them into bringing his brother Benjamin back with them and all the while they had no idea that this was their little brother they had sold into slavery many years ago.

When they brought Benjamin back, Joseph couldn't take hiding his identity anymore and revealed himself to his brothers. They were all frightened that Joseph was seeking revenge, but he told them it all worked together for their good because now they would live and his father would live as a result of the decision they made.

"So," Joseph interrupts, "Why do you remind your aunt of Joseph?"

"Well isn't it obvious?"

"Not really. Joseph was a lot of things packaged in one."

I struggle within myself with whether I should tell him. He's still technically a stranger. A stranger whom I may never see again, so it doesn't matter if he knows my secret.

"I'm a seer."

His face creases with confusion.

"I'm a dreamer."

"Okay. I see," he laughs.

I laugh right along with him, his humor getting the best of me.

"Since I was a little girl, I will have three, sometime, five dreams a night. I try to remember them, but eventually the memory fades. One day my aunt bought me a journal and told me to write them down so I wouldn't forget."

Joseph shrugs. "I hardly ever dream and if I do, I can't remember them."

"Everyone dreams, Joseph, but not everyone remembers. Writing them down has helped me so much." I look off, down one of the book aisles thankful for my Aunt Destine teaching me this years ago. "Sometimes my dreams come true exactly how I saw them, and sometimes they don't, but they all have meaning, or a warning hidden deep within."

"Is this what you were praying about?"

My attention is drawn back to him. His spellbinding green eyes trained right on mine.

"Wow! You were actively listening, huh?"

"It's obvious. As soon as you started talking about how you record your dreams you went somewhere else. Your entire demeanor changed."

This is exactly what Mrs. Rayburn was talking about. I have to stop zoning out.

I confess. "Yeah. I had a very disturbing dream last night, but that is only the tip of the iceberg of my problems."

Moments pass before he finally sits forward and claps his hands together.

"Tell me the dream," he beams. "Maybe I can help you figure it out. I am good at solving problems."

Somehow I feel eager to tell him, but that part of me my mom taught to be reserved and cautious hesitates.

"No, I'm fine. I think I can figure it all out on my own."

Joseph's grin fades. "Have you ever heard the story of the man who was stranded on an island and didn't have any water to drink?"

My head involuntarily twists to one side, knowing exactly where he is going with this. "Yes." I roll my eyes.

"Well, I'm going to tell you the story anyway." He scoots closer towards me, his knee now touching mine.

My heart stills.

"This man came up with a truly wise idea to pray, so he prayed for help out of this situation. As soon as he finished praying," he put his hand out,"—like immediately when he opened his eyes—a man on a boat came along and offered him a ride to the nearest town," he narrows his eyes at me. "Do you know what this man's reply was?"

I purse my lips and I don't bother answering. He continues anyway.

"His reply was, 'no I am waiting on God.'" He sits back in the chair with triumph written all over his face and finishes with, "Eventually that man died."

Looking at his "I'm right and I know I'm right" expression, I feel as though I've known him my whole life. Smiling, I shake my head and ask the obvious question, "So what does this have to do with me?"

He obliges and responds, "You asked for help, and here I am, offering my expertise."

"What makes you think God sent you?" I ask.

"I don't know, but hey," he looks around, "it looks like I'm your only option right now."

Little does he know, he intrigues me and I just want to tell him all of my secrets. I did just meet him, but if I share what's been bothering me, I will probably get some relief from it all. I may not see this guy ever again anyway, how much damage could it possibly do.

I straighten up on the couch and turn to face him. He mimics my body language and there he is, face to face with me—attentive to my every word. I meet eyes with him and do not fight it. I feel calm and strangely comfortable. I melt into his gaze and I feel—at home. Momentarily, I break our eye contact to retrieve my journal. He watches me as I open it up to the entry I made just this morning.

My dream from last night spills over into the atmosphere. My love for Daniel fills the air and gives a sour aroma. I can sense the tension in Joseph's posture. His shoulders have risen and his hands are drawn together tightly. When I finish reading the entry, I fill him in on what my relationship is like with Daniel. I tell of our happenstance love story, but how much we are so different. Then, I tell him about Ms. Rayburn and the warning as best I can: *don't settle, stay away from the tower, and watch.*

We sit in silence for several moments before he speaks.

"I think it's kind of obvious what your dream means. You just may not be willing to see it right now."

My breath catches and I can't bear to look at him. Yes, I do know. I've known since I woke up this morning. Daniel is the first love I have ever had. Although he is hard to love, none the less, I love him.

Joseph continues as the tears begin to fall. "In the dream you were the same way. You had to say goodbye before you actually let go."

He reaches over to wipe away stray tears. His touch settles me.

"Don't cry, Naomi."

His thumb slowly trails down my cheek and lingers on my chin. When my eyes meet his once again, his eyes move down to my lips. Acutely aware of what he's thinking, my eyes dart away from him over to a mom and her two children. Joseph clears his throat then sits back on the couch. I wipe more tears away. "What are you thinking now?"

Stupid—stupid question.

He looks at me, "Do you really want to know?"

"Yes, I do."

"I think you are only with Daniel to fill a void. It's dangerous, Naomi. You have so much to look forward to. Don't waste your time on a relationship you know is going nowhere."

Although I have every reason to be defensive, I take in every word. Joseph vocalizing everything I have tried so hard not to think about is therapeutic. All I needed was for someone to say it out loud—for someone to tell me what I knew all along.

"What about the scenery? Why did it seem like judgment day?"

"Yeah. That piece seems to be very significant. I'm not sure."

I look at him and I can tell he is still thinking about it. After several minutes he says, "This Ms. Rayburn though, she sounds kind of weird, but don't discount her advice. Not settling is what I would advice as well. She also said 'Beware of the tower' or something like that?"

"Right."

"The tower could symbolize an obstacle you may face or an actual physical building. 'Be Watchful' could mean for you to stay on guard, you know, don't get distracted."

"Yeah, the watchful part was the easiest for me to figure out." I give him a side glance and nudge him, "but thanks Joseph. I am glad I talked to you."

He laughs, "No problem."

As I gather my things, he stands to his feet. "Well, I guess I've prolonged this encounter for as long as I possibly could."

I stand up realizing he's much taller than I realized. "I enjoyed it."

He stares down at me. "Me too."

An awkward moment of staring occurs for like the one-hundredth time today. A surge of energy vibrates between us and I almost feel like stepping forward to hug him. Before I can, he smiles and says, "I was just starting to get used to your sassy attitude."

"Oh yeah?"

"For sure."

Gorgeous dimples penetrate his chiseled cheeks.

"Well, I have to go figure this all out. Besides, it's about time for me to be arriving home from school."

"From school? Wait a minute—how old are you?" he asks.

"Now, isn't that a rude question to ask a female?"

"No," he hold up his index finger. "Not if she's under the age of 30."

"Really?"

He exhales. "No. Not really, but tell me."

"Only if you tell me how old you are?"

"Easy. Twenty-two."

"Well, I'm eighteen."

Joseph's beautiful smile returns with a vengeance. "You graduate this year?"

I pull on my book bag, then tuck some stray curls behind my ears. "Yeah, trying to, but if I don't clean up my act in Ms. Rayburn's class, I am going to have to consider online courses for the summer."

He helps to fix my book bag straps on my shoulders, "Well, you better get a move on Miss. Peterson."

"Hey, how did you know my last name?"

He grabs my shoulders and turns me around to face him. "If you don't want strange men knowing your name, it's not a good idea to have it embroidered on your backpack."

I drop my eyes to the floor in embarrassment. He immediately lifts my head and fixes his eyes on mine. His pearly white teeth sparkle as he grins down at me.

He's gorgeous.

I fidget out of the position he is holding me in. Trying not to show my nervousness I say, "Yeah my mom gave me this for my birthday this weekend. It wouldn't have been nice to turn it down."

"No worries Miss. Peterson," he says as he straightens my straps on my book bag once more. "Would it be okay with you if I met you here the same time tomorrow, you know, to continue our conversation?"

"Tomorrow? Tomorrow, I have school."

"No you don't." He laughs out, "Tomorrow is Saturday, but good try."

"Yeah. Right," I say, "We'll see. It depends."

"On?"

"My mood," I blush. Then, I walk away, toward the front of the library—feeling the heat of his gaze on my neck. I turn around to see if my instincts are right. And there he is, watching me, smiling and waving. I wave goodbye.

I float home, thinking of nothing but Joseph. When I reach my house, I hurry to get the door open so I can run upstairs and tell Emmy all about my encounter at the library, but I fumble at the task. When I finally get the key in the key hole, before I can turn the knob, my mom opens the door.

Still in her bathrobe, my mom rants out, "Where have you been? I have been worried sick, Naomi! Your sixth period teacher called. She was concerned about you because she saw you during the day and got worried when you didn't show up to class!"

"Mom, my sixth period class is a joke. All we do in that class is draw fruit and flowers," I say as I threw my backpack on the love seat. "Ms. Rayburn's class is the only class I am concerned about."

She sinks down on the couch to occupy the same spot she has been sitting in, probably, all day. The same spot, where you can see the springs underneath the thinned, faded cushion. My eyes dart from the couch to her and I notice her posture and strained eyes. I swallow hard and I don't feel so happy anymore. The Lord knows I didn't want to add to my mom's tormenting thoughts.

"Naomi, please try not to scare me this way.".

Of all people, I should know how terrified my mom is of losing someone else she loves.

"Yes ma'am. I'm sorry, it won't happen again." I sit down next to her and hug her as tightly as her frail body will let me. She has been through a lot—all of her siblings deceased, deceased parents, and after 20 years of marriage a husband that just up and left her with nothing. It was stupid of me not to think the school wouldn't call. I sit with her until she is fast asleep, then, slowly I guide her head to a near by pillow as I stand to my feet. I pull a blanket over her.

She stirs, "Thank you," she says.

Then, I head up to take a quick shower.

As soon as I get into bed, like a tsunami, Joseph comes flooding back into my mind. I settled on not calling to tell Emmy about him. Maybe I should just keep him a secret for just a little while longer. If I told Emmy, she would surely take that chance to break Daniel and I up. So, I lie there daydreaming and replaying every single word, every single glance, every single brush of his knee. Joseph is the encompassing splendor that saturates my mind until I drift off to a deep sleep.

FIVE

My heels click as I run down a beautiful corridor. The walls are made of the stunning Japanese stone, jade. There are columns every five feet and they extend as high as the heavens. I slow my pace for a moment to marvel at the cloudless sky. The sky, a soft creamy orange and calming pink. The sun is just touching the edge of the earth. The sunlight shines directly through the roofless edifice, reflecting off of the immaculate ivory floors. The tall standing columns are made of pure gold and polished so well I can see my reflection. I catch a glimpse of myself as I continue to run. I almost stop when I see the flowing while gown I am wearing, but I don't. Something is drawing me—like a magnet. The floor is waxed to perfection and I am amazed that I can keep my balance. The train on my gown is so long, so I hold it to keep from tripping. This corridor goes on for what seems like hours until I finally reach my destination. Arms grab a hold of me and up we float into the orange and pink sky, spinning ever so slowly, giggling, carefree, and secure—into the sunset. Our bodies light up as we get closer, and closer, and closer. We saturate its light.

Get UP!!!! Get UP! Get UP!!! Frustrated, I slap the alarm clock, turning off the annoying sound. When I see the sunlight peeking through my blinds, I jump up in horror. Then, I realize, just as I often do on Saturday morning, it's the weekend.

I come to my senses and settle back in bed, relieved I don't have to rush off to school. My morning routine when I wake is to sit in silence, my usual exercise of trying to remember what I dreamed the night before. It takes me some time, but eventually the dreams come flooding back.

Deep in this meditative state, images begin to fill my mind. Contorted images of the breathtaking corridor, the massive columns, the stone walls and *him*. Who was he? I can't bring back the memory of his face. All I can recollect is a blurred image of the figure. I can't even remember what his voice sounds like, but I do remember his words—*I love you, Naomi*—so real, so sincere. Just the thought gives me goosebumps.

Time escapes me while I try to figure out the missing pieces of this dream. I quit trying to make out the face and except that it might just be one of those coerced dreams I sometimes have. I did fall asleep thinking about that guy I met yesterday.

Sitting up in bed, I reach for my journal. It's not in its usual spot, so I get up to see if its on my desk. Then, it hits me, I never took it out of my bag when I got home yesterday. Spotting my book bag on the chair over by the window, I yawn, then trudge over to get it. When I reach my hand down in my bag and wrap my fingers around the spine of my journal, I catch a glimpse out the window. I see Daniel coming up the road on his tiny red scooter.

What is he doing here so early?

He zips into my drive way.

Okay, get it together Naomi. It's just Daniel. No big deal.

I dash over to my drawers to pull on a fresh pair of jeans and a t-shirt.

Just because he is here doesn't mean I have to say *anything* about *anything*. Joseph is just a guy you met and I am not obligated to tell him about everyone I meet.

The doorbell rings knocking me out of my nervous

thoughts. I hear my mom's footsteps and then Daniel's voice.

I'll break the news about our foreshadowed break up later.

I tame my frizzy sleep mangled hair. Then, I turn around and just like that, there he is standing in my doorway—smiling from ear to ear.

"I am so happy to see you, Baby."

Gosh I hate when he calls me that.

"What happened to you yesterday? I called your cell phone 100 times, but I never got an answer," he whines.

Just looking at him I realize just how much my feelings toward him have changed since yesterday. He has no idea everything is different—now. The sudden wave of sadness washes over me because all I have been thinking about is how to break up with him while he has been worrying about me.

"Oh." I have to think quick. "I put my phone on do not disturb. My mom was having a rough day."

"Why didn't you check your phone after she went to bed?"

This time his question sounds like a demand and this time I don't have a quick answer. He walks over to my bed and sits down without asking permission.

I snatch the pillow he sat on from underneath him. "Well just have a seat Daniel." Sitting down beside him, I don't look at him. I tell the truth. "*I* had a rough day yesterday too. Ms. Rayburn asked me to stay after class. She caught me daydreaming again."

"That explains why I didn't see you after her class. Did she write you up for daydreaming!"

"No, I left after that."

He turns toward me. "You left? Where? The school!?"

"Yeah, I just took a walk."

"Wow, Naomi. You surprise me more and more everyday."

He reaches out his arms to hold me. I don't resist. I lay into his chest, thankful, I told the truth and still managed to keep Joseph a secret.

He squeezes me a little tighter. "I missed you, but I'm glad you are okay."

His caring comments only make me feel worse. Daniel tries to pull back, but I stay planted because I know he going to want a kiss and I'm so not in the mood for this.

"Hey, look at me," he gently pushes me back.

His icy blue irises fix on mine—searching for answers. "Is everything okay, Baby?"

I cringe. *Please stop calling me that!* The words don't come out, but I scream it in my head. Instead of answering him, I get up and walk over to the window. Within seconds, I feel his presence behind me.

Okay Naomi, don't chicken out, this is your chance.

"You don't look so well, Baby, are you okay?"

"No. I'm not okay."

I feel like I've been leading him on all of this time. Giving him more time to fall more and more in love with me, while I'm just going along for the ride. It's selfish. Yes, I needed someone after dad left. Daniel is all I know. He's my first love, my first kiss—the only male to tell me he loves me—besides my dad.

"Do you need me to pick you up some medicine from the drugstore?"

His kindness backs me into a corner once again. My heart aches for how awful of a person I am.

"No, I think I might be coming down with the stomach flu."

I chicken out again. Backing away from him because I still want some time alone today, I play the part. I just need more time to figure out how not to break his heart.

The idea of me possibly being contagious doesn't even cross his mine. He reaches for me, "Awe, baby. I'm going to stay with you all day to take care of you."

"No, I don't think it's a good idea. You can't stay. I don't want you getting sick too."

Slowly, I walk over to my bed, holding my stomach.

He attempts to follow me, but pauses, "Yeah, you're right. I can't get sick. I have a wrestling tournament on Monday."

"Oh yeah," I say. "I forgot about that. I don't remember hearing anything about you practicing."

He cocks one side of his mouth up. The cocky smile is one of his signatures. "Babe, please, you know better than anybody I don't need to practice."

"Okay, Mr. Cocky, don't come whining to me on Monday if you get too tired during the second match. You know tournaments are longer than regular school competitions."

"Alright babe, if it means that much to you, I will try to get some practicing in today—since you are temporarily out of service." He approaches me with one of his sneaky smiles, then locks his arms around my waist. Staring down at me, he says, "I love you, Naomi."

He leans in for a kiss, but I pull away. "Daniel, I may be contagious."

"That you may, my dear."

He backs away slowly laughing. As I turn away he gives me a light tap on my butt.

"I've told you not to do that Daniel!" I snap.

He throws both hands in the air grinning as he backs up to the doorway.

"Okay, okay, I'm sorry. I'll call you later?"

"Sure." I roll my eyes—100% sure I am not going to answer the call.

"I love you, Naomi!" He yells as he walks down the stairs.

Under my breath, I respond, "Yeah, me too."

"I heard that," he yells back.

When he leaves, it takes an entire hour for me to decide on something to wear. Joseph asked to see me today and I have no desire in standing him up. I don't want to wear anything that makes me look like I don't care, but I also don't was to try too hard. Back and forth I go between two out-fits before I finally decide on a pair of blue jeans and a red top. Once dressed, I tackle my bee hive of curls. Ten minutes of detangling and twirling my ringlets, I glance over at the clock. If I am not out of here in fifteen minutes, I will be late, and I hate being late.

My hands shake as I gather my cell phone and the books I need to return. Why am I so nervous right now? Is it because I just met this random guy who I'm sneaking to see behind my boyfriends back or is it because I just lied to Daniel about being sick? I don't know. Aunt Destine used to always say, "A lie is a lie. It doesn't matter how little it is." I shutter at the thought of her looking down on my trail of lies. So, along with the butterflies dancing at the thought of seeing Joseph again, I have a large dose of guilt caught in my throat.

With the guilt I put on my gold hoop earrings and some clear lipgloss. Then, I examine my reflection in the body size mirror hanging on the back of my closet. I guess this will have to do. I grab my backpack and head down stairs. My mom is sitting at the breakfast table clipping coupons and drinking her usual first cup of coffee, out of three, for the day. I settle within myself to make our conversation short because I only have five minutes to spare.

"I made a whole pot of coffee Naomi, help yourself."

"No thanks, I'm fine, Mom." I grab a bottle of water from the refrigerator. Drinking coffee with a stomach full of butterflies is just not a good idea. Just as I am closing the refrigerator, my stomach growls and her newspaper folds down just as the door falls shut. She peeks over it.

"Are you okay?"

I stick the bottle of water in the side pocket of my book bag. "Yeah, I am fine. Just a little nervous—that's all."

"About?" She folds the newspaper closed and puts down her scissors.

I never could lie to my mom or keep anything from her, but I have to be cautious on what to share and when.

"I'm going to the library to meet someone—someone I met yesterday."

Her eyes grow wide. "Oh. Okay," she says cooly.

She leans back in her chair and picks up her newspaper again. I lean up against the counter, ready for the next question because I know it's coming.

"So, is this someone a guy or a girl?"

"It's a guy." I pull myself up on the counter to sit and make myself a little more comfortable. "His name is Joseph. We sat and talked for a while yesterday about the story of Joseph and…," I hesitate, "about a dream I had."

My mom turns to me with the same wide eyed expression.

"Really, Naomi?"

This time her voice isn't calm, but filled with disappointment.

"When did you start talking to strangers about personal things? You don't even know this guy—whether he's a predator, a pervert, a serial killer! How old is he any way? Do you even know that?"

"Mom." I roll my eyes. "He's not any of those things. I think I would have figured that out after almost an hour of talking to him." I mean, not many serial killers go around listening to Bible stories.

She exhales, stands to her feet and walks over to face me. At this point, I'm regretting being so honest.

"Naomi, I know I haven't been such a great person to talk to lately, but, honey…," she pauses, placing both hands on my shoulders, "you have to be careful. Are you sure this is a wise thing to do, going to meet a stranger by yourself?"

I turn my head to look out the window. I didn't realize how

beautiful the day was until now. There isn't a cloud in the sky and the sun is shining so bright. All of the sudden images of last night's dream flood my thoughts. I remember the safety I felt and the contentment. I slide down off the counter, put my hands on her shoulders, smile and kiss her on the cheek.

"Yes ma'am, I'm sure."

She grabs my wrist and continues to stare into my eyes. Over the years my mom has learned to trust me. I have basically been taking care of *her* for the past six years. Deep down she knows I wouldn't do anything crazy. She waits a moment, walks back over to the table and takes her original seat.

"Okay," she finally says, then gestures to the door with her hand, as she reaches for her coffee. "Go on and meet your friend." She takes a sip from her cup then says, "Oh, I forgot to ask. Does Daniel know about this—*friend*?"

My mom is very good at making you think about your decisions without controlling your decisions.

"No, and I don't think I need to because Joseph's just a friend. I'm allowed to have friends, right? "

I walk over to hug her goodbye and head for the door.

"I guess," she says. "Make sure you are home by dinner time, Naomi."

Opening the front door, I reply, "I will."

SIX

Although, today, there's a light breeze blowing, I don't risk walking. The weather in Georgia can be a little double-minded—one day it's a cool 70 degrees and the next a hot and humid 90 degrees. I decide on catching the bus to the library which is what I usually do when Daniel isn't around to give me a lift on his scooter. Most kids my age have cars or at least a parent's to borrow, but my dad didn't leave us a car and a mother, who can barely keep a roof over our heads, never had a car of her own. So, local transportation it is.

The streets are busy with vendors, passerby's and bumper to bumper traffic. Saturdays in downtown Augusta are eventful. On any other day, you would think it's a ghost town, but today you can find couples having lunch at local restaurants, people listening to live jazz, and others browsing art galleries and souvenir shops.

I walk one block through throngs of people before I reach the library. When I enter the doors, a cool breeze greets me. I say hi to the usual Saturday crew, Brandon and Sarah, then head back to my already occupied couch and stool. Joseph, looking even more charming than how I remembered, is sitting amongst towering bookcases—reading. He is wearing a pair of black cargo shorts with an orange t-shirt. My eyes scan down to his black flip flops and all I can do is imagine him on one of those Old Navy commercials where all the guys are gorgeous and every part of them are chiseled. A smile creeps to my cheeks just as he looks up and answers my smile with one of his own. He stands to his feet and puts his thumbs into his front pockets—flawless.

"Well, I guess you're in a good mood today, huh," he says with a chuckle. "You showed up!"

"Why, whatever do you mean?" I ask playfully as I take a seat.

He watches me, then sits down in the chair adjacent to the couch. "I'm so glad you came."

I smirk, "Me too."

I sit quietly for a few agonizing minutes, trying to ignore the fact that he is intensely staring at me. Then, I can't bear it any longer.

"Can you please stop doing that, you are really making me regret this."

He leans forward, closing half of the space between us, "I apologize, it's just…"

I finally meet eyes with him. "It's just what?"

He clears his throat, "I don't know what to say. Your presence makes me nervous." He grins, "how about you?"

I'm shocked. He says exactly what he's thinking. I can't tell him I am at a loss for words around him, or that I can't stop thinking about him, or that I think I had a dream we were married. So, I lie.

"I'm fine, just thinking about the books I need to pick up before I leave."

The words leave a bitter taste in my mouth. Truthfully, I am mesmerized by every aspect of him.

"Man, you're tough."

"What?"

"Nothing."

Leaning forward, I crane my neck to see the book lying next to him, "What were you reading?"

"Oh, something for work." He doesn't bother picking it up. "So, what books do you need to pick up, maybe I can help you find them?"

I reach in my book bag and pull out a notebook where I have some titles written down.

"My friend Emmy and I like to read novels together— well, not together, but at the same time. We have our own little book club—sort of. We barely see each other now, so this is kind of our thing that keeps us spending time together."

"Sounds like a good way to stay close," he smiles. "Why aren't you two seeing each other?"

I love how he shows interest in everything about me—I've been with Daniel for two years and he never asks about Emmy.

I cut my eyes at him, "I get the feeling you already know the answer to this question?"

His expression is hard, "Wow. Really? He doesn't like your best friend?"

"Yeah, they really don't get along. I try to spend my time with them separately, but most of my time is spent with him. He is pretty needy."

"So, did you break up with him yet?"

He doesn't look at me when he asks this.

I laugh out, "Way to be direct, Joseph."

He shrugs. "It's the only way I know how to be."

He looks down at his hands patiently waiting for my answer, but I can tell by the tapping of his foot, he wants my answer to be yes.

"No, not yet."

His foot stops moving. He looks up at me.

"What? It's going to take time. One day of realization isn't enough for me to break off a two year relationship."

He doesn't break his stare and I feel exposed—like he can see right through me, every scar and every weakness. I break eye contact with him, ashamed of my weakness for Daniel.

Joseph wraps his hands around mine. His touch sends electricity through my extremities. I shudder.

"Yesterday, you told me you've been thinking about breaking this off for some time. How much more time are you willing to waste?"

I sit back on the couch.

"This bluntness is going to take some getting used to."

Joseph scoots back against the couch. He lets his head hang back as he runs his hands over his face, exhaling into them. "I'm sorry. I shouldn't have said that, I mean this is really none of my business. I just…," he leans forward again, closing the space between us. "I know I barely know you, but I just want the best for you."

He's right, I barely know him, but my heart tells me he's being honest. The look he's giving me right now makes me melt.

Not knowing how to counter this response, I get up, notebook in hand. "Okay, are you gonna help me or what?"

A timid smile creases his face and he rises to his feet, "Sure. Let's do this."

The first book we look for is a romantic novel called, *Tears*. Joseph finds it quickly and we move on to the next book which is a resource book I need to write my research paper for English. This book isn't so easy to find, so we spend about thirty minutes looking in the wrong area. We finally kill our pride and ask Brandon, my very own library Sherlock Holmes, where to find it. The book is actually not in the reference section, but instead the nonfiction section. Brandon directs us to two large bookshelves he suspects we will find the book, knowing full well I do not want him to point it out. Finding my own books is something I pride myself in, plus, I like the adventure. Brandon found this out the hard way when he got this job a year ago.

Joseph and I playfully argue over which book shelf it is on and finally decide to agree to disagree.

"Okay," he says, "you look on the bookshelf you think it's on and I am going to look on the other one. If I find it first, you have to promise to go out to dinner with me tomorrow night."

My mouth goes dry. I can't resist.

"Deal."

I head in the direction of my chosen book shelf. Walking toward the shelf, I hope it's not there. Spending time with Joseph has been a breath of fresh air; no arguing, no pressure, and most of all, honesty. When I reach the book shelf I hear, my name. My stomach turns in on itself.

"Naomi!"

I hear it again. I don't turn around. It's Daniel's.

Turning slowly, I hope it's just paranoia and I am just hearing things.

"Baby?"

The voice is closer now and I know for sure I'm not hearing things. My heart beats so fast I can feel it's rhythm throughout my entire body. I finish my full turn only to find Daniel standing there looking at me as if he has seen a ghost. His cheeks and neck are flushed. Red blotches cover his chest. I imagine the humid thirty-five-mile-per-hour scooter ride wasn't fun.

He doesn't waste time, "What are you doing here?" His question comes out breathy. "You're supposed to be at home in bed."

As all so-called white lies go, you never can stop with just one, because one little lie leads to another. Oh how I wish I would have just told him the truth. I wish I would have told him that I didn't feel like seeing him today, that I wanted to go to the library to meet a friend. Now I'm stuck. But, here it goes—another lie.

"Well, I started feeling a little better and thought some fresh air would be nice."

Then, the tangle in my stomach twists.

Joseph! Where is he?

How could I forget. He could walk up any minute now. How on earth will I explain him away? I look over Daniel's shoulder. Joseph is nowhere to be found. The aisle of bookshelves across from us is completely empty. Daniel notices my quick glance and looks over his shoulder.

"Are you okay, Naomi? I mean do you really think you should be out in public. How did you get here anyway? Baby, please don't tell me you walked?"

My insides recoil at the pet name. I look over his shoulder once more. "No, I caught the bus."

Before he can ask me another question, I counter with my own, pretending to continue looking for books.

"So what are you doing here, aren't you supposed to be practicing for your tournament?"

He grimaces, "Timothy wasn't home, so I didn't have anyone to run through the matches with."

"So what are you going to do? You can't just sit here all day reading *The Spark*."

He smiles and folds his arms across his chest, "I guess I'm gonna have to wing it and spend the rest of my day with you."

Just as he says this, I catch a glimpse of purple in my peripheral vision. I look over Daniel's shoulder and there he is walking towards us. He's so perfect in every way. My heart stills. I hold my breath. Will Joseph be the one to shatter this glass house.

"I'm sorry it took me so long ma'am, but I found the book you were looking for." He hands me the book we were looking for.

Daniel looks at me, then back at Joseph. Then me again. Joseph winks just as Daniel turns to look at me. I take the book from Joseph's hands.

"Thank you Joseph. Daniel, this is Joseph, he helped me find the books I needed."

Daniel turns around and holds out his hand, "It was nice of you to help my girl."

Joseph doesn't extend his hand, he simply nods. "No problem, it was my pleasure." He narrows his eyes at me. "I will see you soon." He winks again while Daniel isn't looking, then walks away.

Daniel watches him as he walks towards the exit.

"Okay, so what was that all about and how does he know your name?"

Daniel makes an exception for my math teacher Mr. Frazier, but he doesn't like when I talk to anyone of the male species. Jealousy and control are two parts of Daniel I just can't deal with anymore.

"Daniel, I just told you. He has been helping me for the past hour, so we did happen to exchange names."

"There wasn't any exchanging of anything else was there?"

"No, Daniel. Now can you please just take me home, I'm actually starting to feel sick again."

As we walk to the circulation desk to check out the books, I do a quick glance around for Joseph. I gush over the fact he kept my secret. At the counter, Daniel mindlessly chats with the other clerk, Sarah. It's perfectly fine for him to flirt with whomever he wants, but it's always a big scene when I even say hello to another guy. My frustration disappears when I hear the door open. I look up and there he is—smiling in the doorway. He has his hand up to his ear. I can't quite make out what he's trying to communicate, but I nod in recognition anyway. Then, just like that, he's gone. I am stuck wishing I could have spent more time with him, or maybe even asked him for his number.

Riding on the back of Daniel's scooter is always the most peaceful time I get to spend with him. It's the only quiet time I have to think without him interrupting my thoughts or him bringing up "his needs" in this relationship. My thoughts replay Joseph standing in the doorway and it hits me! He was gesturing for me to call him!

But, I don't have his number.

Not only do I not have his number and no way of getting it. Frustration sets in and I realize I could have gotten home quicker if I just walked. The temperature has risen and with it the humidity. My face is plastered to Daniels profusely sweaty back and I can only imagine how much he is enjoying this.

Now I really *really* feel sick.

When we finally arrive at my house, Daniel takes one look at my sweat drenched face and he doesn't attempt to come in.

He kisses me on the cheek and says, "I'll check on you tomorrow?"

As he is helping me get off my helmet, I see his concern for me. Guilt from lying to him all day overwhelms me.

"Sure, that sounds good," I say without reservation.

I step closer to him and kiss him on the lips for the first time today. His hands make their way my face and he holds me there for as long as he can. I don't rush him. When he is satisfied, he slowly pulls away, still holding my face.

"I love you."

I whisper back, "I love you too."

When I open the door my mom is sitting on the couch in her usual spot.

She opens her eyes for a few seconds to say, "Your dinner is in the microwave."

I tell her thank you before I head up the stairs knowing she she probably won't respond. When I make it to my room I start to unload my book bag to make sure my books didn't get mixed up with Daniel's. The book Joseph found for me sits right on top of the stack. Remembering the bet I happily lost, I pick up the book we found together. We had so much fun on our scavenger hunt for books. Then his gesture in the doorway comes back, then I realize something. I open the book and there's a note:

Naomi, I am sorry our day was cut short. Text me when you get some time to yourself: (706)985-4444. By the way, I was right and you were wrong. What time is dinner tomorrow???

SEVEN

Sleeping is no easy task after a day like today. I stay up until two o'clock in the morning going over every detail of my day. Sometime past 2am, I fall asleep. I remember staring at the clock, praying to God I would fall asleep soon. Next thing I know I am shaking my head as fast as I can to wake up. It's not the usual horror marathon I have every once in a while, but it's just as petrifying. I pant for breath, blinking my eyes to focus in on the time—5am. I roll out of bed and stumble to the bathroom. My face is covered in sweat. I bend over the sink to splash my face with water. My hands are shaking and all I can think about is the last vision I had before waking up.

I am running as fast as I can, but it doesn't seem to be fast enough. My legs feel as though they have fifty pound sand bags attached to them. There has just been an earthquake in Georgia? I hear on the news that earthquakes are happening simultaneously in other southern states, as well. There has been a power outage for several days. People are losing their minds because they were not prepared for something like this. Stores are out of food, gas stations have shut down and there is no water. In the mist of this, I see myself encouraging everyone else. I seem fine; clean clothing, no appetite, and unusually calm. More days go by and things only get worse.

The sky is a weary purple, streaked with bright orange smoke.

A far off I can see mountains erupting all around me. People are running and screaming to get away, but there's no use, the horror is everywhere. Mothers are running with their children and others are running to their cars to get away, but as soon as they start the car it explodes sending debris in every direction. I miraculously survive several explosions. I continue to run, trying to get to safety, but there is none. After what seems like hours of running and dodging explosions, I hear something that sounds like a thousand lightning bolts striking the earth all at once. The sound is ear splitting. I grab my ears as they ring and fall to the ground. The ground begins to shake and then I see it. The loud noise was the ground cracking right beneath me. The crack is only as thin as a needle, but it is easy to see and notice because beneath the surface, a bright orange glow is shining through. I attempt to touch it to see what is giving off this glow, but my fingers are singed from the steam rising from the crack. I jump to my feet and continue to run. The loud sound strikes again, I look back and the needle size crack is now a yard long. People are falling into the earth, cars are falling, and the ground beneath me is sinking, yet, I continue to run. As I run, all I can think of is the people falling into the earth screaming for help. It's a sound indescribable. I continue on as the ground continues to descend beneath me. Now the crack that was so tiny is no more; the entire world below me is a pit of fire and sulfur. This pit seems to be six miles below the surface and everything that existed has been sucked into it, except me. Running as fast and as hard as I can, with what endurance I have left, I can still hear the screams. Each time I focus on the sound of pain and terror of those people, I become more and more fatigued. It's smoldering hot and I am literally breathless—still I run until all I have left to run on is what is in front of me, there's nowhere to go anymore. When I have run until there is no more ground and I start to fall into that bottomless pit, I wake up.

There's no use trying to regain my sense of reality. I can't get those images and sounds out of my head. It usually doesn't take me long, but I stand in the bathroom until the sun begins to rise. When I feel comfortable enough to record my dream in my journal, I head to my bed, grab it from my night stand, and begin writing. As I sit recalling every significant detail my heart begins to beat faster and faster—I can't catch my breath. My hands tremble. There aren't any hidden messages in this dream. There's nothing to figure out. This is a warning dream. This dream is about the end of days.

EIGHT

I don't bother going back to sleep, so I wait until a reasonable time and decide to use the number Joseph left me in the book. Just as soon as I dial the last number, I hang up. I glance over at the clock—8:45 am—he may not be awake. What if he's at work—wait—it's Sunday. I decide to wait until lunch time and lay the phone down, then I pick it up again. I would love to hear his voice right now and I want to tell him my dream. Daniel will just go into this long tangent about selling my vision to *The Spark* and how much the money could help my mom. With everything that's going on with the government and news that World War III is just around the corner, it's too dangerous to put something like this out there—especially with *The Spark* as the vehicle.

Joseph will know what to do? I sit up on my bed and adjust myself against the backboard. After more thought, I decide to call. Nervous and breathless, I dial the number a second time and wait to hear the ring back tone before I put the phone to my ear. The phone rings once and immediately my palms start to sweat.

"Hello."

I can't catch my breath let alone speak. It takes me gasping for a few breaths before I respond.

"Uh, hi."

"Is this who I think it is?"

I play the field as usual, knowing full well he literally takes my breath away. "The question is—is this who you want it to be?"

"For sure."

My heart explodes.

"I am so glad you called. Are you okay?" he asks.

"I'm fine. I...," words fail me again. What should I say:*I want to go out with you tonight, or I just wanted to talk to you.* Anyone of those would be too much.

"Naomi? Are you still there?"

"Yeah. I'm still here. How are you?"

"I am doing great right now."

I can sense the smile on his face. His words come out so sweet easing my nerves and I find the courage to say what I really called for.

"So, obviously I found your little message. I decided I should keep my end of the deal." I bite my lip, hoping he remembered.

"Deal?"

Oh darn. He doesn't.

"Yeah. You said if you found..."

He stops me mid sentence.

"Of course I will go out to dinner with you, Naomi. I thought you would never ask," he laughs.

"Why are you playing with me, Joseph? Do you have any idea how hard it was to make this phone call?"

Still laughing he says, "I'm sorry. I couldn't resist. It's just that you are so good at playing hard to get, I had to throw you off your game just a little bit."

"Well, good job. You got me." I exhale and brace myself, waiting for his next words.

Joseph exhales, "So what time should I pick you up?"

The question gives me a chest full of fireflies. I have never been picked up by anyone, but Daniel. What would my mom say? I think of an alternative.

"How about I meet you there?"

That fixes the mom issue and the 21 questions she would have for him, but there's still the Daniel issue.

"We would also need to meet somewhere out of town. I would hate to run into anyone unexpectedly again."

"I get it, but how are you going to get there?" he asks.

"I have a plan."

"Can you please let me in on the plan."

"Okay—okay, Mr. cautious. Emmy has a car and she usually works Sunday evenings."

"Okay. Your plan sounds good. Are you a picky eater, because I know a great Thai restaurant right outside of town?"

"Nope. I love Thai food."

"I can text you the address and directions? Five o'clock okay?"

"Sure."

"I will see then."

"Okay."

"Bye, beautiful."

"Bye."

I hung up regretting I didn't say more than just—"bye." Lying on my bed, I rethink every word spoken and replay the sound of his voice booming through the receiver—every word filled with sincerity. I try piecing together several different combinations of out-fits in my mind, forgetting all about the petrifying dream I'd just written in my journal—the ink probably still drying as I lay here consumed with all things Joseph. Then, my cell phone rings with a familiar tune—it's Daniel.

NINE

I let the phone ring a little longer than I normally do, but I eventually pick up. The feelings of deception and disloyalty taint my mood. How much longer can I do this? How much longer will I allow him to fight so hard for me and I am not willing to go to bat for him?

"Hey. Baby? You there?"

I jump at the sudden sound of his voice. I didn't realize I pressed the green button.

"Hey. Yeah, I'm here."

"I am sorry for calling you so early, but I just couldn't wait any longer. You feel any better?"

"Yeah, I do."

What I really want to say is I'm feeling well enough to go out on a date with someone else tonight, but of course, I'm too chicken to say that.

"So, what are your plans for today?"

How much more time are you willing to waste? That's what Joseph asked me yesterday. A surge of courage comes with the memory.

"Actually, I would like for you to come by, I have something I want to talk to you about."

His excitement bites through the phone. "I'm on my way now! I miss you so much it hurts."

Guilt and anxiousness are the only emotions I can feel right know. Guilt that he is misunderstanding my invitation and anxiousness to rid myself of this guilt. I can't stand another minute of this. I have to tell him the truth. I must break this off with him today.

"What time can you be here, Daniel?"

"I will be there in less than twenty minutes."

"Okay. Please don't be late. Emmy is picking me up for church."

"I thought we were going to spend some time together today. You didn't say anything about going to church."

Here we go again.

"I know, but there's no time to argue about this now."

Daniel huffs into the phone. "I am on my way."

I get dressed quickly. I never put any thought into how I dress around Daniel, besides none of that matters anymore anyway. I sit idle for the rest of the time. While waiting, I rehearse everything I know I need to say. Some of the options I come up with are straight forward and in my estimation cruel. Debating on how to sugarcoat the truth, I decide on not telling him about Joseph and to just express how our differences are too much for me right now. Yes, I have given him this explanation before and no it hasn't worked. Just as I am trying to come up with yet another way to say, "I can't be with you anymore," the door rings. I hear my mom greet Daniel and then his footsteps are pounding up the stairs. Before I can sit up on the bed he opens the door and walks right in. He looks at me, then hustles over to hug me.

"Hey, Baby."

Oh how I HATE when he calls me that. He holds me tightly to him for several minutes and I allow it. My heart feels like it is go to burst from the pain I know I he and I will feel when this is finally over. When he peals himself off of me, he looks me in my eyes and recites the words I used to long so much to hear.

"I love you, Naomi."

I silence the guilt raging war inside of me. I don't say anything in return. Those same words just won't come.

"Naomi?"

He looks at me as though he has seen something he doesn't want to see. His arms fall to the sides of me.

"What is it? Is there something wrong?"

"Yeah, there is." I slide to the edge of the bed.

"Did I do something?" he asks.

The pity I've felt for two whole years makes it's appearance and I am lost in a day dream—a replay of the dream I had of him. Tears form in my eyes. My vision is blurred.

He grabs me again. "Aww, Baby, don't cry. Please tell me what it is. Is it a dream you had last night?"

Welcoming his comfort, I cry into his shoulder. I chicken out once again.

"Yeah."

"Tell me about it. Maybe it will help. Was it about me?"

"No."

Should I tell him about the dream I just wrote down? I need to tell him something. Something to completely change the subject because I can't do this break up today.

"I had a really bad dream last night. Armageddon was happening and it started here, in Georgia."

Daniel's icy blue eyes grow colder. He peers down at me. "Tell me about it—" he gets down on his knees in front of me, "give me every detail."

His anticipation causes something to shift inside of me. A huge lump grows in my throat. I can't speak. Maybe this wasn't a good idea after all. If I reveal this dream to him, he wouldn't let me rest until it's published in that stupid magazine.

"Nevermind, Daniel. If I tell you, I won't hear the end of it."

He slowly stands to his feet.

"Naomi, this isn't about you, you need to think of everyone else." He grabs me by my shoulders and I am shuck by his sudden contact. "Come on, Naomi. Tell me."

His grip tightens.

"Ow, Daniel. You are hurting me."

Daniel's eyes glass over, then refocuses. He slowly moves his hands to my face and gently runs his fingers over my cheeks.

"I'm sorry, Naomi. It's just that," he kisses me in between every other word, "this is serious and I think it's about time you take it seriously."

I flinch each time his lips touch mine. At this point I'm annoyed. Please stop kissing me, I want to shout, but instead I push him away and focus on the conversation at hand.

"Oh, please Daniel. All you are concerned about is seeing my dream in that stupid magazine and the money I will get for it. I will not be held accountable for what will happen when people start to get a little paranoid."

Daniel shakes his head. "No. That's not what it is."

He closes the space between us.

"People need to prepare and you are not giving them that chance."

"Guess what, Daniel, you are right. People do need to prepare. What you don't seem to get is that the preparation isn't only physical. Mental and spiritual preparation is essential. There's no way to stop what is coming. The end of all creation is inevitable! Everything comes to an end at some point. All we can do to be sure we are on the right side of things is seek Jesus. He's the only savior in this story."

He releases my face. Pacing the space between me and the door, he clenches his fists.

"I am so sick of hearing about this *Jesus*."

The fear I have turns into anger at the sight of his inflamed face.

I shout, "Well Daniel, you know exactly what to do if you don't want to hear about him."

He stops pacing and his chest moves up and down. The sight of him reminds me of a caged bull, but I'm to anger to back down now.

"Just leave, Daniel!".

Then, I have a flashback of the screams, the fire, the chaos.

"This dream is about what will happen to those who don't know Jesus. It's a warning to all those who do not have a relationship with *him*. Daniel, this dream is a warning to you too."

He looks at me like I have just threatened his life and it sends a chill down my spine. Then when I think he is about to yell at me, he a loud laugh bursts from his chest. He's so loud, I hold my hands up to my ears, hoping my mom doesn't hear. When he stops, he walks over to me, close enough that I can feel the steam rising from his body.

"I am eighteen years old, Naomi, and I have yet to hear from this Jesus you talk about all the time. Tell me, how I am supposed to believe in someone I can't see."

"Can you see love? No! But. you can feel the effects of love, right?" I take a few steps toward him, "Just believe in him Daniel, research him, do what ever you need to do and I promise you will not come up short. It's simple. What do you have to lose?"

"Naomi!"

My mom calls from down stairs.

I pause, stuck between hearing his reaction to what I just said and answering my mom. Daniel is more important in this moment, but I answer my mom anyway.

"Yes, Mom!" I yell.

"Come here for a moment, please!"

"Okay. Coming!" I yell back. "I will be right back, don't go anywhere." I say, as I walk backwards toward the door.

Daniel calmly walks over to my bed and sits.

"I'll be here," he says.

I head down the hallway as quickly as I can. Mom's sitting on her bed holding a piece of mail.

"Naomi, can you read this to me. I got a letter from Aunt Destine's estate lawyer today."

"Mom, can't this wait until after Daniel goes home?"

"No it cannot, Ma'am. Destine has been gone for years. Why is he writing me now?"

I walk over to her, exhaling in the process. If only she knew what was going on in my room right now. Daniel even contemplating changing is life is huge. I talk the letter from her hands and begin to read. Mom fidgets wither her robe until I lift my eyes from the letter.

"He is inviting you to a meeting about Aunt Destine's estate." I hand the letter back over to her.

Confusion creases her already aging face. "Can you come with me, Naomi? I can't keep up with all that lawyer talk. You know that. "

"Sure, Mom. Is there anything else?" I ask, shoving my hands in my pockets.

I hope that's it. I have to get back to Daniel.

Mom looks over the letter again. Reading has never been a strength of hers, but she has always been relentless in trying.

"No, that's it."

"Okay. We can talk more about it later."

I back out of the room and as soon as I reach the threshold I turn around and jog down the hallway back to my room. When I get there Daniel is gathering his bag. He jumps when he hears me close the door.

"Hey, you're leaving so soon. Usually it takes me hours to get you out the door." I laugh.

"Yeah, I just got a text. My mom needs me home right away." He hurries to the door.

"Okay. Call me later."

He doesn't turn around.

"Yeah. Later."

Then, he is gone. Confused that there was no kiss goodbye, nor an 'I love you,' I sit down on the bed hopeful that we can continue this conversation later.

TEN

round 10:30, Emmy picks me up for church which is the case every Sunday. When I get in the car, she immediately knows something is wrong.

"Naomi, you are lying, but I know it's about Daniel."

"Okay," I say, knowing she's right and hoping she just leaves well enough alone.

Emmy—she has been my best friend since eighth grade. We met during the most usual circumstances.

One day, after P.E., I went into the locker room to change and heard someone shouting back by the showers. I ran toward the noise to see what was going on. All of the girls had formed a circle and Rhonda Gillis, the bully of Northside Middle School, was in the center of it. She was staring down a scrawny redhead. Supposedly, her the redhead wanted her boyfriend. I watched the redhead's eyes tear up as Rhonda poked her thick index finger in her face detailing how she was going to beat her up. When the tears finally began to fall from her eyes, I couldn't take it anymore. I pushed my way to the center of the circle and stood right in between the two girls. Everyone was afraid of Rhonda, but I wasn't. I knew her bark was louder than her bite and she knew I wouldn't budge, no matter how many threats she dished out. After a brief stare down, Rhonda slowly began to back away, along with the crowd. When the locker room was clear, I went into one of the stalls to grab some tissue. "Here wipe your eyes," I said to the girl. "She's not going to bother you anymore." I stayed with her until she was ready to face our peers again and from that moment on, we have been inseparable.

Emmy has been with me through everything, but now I need her help. After church is out, I plead with her the entire ride home until she finally agrees to let me borrow her car tonight. Although I didn't tell her what for, she agrees to let me borrow the car on the condition that I pick her up on time. Assuring her I will, I quickly head in the house before she tries to get any information out of me.

According to Joseph's text the restaurant is only a forty-five minute drive from my house and about twenty minutes from Emmy's job. I have no doubt I will make it to Emmy by 9 and home by curfew. When I get to the restaurant, I flip the visor down to check to see if my lip gloss is still giving a glossy shine. my face. Because the air is thick with humidity this time of the year, I decided to do my hair in a tight bun so that I don't end up with a frizzy mess by the end of the night. I feel confident with my chosen outfit—pin-striped ivory and taupe capri-pants and a taupe colored, short sleeve top with a lace embroidered ivory cardigan underneath. Flat sandals to match, with ivory and gold seashells decorating the sash across my foot. Not being much of an accessory person, I went with a simple pair of dangling sea shell earrings and a necklace to match.

Stepping out of the car I scan the parking lot for Joseph. I have no idea what his car looks like so I text him to let him know I am here. As I walk toward the entrance I look at my surroundings noticing how cozy and private the restaurant is, nestled back in sparse woods. It sits cutely on a hill, adjacent to a river lit by lights strung along a boardwalk. Not many cars are parked at the restaurant, but there are at least 50 cars parked along the river. Couples walking hand and hand sends my thoughts back to Joseph.

"Wow."

I hear from just a few feet away. I turn around to see Joseph walking towards me with a wide smile. His casual white, t-shirt and khaki cargo shorts look so good on him. I hold back the impulse to greet him with a hug and try to control myself from smiling too big.

Joseph stops right in front of me—still smiling. I laugh because I don't know what else to do.

"Hey," I say.

"Hey yourself!" He eyes me from head to toe. "Hey, we kind of match!"

An unknown surge pulses through me.

"Yeah. I see that. I wasn't sure how to dress. We got off the phone so quickly yesterday, I didn't have time to ask."

"I think you did pretty good without my help," he says.

From the warmth gathering at my cheekbones, I know for sure I'm blushing. I turn away to watch the river. He steps up beside me, close enough for me to feel his arm brush against mine.

"I love coming here," he says. "It's always nice to get away and come somewhere where nobody knows your name."

"Thanks for choosing this place."

We stand there watching the boats and people move for a while before I feel his hand touch mine.

"Come on, I am starving."

The server seats us near a window that over looks the river. It's so impressive it's hard to focus on anything else. Joseph lets me take it all in and orders for the both of us. He assures me I will love everything on the menu, so I trust him. When he finishes, he reaches across the table with his hands inviting mine to join his. Slowly, I place my hands in his, feeling 100 ways all at once.

Is this okay? Is this cheating?

I don't care. He clutches my hands giving them a gentle squeeze as though he can hear my thoughts. Eye contact is made and I am adrift.

His eyes narrow. "What's on your mind?"

"I'm fine, just enjoying the view."

I remove my hands from his to adjust my napkin on my lap—not that it was needed, but because guilt is looming.

"How was your day?" What is it you do again? I don't remember you telling me."

He straightens up and clears his throat. "I do investigation work for the government."

"What!" My eyes grow big.

"Yeah, well—not officially. Right now, I'm just doing office work to get work experience. I'm still considered a rookie. In two years and after 1,000 examinations," he laughs, "I should be eligible to go out into the field."

"Wow! That's great, Joseph," is all I can manage to get out.

I'm shocked at how much Joseph has accomplished in just a few years after high school.

Our conversations is paused when our waitress returns with our food. As she sits the plates in front of us my stomach growls.

Joseph half smiles and says, "Your stomach is going to thank me for this."

Joseph ordered sweet and sour chicken, fried rice, and some stir-fried beef with carrots and green beans sitting on a bed of white rice—family style. Although these dishes are familiar, everything looks and smells elevated.

"You ready for a flavor explosion?"

"Oh yes." I lick my lips waiting to see if he will decide to pray with me, do a silent prayer, or not pray at all. When the waitress gathers her tray and leaves, Joseph grabs both of my hands, and then, he prays.

"Father, thank you for this day. Thank you for the beautiful company and seeing fit for us to meet. I don't take this for granted. And, God, bless this wonderful meal we are about to eat, in Jesus' name, Amen."

When I open my eyes, Joseph is staring at me.

"What?" I giggle, removing my hands from his.

Joseph is full of smiles. Spooning up a mouth full of his chicken, he stares off at the view. All I can do is wonder what he sees in me. I'm eighteen with a few months left in school. What can I offer him? He doesn't notice my curious stare, so I draw his attention with the most direct question I can muster.

"What are your intentions with me?"

Joseph stops chewing. His eyes dart over in my direction. His adam's apple bobs up then down as he swallows. I don't regret the question, nor do I plan on accepting a vague answer. My Aunt Destine told me once, "If you want a clear and direct answer, ask a clear and direct question, this leaves no room for ambiguity." At the time I didn't know what ambiguity meant, but that's beside the point.

"You sure know how to get someone's attention, don't you?"

I break the only etiquette rule of fine dining I know and put both elbows on the table, propping myself up.

"Well, I am waiting."

Just then, my cell phone buzzes. I hesitate to look at it. I decide against it. Then, Joseph's smile disappears. His face is like a flint.

"Naomi, my only intention is to get to know you. That's all."

My phone buzzes again and I immediately know who it is.

"Joseph, really? No man just wants to get to know a girl—

there's always something more to it," I say, rolling my eyes up into the air.

How stupid I have been thinking this mature and almost established *man* wants me. What have I been thinking. My phone buzzes again and this time it buzzes continuously.

"Sorry." I get up from the table. "I have to take this."

I speed walk out of the restaurant before I pull the phone out of my bag. To my surprise, it's my mom.

"Hey, Mom. Is everything okay?"

"Yes! Why haven't you responded to my texts, Naomi!"

"I'm sorry, Mom. I thought you were Daniel and I didn't think it was as good idea to answer him while on a date with someone else."

"Oh. Well, how is everything going? I just wanted to check on you."

"It's…it's going okay." I peek over my shoulder to see if Joseph is still seated at the table. He is, but he isn't eating. His figures tap on the table in cadence with is right knee.

"Naomi?"

"Yes, Mom."

"Look, you aren't doing anything wrong. You are simply getting to know someone you have found an interest in."

My eyes move from Joseph to the the river. "You're right. I just need to relax. I'm kinda giving him a hard time," I laugh.

"Don't," she says. "You never know. This Joseph just might be the one."

"Mom—I just met him."

"Well, it won't hurt to spend time with him and find out."

I turn back to look at Joseph, who is in the same exact position, tapping and bobbing.

"You're right. Let me get back to him okay, Mom. I will be home after I pick up Emmy."

I hang up with her feeling a little guilty about abruptly leaving him like that. When I return, he stands just as he sees me approaching the table. He pulls my chair out.

"Thank you."

"Everything okay," he asks.

"Yeah. It was my mom. She was just checking on me."

My conscience won't allow me to look him in the eyes. All he has been nothing but courteous and nice to me. Why am I balking?

"I don't know what to say, Joseph. This is all so serial to me. I mean…meeting you the way I did and now we are here… and…"

He leans across the table, his eyes glowing in the dim lighting. "It's okay Naomi. I get it. This is new for me too. I've never been so…I've never felt…"

I wait, but he can't seem to find his words either. Silence hugs our space as we both stare into each other's eyes. I break the stare and pick my spoon up, trying to refocus my attention. Joseph holds his position and then reaches across the table for my hand. I give it to him.

"I'll wait on you," he says.

"What? Wait for what?"

"For you to turn twenty….or thirty, or however old you think you need to be."

I fidget with my napkin. "So you think this is about how old you are and not about how I still have high school to finish and college?"

"Yes, I do think that has something to do with it. Like I said, I will wait for you."

Hearing him say that stops the chaos ensuing in my head and sets my world back on it's axis. I didn't know I needed to hear that, but I did.

ELEVEN

After we take a walk along the river. I check my watch and it's almost eight o'clock, which is good because Emmy doesn't get off for another hour. Now that we have talked about the large elephant between us, I find myself wanting to know more about this guy who is so eager to know all there is to know about me.

"So, Joseph, tell me more about what you do?" I ask. "I've always wondered what FBI agents do all day."

He smiles. "You know, the same stuff you see on television."

"Come on. Like what are you investigating now?"

He hangs his head. "To tell you the truth, Naomi, I haven't been given a legitimate assignment yet. I have only been with the bureau few months. Since I am just a rookie, they send me on coffee and donut runs all day. Most of the time, I sit in the office going through cold cases, searching for undiscovered evidence or taking certifications."

"Wow, I always thought the donut jokes were a myth," I laugh.

"Nope. They really do love their donuts. I thought this experience would be more than just sitting around being someone's secretary."

His tone is solemn and I kind of feel for him.

Leaning into him, I joke, "Don't worry, they will give you a real case soon, I mean, you *are* technically a rookie."

"Enough about me," he says as he captures my hand in his.

At first, I hesitate, considering that he told me he would wait, but I hold on to his hand anyway and it feels good.

"So, how are you and Daniel doing? Did you break up with him yet?"

I steal a side glance at him, "Uh, no. And if I haven't do you think he would be okay with you holding my hand every chance you get?"

He lifts our entwined hands to take a closer look.

"Nope. I wouldn't like it either, but we're just friends holding hands. Right?"

He looks at me for recognition, then clears his throat.

"If you want me to, I can stop."

I smile, knowing I want his hand touching mine just as much as he wants it.

"No, thank you." I softly squeeze his hand. "I think I love this."

He looks over at me. "Good."

We walk in the cool and quiet of the night for what seems like a mile. I imagine us as a couple, in love, planning our future together. Something inside of me tells me he may be envisioning the same thing, but I banish the thought quickly.

All of the sudden Joseph stops walking. He steps in front of me and looks me right in my eyes. He is so close I can smell his familiar cologne. The bursts of sunset in his eyes warm draw me I closer. He lifts his hands to my face then pulls me so close our lips meet. Ice cream. Ice cream is all that comes to mind in this moment—coffee flavored ice cream. Smooth, soft, energizing, and indulgent. It all happens so fast that I have no time to enjoy it fully. Before I know it's over our noses are just slightly touching and I am left feeling like I just ate my last spoon of creamy deliciousness and I want more.

My eyes are still closed, but I know he is close—his breath warming my lips. Still relishing in what I just felt, he pulls me into him. Then, I am spun back into a familiar memory, the memory of me with someone embracing me, and our bodies floating up into the clouds. The shock of it all brings me back down to earth. Maneuvering my way out of his arms, I start walking again. Joseph catches up with me. Silently he walks beside me and his hand finds mine again.

"I'm sorry Naomi, if…if I offended you—I mean…I hope I didn't offend you?" He looks at me, searching my expression for an answer."

Honestly, it was the best moment of my entire life and I want to tell him. I want to share with him how he makes me feel like the only important thing in his universe. I want him to kiss me again and again, and I want him to know that I want him to kiss me just like that everyday for the rest of my life.

But I don't tell him. I mean, what am I even thinking. One door has to be closed before I can open another.

"No, Joseph. I am not offended."

I share a smile with him just to affirm him.

"But, you *did* say you would wait for me."

We walk a little further after that, finding a cozy bench on the river. We talk for what seems like hours, getting to know each other even more. In talking to Joseph, I realize how easy it can be talking to someone who is mature and also spiritual. Who knew a conversation could go on so long without an any arguments, advances, or stray hands finding their way up my shirt.

When we return to Emmy's car, Joseph walks me around to the driver's door and opens it for me. Before I get in, I turn to him and throw my arms around his neck.

"Well, Ms. Naomi, I guess I will see you soon?"

"Of course." I whisper into his ear.

Then, I get into the car fully aware of what can't wait another day.

TWELVE

My mom is fast asleep on the couch when I get home. As usual, I pull her blanket over her and leave her there for the time being. Eventually she'll get up and get in her bed, when she realizes I am home.

Climbing the stairs, I a replay tonight in my head. It all comes back in full color and my companions of fireflies do a dance in my chest. The kiss we shared was so sweet. *Oh my goodness I just cheated and I'm day dreaming about it. How am I going to tell Daniel this?*

I'm not. I say out loud. I will spare him the details. All he needs to know is I can no longer do this relationship thing with him.

Once I shower sleep into my pajamas, then my phone buzzes. I pick it up and notice a from Joseph.

Joseph: I hope you made it home safe.

Naomi: I did. Thank you for tonight. I enjoyed getting to know you.

Joseph: Same! And the pleasure was all mine. Sweet dreams, Naomi.

I lie in bed thinking about Daniel. He hasn't called me and that is very unusual. By this time of day I would have received at least twenty texts if I hadn't reach out to him first. I don't pick up the phone to text him because, now, all I can think of is Joseph. Before I realize it, my daydreaming turns into actual dreams—all about Joseph.

I wake up around 7am grateful I didn't necessarily have to be at school. My first two periods are electives, which I don't really need the credits for, but my attendance is important to me. Emmy has the same situation; classes she doesn't really need to attend, yet we make an effort. I lie back down for a bit, contemplating if I should call her to catch a ride to school and if I should write down the dreams I had about Joseph. I go back and forth in my head about them both before I decide to just get dressed.

On the way to the bathroom, to brush my teeth, I wonder if the dreams about Joseph are even worth writing down. What's the use of writing down 'soulish dreams' as Aunt Destine used to call them. Although these soulish dreams were conjured up by my most dominate thoughts the day before, she did say writing them down would help me remember something I missed. I settled it. Writing them down won't hurt.

I finish in the bathroom, then head back into my room. I grab my phone off my bed to text Emmy in the process. Mindlessly I reach for my dream journal with my other hand and my hand fakes flat. My fingers do a little more searching of their own as I continue to text Emmy. My hand crawls to the left, then to the right, still coming up short. When I hit the send button, I kneel down, sliding my hand further to the rear of the armoire.

It isn't here.

Thinking maybe it fell, I look in the crevasses beside my television and then underneath the armoire.

Still nothing.

Keeping calm, I run downstairs. I look in the kitchen, the living room, my mom's room (even though she would never touch my journal), and still come up short. When I have searched every nook and cranny downstairs, I run back upstairs and turn my room upside down. Then, the panic sets in. My hands start to shake and the room to spins.

Wait!

I haven't checked in my backpack. Jumping right into action once again, I grab my backpack and move my hand all around only to find—nothing. Tired and sweaty, I crash on my bed. Lying flat on my back, I look up at the ceiling, defeated. I try to think through every moment of the last time I had my journal.

"Okay, Naomi, think!" I said out loud. *The last time I had the journal I wrote down the dream about the earthquakes. Then, I placed it right back in its normal spot…but it's not there!*

All at once, the thoughts of having lost something so essential take over all of my emotions. Tears race down the sides of my face.

Please help me, God.

I close my eyes. Then, I get a clear vision of Daniel's flustered face before he left my house in an unusual hurry yesterday. I see him and I arguing over my dream. My eyes shoot open. I call Emmy.

THIRTEEN

In ten minutes, Emmy is at my house beeping the horn like a maniac. I practically fly down the stairs and out the front door. As I approach the car, Emmy gets out and walks around to the passenger side door, mumbling under her breath. My thoughts are racing; *what if this idiot has already submitted it; no one will believe it anyway; where is he; should I go to the school or to The Spark?* I get in the car. Emmy is already in the car reclined in her seat. With her eyes closed she spouts, "So why am I here again?"

"Daniel took my journal Emmy, and I have to get it back before he does something stupid."

"And where are we going?" she asks.

"I am not sure. Sometimes he goes to first period, sometimes he doesn't."

"Okay, wake me up when this is over."

I enter town going ten miles over the speed limit. The streets are busy with nine to fivers arriving to work, so I slow down when I realize I may see him buzzing around on his stupid little scooter. I glance around searching for any signs of him, then I lay eyes on the tallest standing building in downtown Augusta, Spark Towers. In the very first parking space, in front of the tower, is Daniel's bright red scooter. I literally see red and everything goes mute, expect for my heart. It is as though my heartbeat is playing in surround sound. Trying to quickly find a parking space, Ms. Rayburn's voice echoes through, "stay away from the tower." The memory of her warning makes my stomach turn sour.

"Well, how am I supposed to stay clear of the tower when this imbecile has taken *my* journal inside of it!" I shout.

Emmy jumps awake as I whip into a parking space I just found. The momentum and her sudden movement sends her flying back into her seat.

"That idiot got here as soon as it opened," I say to Emmy.

She pulls herself back up. "What is going on, girl?"

I get out of the car, "I will be right back," I say, then I shut the door.

With no hesitation, I sprint across the street, dodging two speeding cars. When I reach for the handle, I am so startled by what I see that I stop in my tracks. Daniel is walking toward the door. When he sees me, he pauses. All of the color leaves his face and he is as pale as a ghost. He looks to his right and then to his left.

Is this fool going to try and run from me?

I immediately pull open the door and there, right in the lobby we face off.

I shout, "What are you doing Daniel!"

The people minding their own business pause in mid stride. Daniel's chest caves in and he ducks his head. He holds out his right hand and there it is—*my* journal. I walk up to him and snatch it away. Every single curse word my mom and Aunt Destine told me never to use comes to my mind. I tighten my jaw to ensure they don't spill out. Daniel's mouth is moving, but I can't hear anything. Aunt Destine's voice stills me, *hold your peace.* So I do. I clutch my journal to my chest, then I turn to leave. When I reach the door, I feel a hand on my shoulder.

Thinking it's Daniel I pull away ready and willing to give Daniel an ear full, but when I turn around there *he* is—the man who has been haunting my dreams since I was a little girl. The sound of my heart beat stops. The entire universe seems to have seized movement.

I take in the man standing in front of me. He is just as hideous as I remember him. His paper thin, silver hair hangs just below his shoulders. It's so thin, I can see right through to his scalp. My entire body begins to shake as he opens his mouth to speak and just like that the volume is all the way up again.

"Miss. Peterson," he says.

The sound of his voice startles me. The rattling of his throat makes him sound as though he hasn't spoken in a thousand years. My insides recoil.

"I have read the premonition you have so graciously submitted. Your contribution is well appreciated, and we here at *The Spark* look forward to seeing your writings in the next edition."

I try helplessly to back away from him, but the door won't allow it. I feel as though I am in a dream. Yes! I must be dreaming. I try to scream, but there's sand in my throat. The words won't come. I can't breathe.

He stares at me waiting for a response, but all I can do is search his eyes—his eyes— milky gray stones. I've never seen his eyes and I wish I never had.

"Do you have anything to say for yourself, Miss. Peterson?" he asks.

I cower on the door willing it to open—willing someone to come wake me up from this nightmare.

"Well, this young man," he points a long bony tentacle at the creep staring at me with pity, "has shared so many interesting things about you?"

Still words allude me.

Then possibly annoyed that I haven't responded, he gives me a vicious glare, "I will be seeing you then, Miss. Peterson. Your dream should give the world something to think about."

He sneers in Daniel's direction, places a black fedora on his head and pushes the door behind me open, leaving the building. His closeness shuts down all faculties to run, so I just watch him walk away, still frozen in time.

Daniel walks over to me blocking my way out the door. "Do you know who that was Naomi? Do you know who you just missed the opportunity to talk to?"

All of my emotions come flooding back and I am in full motion and control of my body again. I push Daniel in the chest as hard as I can. "I don't care!" I push past him attempting to leave.

He blurts out, "It was the owner of Spark, Naomi! The owner!"

I stop in mid stride and turn around to face him once again. "Yes, I know exactly who that was, Daniel" I take more steps toward my so-called best friend. "It was literally my worst nightmare! Or couldn't you see that?"

As I get closer, he extends his hands in front of his face, attempting to block what he thinks might be another blow.

"Naomi, I am sorry, but don't you think you are being selfish? I mean, if your dream really is a premonition of what's to come, shouldn't you warn us."

"God has been warning us for thousands of years! Read the Gospel of Matthew, Daniel, or Revelations, Daniel!" At that moment I realize that every single person in the lobby is still watching this entire scene unfold. Two men in black suits approach us. I lower my head, ashamed at how Daniel has managed to push me out of character.

As they close in on me, I assure Daniel, "I will never trust you again."

He reach out for my hand.

"Don't touch me! And stay away from me!"

The two me reach me.

"I never want to see you again!" I shout.

One of the men says, "Ma'am, you need to leave."

With respect, I turn around and leave quietly.

When I am out of the tower, I take in a chest full of fresh air. I try to blow it out slowly and savor its essence, but my lungs won't allow it. I heave in several breaths of air, willing my heart to slow down so that no one notices me having a heart attack. *Ten, nine, eight…*I try to count down to one. A woman with fierce black pumps stops and places a hand on my back. I can't see her face, but her shoes are the best pair of pumps I have ever seen.

She asks, "Are you okay?"

"Yes, Ma'am." I manage in between breathes.

"Are you sure?"

"I am." I stand up and begin walking in the opposite direction.

I walk for what seems like thirty minutes. Everything in me wants to turn around, walk back into that building and rip Daniel's head off, but I don't.

Cast the care, Naomi. I hear a voice say.

I am reminded of a time when I was a little girl. I was over at my Aunt Destine's house. She was in the kitchen making me some of her famous ramen noodles.

We always sat watching soap operas with a juicy bowl of beef ramen. I hated watching those drama filled shows, but I loved spending time with her. Aunt Destine would become so invested in her shows that she would speak of the characters as though they were real. She'd yell at the television and call up her friends say, "Girl she done left William for that low down Doctor. You think they gonna get back together?" At my young age, I hung on every word, laughing on the inside.

On this particular day, Aunt Destine had to switch over because someone was calling her on the other line. Still listening, I realized she was talking to my mom. She was calling from work and from the looks of Aunt Destine's face, my mom must have been pretty upset.

"Johanna calm down and tell me exactly what happened," she said. "Uh, huh. Yeah. She what!" Aunt Destine jumped to her feet. "Stay put Johanna, don't you dare go back in there," she told my mom, "I will be there in five minutes."

In seconds, Aunt Destine had on her shoes.

She grabbed me by my arm. "Come on girl. We have to go get your mamma before she kills somebody."

Once we got there, I could see my mom sitting in her blue Honda Accord. With her head down and from what I could see she was laughing, we approached the car.

"Oh Lord," Aunt Destine murmured, "I hope she hasn't done something crazy."

We pulled up right beside her car. Aunt Destine throwing open her door just as she put the car in park, leaped out.

"Open this door Johanna," she shouted as she banged on the window.

I remember Mom continuing to grin looking down at her lap. Aunt Destine bangs some more, momma continued to ignore her. This went on for some time.

Sitting in the car, my preteen brain wondered what could be happening. Why was mom ignoring Aunt Destine? Why was Aunt Destine so upset?

"Johanna," Aunt Destine said in a more calm voice, "you know that she isn't worth it, you know that he isn't worth it. Look over there in that car. You see what you have to live for?"

At that moment mom looked at me. She stared right into my eyes. The most unforgettable moment was when she begin to cry uncontrollably and so did I. I kept my eyes trained on hers and after a while of us staring at each other, she pulled her hands to her face and then I saw what she was looking at in her lap. It was a silver pistol. I had seen this gun before. It was the same gun mom kept under her pillow when daddy didn't make it home at night.

"Now, roll down the window Jo. Come on, let's get out of here." Aunt Destine said.

Finally, momma opened the door, falling into Aunt Destine's arms. Slowly got out of the car and ran to the two of them, wrapping my tiny arms around them both.

Mom weeped into Aunt Destine's neck, "I am tired Des. I am so tired."

"I know Jo, I know. Sometimes we have to step back into ourselves and cast all that mess, all the heartache to God. That's the only way we are going to overcome. Cast your care, Sis."

With that memory still resonating in my thoughts, I wait for the coming cars to pass and approach Emmy's car. When I go to open the door, I notice Emmy is nowhere to be found and the door is locked. I scan the sidewalk and the shops on the street and there's no sign of her. Frustrated, I lean against the car and stare down at my journal. I pull the gold string of fabric and open the journal to my last entry. Pieces of turn paper fall to the ground. Shocked, I slam the book closed. *He tore the page out*! I bite back the urge to scream, then I turn around and bang the sides of my fist into the hood of the car.

"Is everything okay?" I hear a familiar voice say.

I ignore the voice. The sound of my heartbeat has returned and now the voice is muffled.

Cast your care, I hear Aunt Destine's voice push through the base in my ear drums.

I feel a presence behind me lifting me from the car. The voice is closer now, "Naomi, are you okay?" Arms are now holding me and tears begin to flow. I can barely see his face. His hands cup face and lift it to his. It's him.

"Joseph?"

Then, the ground falls from my feet.

FOURTEEN

In the darkness I hear Emmy's voice.

"Is she okay?"

Many voices are speaking at the same time, but there's one voice that rattles me. I hike my shoulders at the sound of the voice and they all fall silent. A warm embrace envelops me and I hear Joseph's voice.

"Shhh, I think she's coming back to us."

I open my eyes to see a throng of people surrounding me. Joseph is the first face I see, so I smile, then Emmy, two men in black suits (the same men who threw me out of Spark Towers), a lady (possibly the one that asked me if I was okay), and *him*. When I lay eyes on him, all I want to do is punch him in the face.

"Hey, Naomi." Joseph asks, still holding me in his arms. "Are you okay?"

Emmys whines, "I am sorry I left the car Naomi, it was getting too hot. I…"

I groan as I sit up on the ground, disregarding the rest of what she has to say. "I am fine. What happened?"

Joseph starts, "Well, you were over here beating up this poor car when you caught my attention, so I came over to see what was up. You started crying and then you just collapsed."

"It's my fault," Daniel moans. "I shouldn't have..." and he stops mid-sentence and looks around at all of us.

"Yes, you are so right. You shouldn't have," I say.

Joseph helps me to my feet and asks, "He shouldn't have what?"

I turn to him, getting in between his glare and Daniel's face. "Can you take me home, Joseph?"

"Yeah. Sure I can."

His eyes are soft and caring. I can stare into them for a lifetime, but Daniel's words pierce through my thoughts.

"Wait a minute, you two know each other?"

"Uh duh. He's said her name like three times already." Emmy chimes.

Joseph adjusts my limp body against his and places my arm around his broad shoulders. Emmy and Daniel stare at each other.

Joseph addresses Emmy like he has known her for years. "Just head to school Emmy, I got her from here. He ignores Daniel, beginning to guide me towards his car.

"Wait a minute," Daniel broods. He jumps in front of Joseph to block his path.

"Wait for what? For you to make her so upset again that she passes out? I don't think so."

Joseph pushes past him and I avoid eye contact. I allow Joseph to take half of my weight on himself, too weak to respond. Holding my journal tightly to my chest, I don't bother to look to see if Daniel is pursuing us. Once in the car, the weight of it all hits me again. Eventually the its too heavy to think about anymore and I doze off, losing myself to the darkness.

The sounds of laughter interrupt my dreams of running over Daniel with an eighteen wheeler. I wake up frustrated that I couldn't see it through to the end. I sit up slowly, realizing I am in the my living room. A little light-headed, I recognize the voices coming from the kitchen—Joseph and my mom. I get up, cautiously, and walk to the kitchen. There, Joseph and my mom sit at the table with two coffee mugs. Mom is in good spirits and she doesn't seem the least bit angry that some strange *man* brought me home. Joseph is in the middle of telling her some story about a kid who manages to send his unit on a wild goose chase. She is laughing so hard tears are filling her eyes. She stands to her feet, staggering, because the bitter sweet pain of the laughter won't allow her to sit anymore. She leans over the sink to keep herself standing. I reach the threshold of the kitchen and Joseph notices me, but he continues to tell the story.

"...so when his mom got to the school to pick him up early and the attendance secretary told her he was marked absent by all of his teachers. Little did we know, he was right there in our station."

Mom explodes into another fit of laughter. I lock eyes with him, admiring how he has managed to win my mom over without any help from me.

Joseph continues, "Well, the mom and the administrators had no idea, 'little Johnny' only wanted to spend the night in a real FBI station, so he pretended to get on the bus after his mom and dad left for work and made his way downtown. Yep, that's how I became Rookie of the Year. Returning 'Johnny' back to his mom."

Mom manages to get a grip of herself. "Wow, I haven't laughed like that sense Destine was alive."

Wiping the tears from her eyes, she notices me.

"Hey, Naomi," she says breathlessly. "As you can see, I met the famous Joseph. I mean, I just found out his name because someone never told me, but this is the friend you went to meet the other day, right?"

I walk over to the table and pull out a chair. "Yes ma'am, this is Joseph."

"Well, he is pretty funny. I never met a real FBI agent

before." She says raising one eyebrow, which usually means, we have to talk about this later.

Joseph gives off this shy grin I've never seen before. Mom on the other hand is glowing. Her hair is done, she has on fresh clothes and not that raggedy old bathrobe I can't seem to get rid of. She actually looks happy.

Mom gives me this enormous smile, then looks over at Joseph. So, how long have you been an agent?

"Ah, Ms. Peterson I told you I'm just a rookie. I haven't had a big case yet," he cuts his eye at her, "except for the case of the 'Runaway FBI Fanatic.'"

My mom bursts out laughing again, and I still, for the life of me, can't figure out what is so funny about the story. She finally calms down, probably noticing that Joseph and I haven't said one word to each other.

"Okay you two. I will get out of your hair. And Miss. Secretive Peterson, we need to talk."

I glare over at her and ask, "About?"

With both hands on her hips and a roll of her neck, she spouts, "How about, Mr. FBI bringing you home passed out."

"Okay, we can talk about that as long as afterwards you can talk to me about why you are all dressed up."

She smirks, does one of those struts she used to do when she was flirting with my dad and says, "Deal."

Joseph and I sit in silence for a few moments after my mom leaves. He sips from his cup, patiently, while I find the words to tell him how my so-called "boyfriend" submitted the most profound dream I have ever had, to the most corrupt magazine in the country.

"So how did you get me home seeing as how I was passed out and you didn't know where I lived?"

He sits his cup down, "First of all, I have training on how to find people, and second, you were smart to put your address on the inside of your journal." He chuckles, "I just put the address in my GPS and here we are."

"Please tell me you didn't read anything else from my journal."

Joseph straightens his face, "Naomi, I would never do something like that."

I hang my head, ashamed I even said that.

"I know you wouldn't. It's nice to hear some people respect other people's property."

Then, I hear a melody coming from the kitchen counter. A familiar tone that makes me cringe. Joseph gets up from his seat to get my phone for me.

"Oh, it's Danny boy."

I drop my face into my hands. "I am done with him."

I feel Joseph's warm hand touch my shoulder. "So are you ready to tell me what happened?"

My hands muffle my words. "It's a long story."

He moves his chair right beside mine. "All I have is time."

After several minutes and a pool of tears on the floor, I get through the entire story of how I ended up kissing the concrete in front of Spark Towers. When I finish, Joseph sits back in his chair—wide eyed.

"Why didn't you tell me about this dream?"

"I tried the night of our first date."

"And what stopped you?"

I can feel my face heat up as the words come out. "A kiss."

A small smile curls his lips. He leans into me.

"Oh. I guess that must have completely made you forget."

I push him off me and we laugh lightening the moment.

Then he straightens his posture, as though he wasn't just laughing, and becomes this stoned-faced FBI agent.

"We are going back to get your property. Their acquisition of this document was fraudulent."

My eyes light up at the thought, but then the image of the man I can't bear to face again fills my head.

"I can't Joseph," I whine into my hands.

"Why not, Naomi? You have every right. This dream is definitely important, but *The Spark* is not the right channel for it.

"It's not that Joseph," I stare down at the floor. "It's the man we have to see in order to get my property back."

"Who is he?"

I plant my face into my hands again. "That's another long story in itself," I whine.

FIFTEEN

After telling Joseph all about the owner of Spark and sharing the terrifying dream I have had since I was a little girl, he understands why I never want to go back to that place. I'm grateful because if it was Daniel, we would spend the rest of the day arguing about how stupid my fears are. Joseph and I agree the dream is a warning. Surprisingly, he remembered Ms. Rayburn's message for me, so we also agree to wait it out to see if we can fight this from a distance.

After Joseph leaves to head back to the office, I look around for my mom. First, I check in the living room to see if she was in her usual spot watching television, but she isn't. I go upstairs to find her in her bedroom, sitting on the edge of her bed, head down. She's holding something in her hand. I slowly push open the door, trying not to disturb her, but the creak draws her attention my way. When she looks at me, I can see the tears in her eyes.

I walk over and sit next to her. "Mom, what's wrong?"

Now, I see she is holding a picture of her and Aunt Destine. In the photo they are around my age posing cheek to cheek with their arms wrapped around each other. Their smiles are so big. I never seen my mom smile like that.

"I just miss her so much." She traces Aunt Destine's face with her finger, shaking her head.

"She's still with us, Mom. I feel her every day."

She turns to look at me, like she isn't sure of what I just said. Tears run down her face, "You can?"

I tell her the whole story, about the dream I had the other night. Then, I tell her all about Daniel stealing my journal and submitting it to Spark. I tell her how angry I was and how it led me to my memory of her sitting in the car holding the gun.

"You see mom, I believe that was Aunt Destin's way of reminding me of how anger can only lead to trouble. She may not be here physically, but she left us with so much of herself. The example she set will never die. She may not be here physically, but her wisdom is still in our hearts."

She nudges me, "You know, you are right, kiddo. Destine always said you are wise beyond your years?" Then, she throws her arm around me. "Do you know why I was sitting in the car that day holding the gun?"

"I have thought about asking, but I just never found the right time." I grab her hands and hold them in mine, the creases and ridges telling a story of their own. "You've been through a lot, mom. I never want to bring up something that could…" I stop mid sentence. Once again, holding back to avoid reminding her of the past.

She picks up the picture again. "It was a month before your dad left us. I had been hearing rumors about him being with another woman, but as usual I just ignored it. One night, I received a phone call from a strange woman. She said, 'Your husband is sleeping here on my couch, you might want to come and pick him up.' I was dumb-founded and thought some kid was doing prank calls, so I just hung up. A few minutes later, the phone rang again, the same number appeared on the caller-id, but this time it was your dad. From the sound of his voice, I knew he was drunk, so that immediately became my justification for him being at this women's house. I didn't want to accept the truth. He told me he would be coming home soon, but in the background I could hear her. She yelled, 'No you're not. I will kill you and her if you leave.' I dropped the phone. You see, she called just to let me know he was there, she didn't want me to pick him up, she wanted to let me know what was going on to of course—end our marriage."

"Is that why you brought the gun to work? Were you going to follow him?"

She stares straight ahead at the wall, as if she is right back there in the car that day.

"Your dad did come home that night, and before he did, I realized who the lady was that was calling my house. She was the same lady that was spreading the rumor at work. I recognized her voice.

"What did dad say when he got home?"

"We argued but not enough that it would wake you. He admitted that he was having an affair with her, but I was in denial. I just wanted to keep our family together. I went to work the next day anticipating she would get in my face, but she did something worse, something I never thought any human being would do."

"What did she do?"

"She pretty much told all of our coworkers things that only a wife would know about her husband. By the time the third co-worker came up to me to tell me about the new rumors, I was in a rage. I had to get out of there. That's how I ended up in the car. I knew if I didn't call Destine I would do something that I couldn't take back."

My dad, I know he did some hurtful things to my mom, but I didn't think he had the capacity to hurt my mom this way. All these years, this pain has consumed her, taking up every breath, leaving only a blurry image of her former self.

She finally blinks. Then she gets up and walks over to her dresser. She picks up her pearl earrings and begins putting them on.

"If you can remember, Naomi, two days later, I had my first nervous breakdown. I had to let go of the job, thank God, and was deemed disabled to work. Two months later, your dad left. I told him but, deep down, I didn't want him to. Shortly after, I had a second breakdown." She turns to face me, "I didn't want you to grow up knowing, I accepted a man cheating on me."

I stand to my feet, looking her straight in the eyes, "but Mom, you have been so unhappy without him, " and the tears start to flow. "I would have wanted you to be happy, Mom."

She walks over to me and wraps her arms around me.

"No, baby girl. I don't think I would have been happy continuing to live like that. I couldn't live knowing I let you, Destine and myself down." She squeezes me a little tighter, "But I am coming out of this pit I have been in. I now have something to look forward to." Still holding on to me she says, "Today, when I realized you weren't here to go with me to see your Aunt Destine's Attorney, I went on my own." She let's go of the embrace and walks back over to the dresser to put on her pearl necklace.

"Oh mom, I'm so sorry. I was trying to catch Daniel before he did something stupid. I completely forgot." I ball my fist up, my nails biting into my palms, just another reason to hate the very thought of his name.

"No. Don't be sorry. I needed to go on my own. The attorney had good news. She turns around, presenting a smile I haven't seen in years. "After years of draw backs and confusion about your Aunt Destine's estate, they finally worked out all of her debts." She walks over to me and grabs me by both of my shoulders. "Do you know your Aunt Destine saved over a half million dollars in her life-time!"

My mouth goes dry. I try to swallow, but I can't. My breathing is shallow. Mom laughs and begins to rub my back. I'm stunned.

"Yeah, baby girl, our struggling days are over! She left us a letter too. The lawyer said that she only wanted me to have it once I received the money and not before."

Still trying to catch my breath, I sit down. "Why?"

"I'm not sure honey, but what I am sure about is she had good reasons."

"When will we get the money?"

She goes over to her closet and pulls out some black pumps that I haven't seen her wear in at least a decade.

"Soon, baby girl. Soon." She smiles big. "Now, go get dressed. We are going out for dinner. We both need a pick-me-up." She grins and slides her feet into the pumps. "Wow, they still fit," she says as she prances to the body length mirror in the corner of her room. "So, what are you going to do about this thief issue, is Mr. FBI going to help you out?" She walks over to the doorway and turns off the light.

"Yeah, I hope we can figure something out, or the world is in for a huge scare."

She looks as if she is listening, but from the looks of her face and what I just said, she doesn't have a clue.

SIXTEEN

THREE WEEKS LATER

The birds singing a new song outside my window, annoying me to the point of submission. I drag myself out of bed, staggering to the bathroom. It's graduation day. Although this week should have been the most memorable considering it was my last days of high school, every morning I dreaded waking up. On Monday the newest edition of Spark hit the stands. And yes, my premonition was not only published, but it was the cover story for the month of May. After hearing about all of the legalities of retrieving my journal notes, I gave up on the pursuit and settled for it being published as anonymous. My mom was ready and willing to put up the money for the suit, but I didn't want Aunt Destine's hard earned money to go to waste, nor did I want Daniel to suffer through this either, even though I felt he deserved it. I was content with what they had, which was not the dream in its entirety. All I had managed to write down was the occurrences of the three earthquakes, where they hit, and the chaos afterwards. In the process of them ripping it out, they missed a page. There was so much more, but I thank God that was all I they stole. Tuesday crypt up, which was the day my mom announced she wanted to have a graduation party for me. This was completely unexpected, considering how much was going on, but Joseph Emmy and my mom all agreed that it was more of reason to have a party. They insisted it would cheer me up. Wednesday, Joseph and I had our second date, where we ran into Daniel at a local diner. I was dressed casually but cute. Joseph and I were just walking through the door, hand in hand, when we ran into Daniel as he was coming out. At first, a feeling of gratification filled me, but the look he gave me turned my stomach inside out just as quickly as the gratification came. It was a look of despair, a look you only see when someone you love has breathed their last. He stood motionless in the doorway looking at me as though he was truly watching me die, yet, I was in the happiest state of my life.

"Hi," was all I could manage.

Without a reply, he pushed the restaurant door open gently, disappearing into the night. Although Joseph and I hadn't as much as kissed each other on the cheek since our first date, the guilt of it all consumed me that day. Later on that night I called Joseph to ask if we could take it slow for a while, which included no more public appearances. He agreed with me even though I knew, deep down, he didn't want to. Deep down, I didn't want to either, but for some reason I still wanted to spare Daniel's feelings, even if it meant mine had to take a backseat.

Because of this, Thursday was painful to endure. Emmy, my mom, and I spent the day together, arguing over décor for the party, the food and any other menial detail I could care less about. All I could think about was Joseph. Hoping he would call me, text me, or maybe even email me. For him, not going out in public together, meant no more contact during the day. To go through an entire day without speaking to him and waking up the morning of my graduation without a voicemail or a text was even more heart wrenching. Now it's the day I close the book on my high school years. All of the events of the day before have led me to one conclusion: this is also the day I tell Joseph I want to be with him no matter who I hurt in the process. This is the day I tell him how I truly feel about him. Daniel and I had been on the brink of breaking up since our relationship started. Guilt has to take a backseat today. Although my feelings for Joseph are fresh, my feelings for Daniel are not important anymore. It hurts to lose someone you have grown to love, but I believe Joseph is my soul mate. Nothing is going to stop me from expressing that to him.

Sitting through graduation ceremonies has always been agonizing, but sitting through my own, with my best friend right in front of me, is something I will remember for the rest of my life. The speeches given are memorable, but the time we have all been waiting for—our names to be called—is finally here. Bitter sweet anticipation fills the air. When the person right in front of me name is called, I glance to where I know my mom is sitting. In a powder blue dress, she waves frantically. My eyes float to her right and there's Joseph. *He came.* In his hands is a large bouquet of white roses. His gorgeous smile illuminates me from the inside out and I feel an overwhelming emotion fill my heart. Everything in me wants to run to him, to hold him and to feel his arms around me. One day without him feels like centuries.

When my name is called, I walk across the stage I hear Emmy's voice chant my name, a few cheers here and there from friends. Then, I hear my mom and Joseph chant in a chorus, "We love you Naomi!" as I shake Principal Townsend's hand. Walking down the stairs, I hear a faint whisper from a familiar voice, "Well done, Baby Girl." Tears burn the edges of my lids and I look up into the rafters, which is as far as I can see in the moment, and I reply, "I love you, Aunt Destine."

Emmy and I try to say our final goodbyes to some of our favorite teachers, and invite a couple of more friends to the party, before we head out. As I am talking to my journalism teacher, Mrs. Reynolds's, Ms. Rayburn's, now burnt orange afro appears in the crowd. I hesitate to approach her. Then, I think, *what the heck*. I notice she's talking to another graduate, but she abruptly turns around and looks directly at me.

She is one weird character.

I almost turn around and walk away. But, this is just like her, finishing your sentences, calling out the answer to your question as you approach her desk, just flat out weird.

Smiling from ear to ear, in her thick Jamaican accent she says, "Miss. Peterson."

"Hi Ms. Rayburn. I just wanted to say goodbye, and thank you for the extra point you so graciously gave me."

"Well, you earned it," she bows her head. "I couldn't let my number one daydreamer graduate from high school with a 79 in Chemistry, now could I."

"Well, I appreciate it Ms. Rayburn."

I turn to walk away. Then I hear her excuse herself and my legs seem to move a little faster, but not fast enough. I feel a light touch on my shoulder.

"Miss. Peterson."

It's her. I stop in my tracks, but also beating myself up that I couldn't get away fast enough.

"Yes, Ms. Rayburn."

She dressed in a black gown just like every other teacher, but her's appear to have been stuffed somewhere tight and pulled out in haste, never pressed or steamed for such an occasion as this. She gives me a stern glare then cocks her head to the side.

"Did you take heed to my warning?"

I look at her and words escaped me.

She asks again, "Did you?"

"I tried, but some things were out of my control"

"I see," she says, then nods, "I see." She looks down at the floor.

"You see what."

Her head snaps back up and she fixes her eyes on mine. "You don't have control of what is about to happen, Naomi, but what you do have control over is how you handle what is set before and the people you surround yourself with. Don't be discouraged, stick with what God has given you and love as though there is no tomorrow. Time is of the essence."

And just like a vapor, she's gone.

I decide to ride home with mom because I know Emmy will torture me about my conversation with Ms. Rayburn. I never talk to my mom about Ms. Rayburn and the crazy things she says and does. She trusted me to bring up my grade, so there was never anything else to say. I'm grateful because God knows I do not want to talk about her right now. Plus, I am so aggravated our conversation caused me to miss Joseph. Mom said he waited around for me after the ceremony and eventually left. He was gone before I could even lay eyes on him again, but Mom assures me he would be at the party tonight.

Once home, I run up to my bedroom to get a few moments to myself before the chaos of the party begins. As I sit down on my bed, I hear Ms. Rayburn's words again.

Love as though there is no tomorrow…time is of the essence.

I look over at my night stand. On it is a small black safe. My mom bought it for me to keep my journal in. "Never give the combination to anyone, not even me," she said. I put the three digit combo in, and turn the small silver nob. I retrieve my journal and open it up to the missing page. Staring down at the page they missed evokes a sinking feeling. My stomach churns and I feel as if I am going to be sick. It's the same feeling I get when something awful is about to happen, the same feeling I got the day Aunt Destine died. At this moment, I decide to rip out the page. Holding it in my hands a say a silent prayer, then I tear it into tiny little pieces. Although I have a safe now and I'm much wiser, it's too risky. On the empty page looking back at me now, I write Ms. Rayburn's words down, then I place the journal back in the safe and turn the knob until I hear the click.

SEVENTEEN

At 6pm the guests begin arriving downstairs. It's obvious Emmy has arrived because I can hear the music blasting as loud as it can go. As soon as I slip on my shoes, I hear a knock at my door. Without a word from me, Emmy bursts through my door.

"Girl, what is taking you so long? Everyone is starting to show up."

I am taken aback by Emmy. She is wearing her favorite color, emerald green, which glows against her bright red hair. Her tightly curled hair drapes around her round face. She is beautiful. It took her four hours to decide on a dress, but I knew the strapless dress she picked would look good on her. Because she has such great taste, I allowed her to pick out a similar crimson dress for me. The only difference in our dresses is the color and the cubic zirconia studded design at the top that I absolutely had to have.

"Naomi!" she gasps. "You are stunning! You really need to get all dolled up more often!"

I blush, but there's only one person I can't wait to see me like this.

"Is Joseph here yet?" I ask.

"No," she says as she walks over toward me.

She sits down on the bed in front of me and the excited once present in her cheeks, has faded.

"What is it?" I step towards her. "He's not coming?"

She grabs my hand. "Daniel's here."

"What! My mom let him in?"

"I'm sorry." Her face is now the color of my dress. "It's just that we arrived at the same time and he started going on about how he didn't mean to hurt you and how he was just trying to save the world and ..."

"You got here at the same time!"

Just as I am about to lay into Emmy, my mom knocks and opens the door. I shoot my mom a harsh glare, and I can tell Daniel has gotten to her too.

I throw my hands up, "Mom, I don't want to hear it! You know I don't want to see him or hear his excuses." I look over at Emmy, then back at mom. "This is supposed to be our day! How could you allow him in our house, to *my*, party!"

I fold my arms then sit down on the bed. My mom walks over to me. She kneels down in front of me. She's dressed in a flowing white romper. Although she looks great, I'm so mad at her I can't bring myself to tell her. What amazes me is how quickly the absence of lack and worry has changed my mom for the better.

With the most gentle voice she says, "Look baby girl, you can't run from confronting him forever. Now, he has a good reason for coming here this evening. I suggest you hear him out."

"Mom, I told you I don't want to see him!"

At the tone of my voice she stands up slowly, lifting my head with the tips of her fingers. She glares at me.

"Now you listen, I understand you are hurt, but you know good and well you are on the verge," she whispers now, "of falling for someone else. You can't open another door without closing the other! You need to talk to this boy. He has lost weight and to tell you the truth," she whispers again, "he looks like he is going crazy. I know you love him, and I know he loves you, but if you truly want to move on, you have to give yourself closure and he needs it too. Take it from me, it's horrible living in a messy chaotic house, especially when you continue to sweep all your trash under the rug. Eventually, there's going to be too much under that rug and nothing else is going to fit."

I look at my mom with a half-smile because she knows and I know she sometimes gets carried away with her metaphors.

She props her hands up on her hips. "And when nothing else fits, everybody is going to see the big mess you made and how you didn't bother to clean it up."

"Okay, okay, I get it!" I shout.

"Well, you asked for it," she says. "Now talk to the boy, tell him how you feel," she whispers again, "tell him you are finished."

Mom gives me one of those priceless smiles, then kisses me on the forehead. Within seconds, as if he's been standing at my door the entire time, Daniel pushes the door open.

"Excuse me," Emmy says as she finally breaks her silence. She walks out of the room, placing a hand on Daniel's shoulder in the process. He gives her a half-smile as she does this and just like that—we are within ten feet of each other.

EIGHTEEN

Standing there Daniel looks at me, stoic and firm. I stare back reminded of a dream. I remember a veil, ginormous angels and gaining the strength to tell Daniel goodbye. With that memory burning bright in my mind it ignites a fire within me, a desire, but also the courage to finally say goodbye. Now, I know with certainty, I am ready to face the boy I have grown to love, with the words I have held back for far to long. Daniel shifts from one leg to the other, his eyes now trained to the floor. I approach him, moving with caution.

"Daniel," I say in a whisper.

His eyes don't leave the floor. "Yes, Naomi."

"Can you please look at me?" I ask.

He looks up and there in his eyes, I see the pain my mom described. I can also see how his body has changed, his head now appearing much bigger, his once bulky arms now just long and lanky. *How can I hurt him anymore than I already have*, I think. Another part of me says, h*ow can you allow him to continue hurting you?*

"Wow," he says with a strained voice, "you look amazing."

I smile gently, "Thank you, Daniel."

Now that I am within three feet of him, I reach out my hand and he meets mine with his. I guide him over to my bed to sit. We speak simultaneously.

"Naomi, I am so…,"

"So what…,"

We laugh and he says, "You go first."

I reach for both of his hands and cup them in mine, then I look directly into his weary eyes.

"Daniel, I know you are sorry for what you did, and I also know that you feel what you were doing at the time was the right thing to do."

His eyes move to towards mine. A million questions crease his face.

"I don't want you to apologize anymore. I want you to know that I forgive you. Even though, when I think of what you did to me, I feel anger and hurt, I FORGIVE YOU."

I hold my stare hoping my words will free him from his pain. Daniel's eyes twitch into a half smile. He reverses the grasp I have on his hands and cups mine with his. I continue, ready to close out this chapter the best way I can.

"Daniel, you are all I have ever known when it comes to a companion. I have grown to love you so much because I have always felt safe with you, but for the past few months, I haven't felt that way."

Daniel's forehead creases. His body stiffens. I keep going.

"I realize now that we are so different from one another. Our beliefs, values and goals are not the same and that's okay. We both…"

Before I can finish, Daniel jumps to his feet. "Is this because of that half breed I saw you with!"

Shaken from his abrupt change in mood, I stand, slowly creating space between us.

"So is that what you think of me? Am I a 'half-breed' too?"

He shouts back, "He doesn't love you like I do!"

He closes the space between us and grabs me by my arms

walking me toward the door. Good being close to the door is good. At least there's hope someone will hear me if I scream.

Through gritted teeth he says, "I need you, and if I can't have you no one else will!" He slams my body against the wall. His face is red with rage, his shaky grip on my arms tighten.

"Let me go, Daniel!" I shout out as loud as I can.

He doesn't listen. He is in a trance, repeating over and over again, "I love you, I can't live without you." He presses his body against mine. "I need you, Naomi."

The music blares downstairs as the voices and laughter grow even louder. Knowing no one will hear my screams, tears stream down my face.

He breaks from the recited phrase momentarily and looks me over. "Have you kissed him? Has he been this close to you?"

I don't answer, I look away and he immediately grabs my face with one hand and turns it back to his.

"I love you girl," he says through his clenched teeth.

Then he kisses me violently. I don't fight him. I just let him. I let him, because I'm scared. I let him because I know this is how he gets when he is upset. The kiss continues for what seems like forever and my whole body wants to reject him, but I stick with it hoping it will stop soon, hoping this will calm him down enough so that I can escape. Then, maybe, I can officially, call him and break this off forever, yet the kiss continues. He begins a steady rhythmic movement against my body. His hand caresses my face, then my neck, on to my breast, and finally my hip.

I open my eyes, panicked. *What is he trying to do.* Then, his hand move from my hip to the hem of my dress. He begins to hike up my dress, the he forcefully presses himself against me, even harder. At this point, I can't pretend anymore. I tear my lips away from his and shout, "NO!" with the little air I can breath in. With all of my strength, I try to push him away, but it does no good. Even several pounds lighter, he is still all muscle and manages to keep his body pinned against mine. He lifts my body from the ground, pinning me to the wall with his body weight.

"I won't... let... you... go... EVER." He says in between breaths.

He fumbles with one hand trying to undo his pants, but I fight all the more. Thoughts run through my head, *why did I agree to talk to him—no one knows him like I do? Why did I think he would take this well? He has lost his mind! Jesus, send help for me!*

Then, everything begins to shift around me. *Am I blacking out again?* I see faces: Joseph, Emmy, my mom, Daniel. Suddenly my body drops to the floor—hard. I hit my head on something on the way down. In the darkness, I hear screams, I see blood. The floor shakes beneath me. When I open my eyes, I see running feet go slanted. My dresser hits the floor beside me just missing my face. "IT'S AN EARTHQUAKE," I hear someone yell. Just before I give in to the darkness, someone hovers over me. "You're okay, Naomi, I got you."

NINETEEN

BEEP…BEEP…BEEP… the slow steady sound fills my dreams. Then, the constant sound is interrupted by a flood of voices surrounding me. I stay under the shade of my eyelids, listening, until I hear that voice. The voice that causes my heartbeat to drum a little stronger.

"She will be fine, Ms. Peterson. Don't worry."

My mom replies, "Joseph, she's been sleeping for over 24-hours. I'm starting to get a little scared."

Another voice speaks, an unfamiliar soft baritone. "He's right. She is doing fine. Her heartbeat is strong and her test results are all normal. With a concussion, the brain needs time to rest."

"I get it, but if she would only open her eyes I would feel so much better. How come she won't open her eyes!"

"Okay, okay," I say, and finally open my eyes. "Are you happy now?"

To my left is a man dressed in a white coat. He has jet black hair wavy hair and a beard dripping down over his upper lip to match. Mom is at the foot of my bed with an expression I know all too well—worry. Joseph stands over me, looking into my eyes. He traces my face with his fingers.

He says softly with a smile, "You're awake."

Mom comes around to where the doctor is standing. He looks over at her.

"Well, there you go, but my answer to your question would have been 'when she's ready,' and I guess she is ready." He gives her a friendly nudge and she returns his gesture with a gentle smile, then walks out.

"He's kind of cute," I giggle.

"Girl, hush, you playing around after scaring us like that."

She moves in closer to me, then she gives in to a giggle as well.

I ask, "What happened?"

My mom starts, "Well, your friend over here," she winks one eye at me, "beat up that lunatic you used to call boyfriend. When we burst through the door, you fell but not before you hit your head on your dresser."

Then Joseph chimes in, "As I was trying to restrain the maniac," he looks up at Mom and winks, "an earthquake hit."

Mom sits down on the edge of the bed, "Well, your restraining techniques are perfect because a bloody nose was just what the doctor ordered."

They both share a smile, but I am still stuck on the last words Joseph said.

"What!"

The screams, people falling to the floor and everything going topsy turvy suddenly comes back to my memory. Everything comes into full view. It's like someone has turned the volume all the way up and I realize there are at least six news reporters standing outside the room, along with others who are holding their phones up, I guess, to take my picture. I look at my mom and then over at Joseph.

"Two more earthquakes hit simultaneously, one in New York City and one in Iowa," Joseph confesses.

"Once word got around the country that a teenager saw these earthquakes in her dreams, people wanted to know who you were."

Fear grips my lungs and I can't breathe. A loud beeping noise begins to come from the machine near my bed. Before I know it the doctor is back. Mom covers her mouth as he gently coerces me to lay back.

"It's okay Naomi, security is on their way to remove these people. Just calm down—take a deep breath."

I do as I'm told. Mom comes back to my side as the doctor presses silencing the noise.

"Who told them who I was, Mom?"

She cuts her eyes at Joseph. "We are trying to find out. Lord knows if it was that Draegon man, he is in deep trouble. It seems like the whole country is in an uproar. Who knows, maybe the entire world. They want to know what's next and if the world is coming to an end. Well, at least that's what the news reporters are saying, but we know we can't trust them."

Mom gives the news reporter, who are being escorted out, a stare I usually tremble at.

I look over at Joseph and without me having to ask he says, "Don't, Naomi. I'll get you out of here."

The essence of fear floods my entire body as I lay here, thinking through how many ways this all can go terribly wrong. Eventually, words come, and I look up at Joseph, who is still giving me firm eye contact. "I'm scared."

He replies, "God has not given us the spirit of fear, but of power, and of love," he pauses and places both hands on each side of my head, "and a sound mind."

When night falls, and after Joseph has run all the reporters out of the hospital, he comes back to my room. Mom is curled up on the sofa near the window, asleep. He sits in the chair next to my bed. Gently he takes my hand and pulls it to his lips.

"What am I going to do, Joseph? I don't know what to tell those people. I mean, if I tell them the rest of the dream it would probably only make things worse. What if the last part what doesn't even happen."

Joseph just listens. At this moment, I appreciate his calm and his ability to make every situation seem bearable.

"Everything is going to be fine. You just keep the rest of the dream to yourself. Don't even share it with me until God himself gives you the okay."

He stands up and sits on the side of my bed, then he leans down, placing a soft kiss on my nose. I look up into his evergreen and hazel eyes.

"I thought I lost you for a minute there girl. I didn't know if that psycho had killed you. I just can't get the sound of you crying for help out of my head. All I can think about is you lying there unconscious." He shakes his head and leans in to kiss me.

My entire body is warmed at the touch, and I feel safe. I reach up to hold his face, wanting this moment to last a little longer. Then, an emotion rises in me. An emotion that sets my heart at a rapid pace once again. He kisses me with that same energy. Tears run down between our cheeks and I know this is where I want to be. With him.

After we have expressed our feelings through a single kiss, still staring down at me, he says, "We have to get out of here tonight. The FBI wants to question you."

I'm not surprised. "I wouldn't mind talking to them. I don't want them to think I have something to hide."

Joseph purses his lips, "Naomi, you do have something to hide and when the FBI questions you, they want answers." He shakes his head and then looks out into the lobby of the hospital, "We have to get out of here—tonight."

"What about my mom?"

"We talked about it while you were sleeping. She knows and agrees we have to leave, maybe take you to another state or something. Just for a little while, until this dies down."

I gaze toward the city lights beaming down over the parking lot. I can't see the chaos looming in the darkness below, but I sense it. In such a short time, so much has changed and there's nothing I can do about it. Maybe that's what the huge clock symbolized in my dream. Time is fickle and once it is gone you can't get it back.

"Your mom purchased two tickets for us." Joseph says and he shoves my clothes in a backpack.

"To where?"

"I can't tell you now, but I will. Soon."

My mom left hours ago. We said our "see you laters" and she promised she would come to see me as soon as everything cools down. Although she didn't tell me where I am going, her words settled me. While I sit on the edge of the hospital bed, thinking of the events leading up to my current situation, Joseph paces the floor—phone in hand. After watching him for quite some time I finally ask, "What are you doing?"

"Trying to organize our flight schedule, we need to leave as soon as possible, but your mom and I were only capable of getting a flight for Tuesday."

Then I ask a question that I have been pondering all day, "So does the Bureau know that we...," I hesitate with what to call our relationship, "...know each other?"

He stops in his tracks and stares at me with a grin, "No, they don't know we are together."

I smile at his word choice. His dimples melt my worries momentarily. Then, the sweet sensation of this moment is ruined with one thought: *how are going to get out of here undetected.* Joseph shared half of the plan with me, but he is keeping a lot of the details. I know an FBI agent is coming tomorrow to take me to be interviewed. I also know Joseph is totally against it. Joseph looks pretty preoccupied still pacing the floor and strolling through his phone, but I needed answers.

"Why are you so against me going in to have this interview?"

He doesn't stop what he's doing. "Naomi, the country is in a state of emergency and you are caught right in the middle of it. Have you looked out the window, or even the news since you've been awake?"

"*No*, I haven't."

He continues, "All three states where the earthquakes hit," he pauses and the look in his eyes scares me, "the damage was catastrophic, this country has never seen anything like this before."

Swallowing hard. I don't know what to say. I've been trying to minimize everything in my head, but he just made it all very clear.

He walks over to me.

"I apologize if I am scaring you, Naomi."

I get up and go over to the window. "I am fine. You are only trying to help me see how serious this all is.."

I then draw the curtains. Even at midnight the streets are busy, which is very unusual. I can see police officers directing traffic, a few power lines are still being repaired and workers are working on cleaning up debris from collapsed buildings. It's raining and I see hundreds of people flooding the streets on foot and in cars.

"Where are they all going?" I ask.

"People are trying to leave the state. Some dooms day prophets are saying this is only the beginning of the earthquakes here in Georgia. They are trying to go further west."

Down in the parking lot there are people everywhere—lining the sidewalk, in tents, in their truck beds. I try to keep the panic at bay, but a chill races through me. Joseph comes up behind me. He places his hands on my shoulders, warming me from the inside out.

"How is my house?"

"It's fine. Actually, your house is one of the few on your block that didn't crumble to the ground. What you are looking at is the worst of the results. Georgia didn't get hit as bad as the other two states."

I recall seeing everything around me crumbling in the dream, yet, I was still standing. A tall white steeple, across the street, catches my eye. Joseph sighs, wrapping his arms around me.

"God chose you, an eighteen-year-old from Augusta, Georgia."

I close my eyes and lean into him. Seconds pass before I hear the church bell toll. My eyes open.

"It's midnight."

"That it is," Joseph says.

I peer down into the parking lot as I close the curtains. I notice a shiny black Mercedes pull into a parking space.

"Let's go, Naomi."

Backing away from the window, I pray it's just a doctor late for work.

TWENTY

The hospital is a buzz with all the extra patients they have tonight, so our movement goes undiscovered. No one notices Joseph and I getting on the elevator. I wipe my sweaty palms on my jeans, then I grab Joseph's hand. I peer up at the lights counting down the floors much slower than I have noticed before. Nine, eight, seven, I am acutely aware of every floor descending beneath my feet. When we reach the sixth floor, the elevator stops. Two doctors get on. They are having an intense conversation about the news, so they don't even make eye contact with us. The veil of rising gas prices, people migrating to "safe states," and rioting keep us hidden.

Finally, we reach the first floor. The two doctors exit first and we follow. We turn the corner and I run straight into Josephs back.

"Rook!"

I hear a voice call from a few feet away. I immediately put my head down, remembering what Joseph told me to do. Peeking from around his arm all I see is a pair of very large pair of patent leather shoes. My dad used to have some just like them.

"What are you doing here, Rook?" Another voice asks.

I lift my head just to peek and notice a tall man, who appears to be about Joseph's age if not older. He's a ginger and has the body of a boxer—board shoulders skinny waist. The other guy with him is dressed in an identical black suit, white shirt, and a skinny black tie. They look like stunt doubles from the The Matrix. The guy talking to Joseph is much shorter and looks to be a lot less serious than his counterpart.

The short one slaps Joseph on the back, "You headed out to go get our coffee ready? It's going to be a long night."

He laughs, but the taller one doesn't. He's too busy watching me.

"Yeah, fellas. That's exactly what I'm doing," Joseph says.

He gently pulls me behind him. I turn around and walk toward a television affixed to the wall. The news is on and they are showing clips of what is happening in New York which looks much worse than what I am seeing here.

"I was just checking on a friend of mine. Trying to may sure she gets home safely."

"Is that her over there?" I hear the tall one ask.

"Uh, yeah, that's her."

Joseph continues feeding them a vague, but true story as I try very hard to keep my eyes trained on the TV. Like Joseph is under an investigation, the two agents press him for a more detailed explanation. I listen as Joseph diverts every question.

"Oh, hi, Joseph!"

A familiar voice calls out and I turn around to see my doctor.

"Hi. Dr. Ward," Joseph responds.

"Are you leaving so soon?"

I can hear the panic in Joseph's voice when he chokes out, "No, just…getting a snack."

The short agent is quick to call Joseph out. "You said you were leaving. You and your friend over there." He leans in and whispers really loud. "What are you doing, Rook, sneaking pretty girls out of the hospital?" He laughs out loud. "She must be a very close friend!"

Is this what he goes through every day.

Just when I think we are about to get rid of them all, the doctor laughs too and says as he boards the elevator, "Well, I am sure Naomi is ready to get back home. Are you picking her up in the morning?" He asks as he boards the elevator.

Joseph stalls. I hear him fumbling over his words, trying to maneuver his way out of this one. The doors shut on the elevator before Joseph can formulate an answer.

There's an awkward silence.

Then the short one asks the tall one, "Did he just say *Naomi?*"

In my peripheral, I see the tall one nod and then cock his head over in my direction. The short one then digs in his pocket and pulls something out. I wipe my hands on my pants. My stomach lurches. They both begin to examine whatever it is.

"Well, well, well. Rook, you sure have a lot more explaining to do." The short one says.

We are caught and I know it. I turn around and finally look in their direction. The talkative one holds a cell phone that he is still examining for good measure.

"Yeah. That's her," he confirms.

TWENTY-ONE

The two men, who now have names, agent Sylvester (the short one) and agent Baynes (the tall ginger), put me in the back of the same car I saw pull into the parking lot earlier. They explain that they only need to ask me a few questions, so I agree to go with them. They order Joseph to follow them even though he's not on duty. Sylvester makes pointless jokes about Joseph for the first few minutes of the drive. I ignore him and I guess Baynes does too because I don't hear a peep from him. Eventually, Sylvester shuts up, realizing he's the only person laughing.

I am surprised to see how far out we have driven from the city. The office Joseph told me he worked for was just off of Broad Street. We've been driving for about two hours now and from what I can tell, we are somewhere near the outskirts of Atlanta. Dark shadows of trees surround us on every side telling me we are nowhere near a city or town. It is so dark I can't tell Joseph's car from any of the cars on the road. We get off on exit 147. We travel a couple of miles down a dark road with nothing but an abandoned gas station. As soon as we pass it Baynes makes a quick right on to an unpaved one way road. The road ahead is narrow and I can only see as far as the hood of the car. Wherever they are taking me, it sure is in a strange location.

I think through my answers to their possible questions, just as Joseph and I rehearsed, hoping it will all be over soon. The trees on both sides of the car become more and more dense the further we drive, giving me the feeling of falling deeper and deeper into a black hole. Breathing is becoming difficult. Trembling, I turn around to look for Joseph's car, hoping to see his beaming headlights. When I turn around light bounces off the dashboard. I exhale in relief, continuing to focus on the road ahead.

Minutes later, Sylvester retrieves a cell phone from the console. He calls someone. It's a lady's voice I hear on the other side.

"Are you in the vicinity?"

Sylvester replies, "Yes, Ma'am we are one minute out."

He hangs up without saying goodbye. Baynes makes a quick left and as soon as he completes the turn, I see it. Nestled in the middle of nowhere, a robust building stretches the span of maybe 60 yards. Three floors high, complete with gray cinder blocks and enclosed by thousands of trees, this edifice appears to be out of a movie. As we get closer, I realize this there's four floors, not three. The top floor is mirror glass reflecting the murky sky.

Six armed agents stand at the single door entrance of the facility, all of which are dressed in the same black and white suits.

All they need are black sunglasses, special effects, speed and I would be convinced I am having a nightmare about *The Matrix*.

The car stops. Baynes gets out, then opens my door.

"Miss. Peterson," he says.

Sylvester stands stoic outside the car, his jolly demeanor obsolete and now I am irritated. Why is he being so mature now?

They lead me toward the entrance and I see Joseph already standing with the other agents. Once we enter the building, the six agents fall in line right behind us. As Joseph passes me, we briefly make eye contact and my nerves are calmed just knowing he is nearby.

The inside of the building surprises me because it doesn't look like a prison at all. The six agents walking behind me sound like twenty in the empty hallway. I walk to the sound of their shiny black shoes clacking on the polished white floors. Everything is white, making the hall intensely bright. I squint, shielding my eyes to keep from running into one of them. The long hallway seems to go on forever and the longer we walk, the more unsettled I become.

Why is it necessary to have eight agents escort me, I think.

Finally we turn a corner and approach a door. Joseph pulls out a card, then slides it through a raised panel on the wall. The door beeps, then slides open. I am taken aback when I realize we are entering an elevator. Only Sylvester, Baynes, Joseph and myself board.

Sylvester attempts to start up a conversation which is what I expect when we lose our entourage.

"So what were you and Miss. Peterson doing together, Rook? You know the boss is going to ask."

"Sylvester lets leave the questions to the real investigators, please?"

The elevator stops on the fourth floor and the doors open to reveal a dark-haired woman, dressed in a navy blazer and black pencil skirt. She is striking, but not in a good way. Every hair is perfectly placed in a tight crisp bun on the back of her head. Her skin is almost as white as the walls and her bright red lipstick is flawless. Her angular face draws and maintains your attention.

Taking her in, I lose sight of Baynes and Sylvester. They have disappeared from view. My eyes dart around looking for them, but I am drawn back in when I hear the woman giving Joseph orders.

"Your services are no longer needed Peters. You may go."

The she looks at me and I am instantly disturbed. Her eyes just as dark as her hair. I pray she isn't the agent interviewing me.

Joseph looks as though he is going to speak, but instead, gives me a reassuring look that he isn't going far. As she leads me to a glass door, I try catching another glimpse of Joseph, but he is already on the elevator and the door is closing.

"This way, Miss. Peterson," the woman demands.

I follow her orders, still praying she is not the agent interviewing me. Once I enter the room, the air is sucked out of me. The room spins as I take it all in. It is dimly lit encompassed with floor to ceiling, wall to wall, windows. My heart stops. *Am I dreaming.*

"Please, have a seat."

She gestures toward a small steel table in the center of the room. I will my legs to do as I'm told and as I do this I notice a cot in a far off corner. More fear courses through my veins. *Is that for me.* My chest tightens. *This is not an interview at all.* I fight back tears.

The woman watches me intensely. I sit, trembling. In the center of the table is a manila folder which she begins to flip through. She purses her crusty red lips as she focuses on a single piece of what looks like notebook paper. My foot begins a slow tap on the floor. The sound is magnified in this frigid empty room. She peers up at me from the paper then slowly turns it over.

It's my handwriting.

It's the page Daniel tore from my journal!

Finally, she speaks.

"Where's the rest of it?"

My eyes are trained on my stolen property. I don't respond.

"Miss. Peterson, the reason we have summoned you here today is to gain an understanding of how you obtained the information about the catastrophic events that have occurred in the past few days. I understand you submitted this information to a local magazine a few weeks prior?"

"No, Ma'am," my words come involuntarily, "I did not *give* that information to anyone."

She leans back, and folds her arms across her chest, "Well, how did you get this information?"

I think back to what Joseph and I rehearsed, which is the truth, nothing more, nothing less. "I dreamed about the events. And as I always do, I then decided to write the dream down in my journal. I told a friend the dream and he decided to steal my journal and sell it to *Spark Magazine*."

Her eyes slice through me. "So, you dreamed about these natural disasters weeks before they happened?"

"Yes, Ma'am."

"Is there more to this dream?" She unfolds her arms, leans forward and begins to flip through the papers in the folder again. "It seems the transcribed version of your dream is incomplete."

Stick to the plan, Naomi.

"That was all I could remember at the time."

She leans back in her chair, folding her arms across her chest again. "Well?"

"Well what, Ma'am?"

"Do you remember the rest?"

I flip through the script in my mind only to realize there's only one more line left to recite.

"I don't remember anything else. I woke up after the earthquakes happened."

Suddenly she stands up sending the chair backwards with a screech. She walks over to one of the many windows and glares out. I wait—hoping to hear her say, "okay, you can leave now," but those words don't come. She turns around, walks over to the table, picks up the folder and approaches the glass door.

"Well, can I leave now, you know, since there isn't anything else to tell." I ask.

"Your presence here is indefinite, until you remember or dream the rest of what happens."

The door beeps and she exits through the thick glass door. It shuts with a menacing thud. Reality begins to set in. I am never leaving this place unless I reveal the rest of my dream. I take in the room again and see that it's just a cell with windows. Now that *she* is gone, I can relax. Without warning the lights that were was casting minimal light in the room, turns off. I jump as a blue spot light clicks on and shines down on the steel table. I now hear, in full volume, sounds of nature all around me. I walk over to the glass. Gazing up at what should be a bright midnight blue sky are dark gray clouds. Drops of rain hit the window just as tears begin to fall from my eyes. A flash of lighting brightens the landscape and I am transported back to a dream. I take all of the images and sounds in at once and it hits me, I am living out my worst nightmare.

TWENTY-TWO

Images of that haunting dream flash through my mind. I fall to my knees and I cry for what seems like hours. Eventually, I run out of tears. I sit up, scooting to a corner near the window. For hours I stare out the window, counting the cars that come down the path. Five is the number I end up with before I grow tired of watching. None leave. Whenever thunder rumbles through the clouds, I turn to the door, hoping it's someone to rescue me: my mom or Joseph. That's it. There is no one else. My absent father probably has no clue where I am and probably doesn't even care.

Joseph. I wonder where he could be and why he hasn't come to see me? My heart stutters. I hope he hasn't abandoned me. My heart couldn't handle another man leaving just when I need him most. The feeling of despair begins to infiltrate my entire body. I slowly lie on the cold black marble floor. The rain starts to fall harder, creating an intimidating sound on the roof. I rise up to look out the window, fixing my eyes on the path now darkened with mud, and I I will someone to come save me. Then, I see a large four door gray Buick pulling on to the compound. *Six*, I say to myself. I don't get excited because deep down I know this isn't my savior. Two men get out. One of the men walks to the back door passenger side and opens it. I can't make out who it is, but who ever it is must be important. The men cover him with an umbrella further blocking my view. I strain to see what the figure is wearing and I catch a glimpse just as they approach the single door. The trench coat brushes the ground and the bowler hat is removed when he enters the door. My chest rises in quick pulsing movements and just as the umbrella comes down, the man under the umbrella stops and lifts his face up toward my window. Almost most falling backwards, I cower to the corner across the room.

Oh God, please. No!

I blink several times to see if maybe I am dreaming or maybe evening seeing things. Maybe I'm hallucinating. It's from sleep deprivation. All of this is too much—his room—the windows. I wipe the sweat from my forehead, whispering prayers to God. Taking deep breaths in and then out, I ease up from the floor. My heart rate slows. Just as I make an attempt to walk back over to the window, I hear voices coming up the hallway. I run over to the door and press my ear to the glass. The voices are closer, and I swear one of the voices belongs to Joseph. With hope, I back away from the door, praying.

Father, I know you are with me, I whisper. *You have not given me the spirit of fear, but...* the door opens.

It *is* Joseph. I fall into his arms. He wraps his arms around me and I can feel his heart beating almost as fast as mine.

"Oh Joseph, I am so glad you are still here."

He squeezes me even tighter. "Did you really think I would leave you? I have been trying to cut every corner I could to get you out of here."

I pick my head up from his chest. "Are they going to let me go home?"

Joseph gently holds my face. I can tell from the look in his eyes the answer.

"Naomi they have orders to keep you here until their

questions are answered. The FBI has called in the owner of *SPARK* to see if he could get you to talk. Naomi," he pauses, "they want to keep you here until you tell them what will happen next or give them an explanation of how you knew this would happen."

I pull away and walk over to the place that has brought me some comfort during my time here. I look out into the landscape. Why did he have to do this? Why did he do this to me! If he would have never stolen my journal the earthquakes would have occurred and no one would have ever known I knew about them. Just as I am spiraling I feel Joseph's body lean into me, he kisses the back of my head.

"I will get you out of here Naomi. I promise."

I turn around to face him, "But how when…" I barely have time to finish my question when the women from earlier walks in.

With irritation in her vocal cords, she demands, "Agent Peters, you may leave now."

Joseph kisses me on the forehead, then whispers, "I promise."

He obediently turns around and leaves the room. I fix my eyes on the shiny black tile, unwilling to look at her. Two sets of footsteps move around the room, now. The sound of the heavy glass door shuts and I look up. There, standing right in front of me is the last person I want to see. He gives me a sinister smirk, just as he did the first time I met him face to face. His voice comes out scratchy and morbid.

"Aren't you going to sit down?"

He gestures toward one of the two chairs, but I don't move. I want to stay as far away from him as possible. Glancing around a hopelessly empty room, I look for an escape route and notice a mirror on one of the walls. It looks like a mirror, but I'm willing to bet it isn't. It looks to be one of those things investigators use to look in on an interrogation. I recognize it from those detective shows my mom watches.

When he notices my attention is no longer on him, he clears his throat and sits down. I fix my eyes on a spot on the tile again, vowing not to make eye contact.

"Look, my dream ended after the earthquakes. I willed myself awake after that. I don't know what else you all expect me to do or say."

He doesn't respond right away. I can hear him shuffling through some papers.

"Miss. Peterson, I am here to offer you an alternative. If you agree to publishing the rest of your dream in my magazine, this will all go away. You could go home and continue living your life, with a quarter of a million dollars."

The offer knocks me off balance. I'm disgusted.

"So, you are going to bribe me to tell you something that may or may not be true?"

A haunting laugh rips through the air and my fear of him turns into pure wrath. I clench my fists.

"I know you wouldn't allow a false prophesy to be published, sending the entire country into a further state of mayhem."

He continues to laugh like this is all a joke. The rage inside of me pushes me toward the table. With caution to the wind, I slam both hands down on the table.

"Look, no amount of money is going to make me tell you anything, so leave me alone!"

He stops laughing and his face turns into a pale cracked stone.

"Well I guess you will rot in here until you dream the rest of it."

Without another word, he knocks at the door twice and just like that—he is gone. I let out a huge breath bracing myself on the table for support.

He wasn't so scary after all.

There's no clock in the room, so it's difficult to keep track of time when the sky has looked exactly the same all day—dark and gray. When the blue night light click on and I realize it is darker outside, I know it's been close to 24 hours since I slept. Lying on the cot, I will myself to stay awake.

I listen to the footsteps coming up and down the hall for what seems like hours, but none of them are coming for me. I listen to them get closer and then fade just like they have been all day and all night. Finally, I hear voices. They sound pretty close, so I get up from the cot and walk over to the door to see if I can make out what is being said. Putting my ear on the door, I strain to hear something, but the voices have stopped. *Wait.* I hear something that sounds like buttons on a telephone. Now there's a loud click. In an instant the door opens and I stumble backwards, but I am caught by whoever has unlocked the door. The scent tells me exactly who it is.

Joseph! I look up.

"Shhh," he says.

"What's the plan?" I whisper.

He walks quickly to the windows, looking down at the cars on the compound. "Medusa just left so it's as good a time as any to get you out of here."

"What do you mean 'get *me*' out of here? Aren't you coming with me?" I ask walking over to him. "And is her name really 'Medusa'?" I smile for the first time in the past few days, trying to calm my nerves.

"Nah, we just call her that behind her back. Agent Castro is her name. None of us like her. She is hell personified."

"She is a presence."

Joseph continues to silently look out the window.

"You didn't answer my first question."

"I know." He moves swiftly to the door again and sticks his head out. He looks to the left and then to the right. "Although they are holding you, you are not a criminal."

"Okay, what does that mean and what does that have to do with you coming with me?"

He walks back over to me with urgency in his eyes. "That means, since you are not a high profile criminal there aren't many guards around. You are harmless. The agent they have guarding you tonight is my friend. He's doing his rounds right now and agrees he didn't see me tonight."

"What about the cameras?" I ask.

He whispers now, "Let's just say I have more than one friend who can't stand Medusa. Now come on. We have to leave right now if you want to make your flight."

He takes my hand and guides me slowly to the door. Again I ask, "What about you?"

"You have to leave on your own. I will catch up with you after I cover our tracks. We have to get you out of the country until this all dies down."

"The country!"

"Yeah. Don't worry. You mom knows and she agrees this is our best chance to keep you out of this place."

That settles it, I stop asking questions because I don't want to spend another moment in this place. I follow Joseph out into the long, empty hallway. We speed walk to the elevator and Joseph slides his card to open it. Voices echo up the hallway as we wait for the elevator doors to open. My stomach drops. We press our backs up against the elevator hoping for a miracle. The voices get closer, and closer. Joseph braids his fingers through mine. Our chests rises and falls in harmony as the voices get ever closer. Then, voice yells out from a further distance.

"Hey did you guys sign out?"

Joseph looks over at me and we both hold our breath. The footsteps pause, then retreat in another direction. Finally, the elevator doors slide open.

"That was James. He works in surveillance," Joseph confesses in between breaths.

I press my hand to my chest. "God bless James and his entire family. Amen."

Once we reach the first floor and the door open, Joseph sticks his head out to see if anyone is in the foyer.

He whispers, "It's clear."

As we walk out of the front door, Joseph gives the camera facing the foyer a thumbs up. Every step we take, I feel a weight lifting from my shoulders. When we reach the car I feel even lighter.

Joseph looks over at me. "Don't get too excited yet. We still need to get out of this clearing and back on the highway."

The dark path is slick with mud from all the rain, so Joseph drives extra careful. At this point, I can tell he is panicking. He checks the rear view mirror every few seconds, then his watch. After five miles of praying to God that we don't run into anyone, we reach the intersection of the path and the road. Joseph waits for one, two, three cars to pass before he turns onto the road. I look back just to be sure we aren't being followed and I exhale in relief when I see no one.

"So where are you sending me?"

Joseph keeps his eyes on the road, "Don't say it like that."

"Like what?" I mean, you are sending me somewhere."

"Your mom and I planned it all out this evening. I went to the house to reassure her that you were fine and they just wanted to keep you for questioning. I let her know that they couldn't keep you for more than 24-hours, but I wasn't sure what laws would have been broken with Medusa heading this whole operation. We bought you a one-way ticket to London. You should be safe there until this whole situation dies down."

"Well, what do I do when I get there—like where am I going to stay? What do I do for money? How do I get around, I don't know anyone in LONDON!"

I am hyperventilating at this point, confused and angry that they have basically done all of this without my consent.

"Naomi," He pats my back. "Breath."

I lean forward panting for air, panic attack in full swing.

"You will be fine," he says. "Your mom and I have packed you a bag with everything you need; an account number with enough money in it to get you through an entire month, and your passport. A car is picking you up from the airport when you land and it will take you to the hotel we have reserved. I will come to check on you once I tie up loose ends here."

"How?"

"Just breath, Naomi. I promise I have everything handled." He rubs small circles on my back. "You are going to be okay."

Once we reach the airport, Joseph reaches over the seat to retrieve the bag my mom packed for me.

"Okay," he exhales. "Put this hat on and this jacket. Don't start a conversation with anyone. Agents, if they are here already, blend in with the crowds. Don't tell anyone your real name and don't try to contact your mom, Emmy, *Daniel*, or me. I will get in touch with you as soon as I can. There are some letters in the side pocket of the back-pack, one from your mom and Emmy, don't try to read them until you are in flight."

Then, he hops out of the car. Before I reach to open my door, he sticks his head back in the car.

"Oh yeah, there is also a small envelope in the bag with spending money. Try not to spend it all in one place." He winks.

We both exit the car and head for the International terminal. I pull my blue cap down snugly over my tangled head of hair, tucking in stray hairs. As we enter the sliding doors, a light drizzle wets my face. We retrieve my ticket and head for the Amtrak, it is apparent that my flight is boarding soon because Joseph is practically dragging me through the busy Atlanta airport. Just before we board the train that will take us to my gate, I hear a familiar voice.

"Agent Peters!"

Joseph doesn't look back, but he looks at me, "Come one!"

We sprint for the train door. I peek over my shoulder and catch a glimpse of the two male agents, Sylvester and Baynes, hot on our trail. Running on barely any sleep, I'm thankful for the busyness of the airport.

Joseph and I glide through the crowd, but from the sounds coming from behind us, Slyvester and Baynes are not as successful.

Joseph yells, "It's just up here Naomi. We are going to have to part ways. Get on the train and run for gate 23."

Still running, I catch a glimpse of his face. He is flush red and all I can think about is how much I want to say, and the things I haven't had a chance to say. I reach the train and in a blink of an eye the door opens. Joseph boards along with me and I turn to look at him as the audio voice rings out, "This train is departing in thirty seconds." Joseph throws his arms around me and presses his nose against mine.

He breathes out, "I love you Naomi," and kisses me softly.

And just like that—he's gone.

In utter shock, I watch him as the train departs and the two agents finally catch up to him. I watch as they hold him by both his arms and the image fades as we enter the dark tunnel.

Just as Joseph instructed me, I sprint for gate 23 and check in. I board the plane just in time. Squeezing my way through several passengers placing their bags in the overhead carriers, I finally find my seat. I smile at the thoughtfulness of Joseph getting me a window seat. When I sit down, I feel as though my entire body is quaking. I hold on to my bag for dear life, hoping my heart will catch up with my body before my seat mates show up. Taking three deep breaths, I am capable of focusing my thoughts again. I unzip the back-pack Joseph gave me to inspect its contents. Inside, I find three maybe four outfits, another pair of shoes and a few snacks. Thinking about my mom packing this bag and now being left all alone, tears begin to flow.

I push my hand deep into the bag, feeling the envelop Joseph said would be there. deep down in the bag for the small envelope Joseph said would be there. *It's there.*

As I pull my hand back up through the bag, I feel something else. I run my fingers over the smooth cover, then I grab a hold of it.

My journal!

I hold it to my chest, grateful my mom packed it for me. For a slight instance I questioned how she got into the safe, but it doesn't matter, as long as I have it. A smile forms on my face just as my neighbor for the next several hours arrives. A small silver haired woman sits down next to me. A smiles creases her face as she takes me in.

"Hello," she says. "Taking a long trip by yourself like me?"

"Yes, Ma'am," keeping it simply, remembering what Joseph told me.

"Well, I am going to visit my grandchildren. I am so excited to see them."

She looks over at me, waiting for a response, but I just smile gently at her, place my journal back at the bottom of my bag and adjust myself in my seat. I gaze out the window, watching the rain drizzle down. I reflect on the words Joseph whispered to me several minutes ago, *I love you.* I close my eyes to catch a glimpse of his face once more. Then, I think of my mom again and the letters come to mind. In the front pocket of my bag, I find them. I open the first letter, realizing it's from my mom.

Hey Baby Girl,

I know this is all a very sudden thing, but you are in good hands. Joseph seems to be very capable and there is no doubt in my mind he cares about you. I'm okay. Don't worry about me. I will see you soon. Be strong, Baby Girl.

Love,

Mom

P.S. I know you are probably thinking, how did she get my journal out of the safe? Ask Joseph, he is very good at what he does.

The last line makes me giggle to myself, disturbing the sweet lady sharing this space with me. She glances over briefly and giggles too. The flight attendants begin their flight instructions about seat belts and what to do during an emergency and I am just eager for the plane to start moving. When it does, the captain comes over the intercom.

"Good evening, Ladies and Gentlemen. I am going to be your captain for this flight. We should have a smooth flight with light rain for the first few hours…"

I listen as I hold the second letter open in my hands. Once he finishes, I fix my eyes on the handwriting. Right away I recognize it.

Naomi,

I am not sure this letter will ever get to you, but I needed to at least try. I asked Emmy to get this to you. First of all, I am sorry for everything I have put you through. My judgment has been clouded lately, but there is no excuse for what I have done. I hope you can forgive me because like you have always told me, forgiveness is the first step to healing. You are the epitome of love for me. I don't know how I am going to live without you, but I pray one day you will forgive me and we can at least be friends. I wish you all the best Naomi. I love you and always will.

Daniel

Stunned, I fold the letter back and place them both in the inside pocket of my jacket. Why would Emmy have done something like this for Daniel, let alone made contact with him. With a million thoughts and emotions running through my mind, I lean the seat back and close the shade on the small window. Then, I feel the plane lift beneath me and before I know it, I am a drift. I am dreaming of someone familiar carrying me in their arms as I whisper goodbye to a boy with golden straw-like hair.

BOOK II

THE OPEN DOOR

THE OPEN DOOR

BOOK II

ONE

Joseph

Three months have passed. It's painful to be away from her. All I think about is her. Is she okay? Is she eating well? Is she scared? Does she miss me? Then, I realize how selfish I'm being. Her mom seems to be taking this all in stride, and I am the one acting like an overgrown baby most of the time. I try to visit Ms. Peterson as often as I can, but since I was picked up for supposedly helping Naomi escape, the agency is keeping a close eye on me. They still haven't been able to prove I helped Naomi flee the country. They also can't prove who I was running with that night. It could've been anyone in the blue hat. No one witnessed seeing her face, and for all they know, that girl I was running with, was my cousin, at least that's what I told them. So, I lied. Although sometimes the guilt itches it's way up to my conscience, begging for my attention, I don't feel any regret for what I did.

When I think of why I don't feel remorse, I remind myself of a woman named Rahab. She lied to the King of Jericho. She hid two spies in her house and helped them to escape to safety. Rahab's story is short and often not remembered, but it brings me peace knowing I did what I could for the safety of Naomi and—love.

Ms. Peterson, during our short visits, tries very hard to encourage me to bring up Naomi's constitutional rights, or she will. I'm trying to keep my job and keep this whole situation under a low profile, so I reassure her this will all die down, and to my credit, it has. Naomi's name hasn't been associated with *The Spark* or the prophecy. Agent Castro moved me to a different office a few weeks after Naomi left. She couldn't stand to look at me. Her flame of disdain for me growing wilder and wilder every single day made it very uncomfortable for the both of us. By the time she requested my transfer, I was more than willing to leave.

The new office is smaller and is further from Augusta. Some days, I feel like I have been demoted, but I am optimistic about my new colleagues. They have yet to call me "Rook" and they seem to be even tempered. For the most part, we all sit around thumbing through cold cases and typing up reports for the main office. There's only five of us and there doesn't seem to be anyone who is taking the leadership role. I mean, there's really nothing to lead unless someone wants to step up and create a schedule for who is going to pick up donuts and coffee every morning. The bright side is, we all kind of hide out in our cubicle, not really getting in each other's way and I will be transferring again soon. Virginia is my next destination.

Ms. Peterson and I have gotten pretty close over the past months and it will be hard leaving her, but at least she has someone to keep her company. She reminds me of my mom and I will miss her. I plan on taking a vacation to visit my mom soon. I figure, getting away to let everything cool off would be nice.

TWO

Naomi

Three months have passed and I have come to terms with what my life is like now. I realized "The Window Dream," was simply a warning of what was to come. Sometimes dreams can do that, but they can also inspire, or show you a glimpse of the future. So much has happened. So much has changed. Now, here I sit. In London. Alone.

My pulse speeds up at the thought of how I got here. The only way I could have ever avoided all of this was to not have met Daniel at all. How stupid of me to trust him. When I try to forget what he did, or try to forget him, it all comes back to me like someone is pressing the rewind button and replaying all of the bad parts. Daily, I relive all of it. Part of me feels like it's best that I am far away from home— far from Daniel. He's safer that way.

Joseph says to be careful when I call home because our phones could be tapped. We make sure to keep our conversations under two-minutes, which is very frustrating. I miss my mom so much. She seems to be doing okay. She calls every other week, but she always calls from a different phone: her cell, Joseph's cell, or on occasion, an unknown number. Once, I asked where she was calling me from. She just laughed and deflected the question. Which told me everything I needed to know. I'm ninety percent sure she is seeing someone. She can be pretty sneaky at times, but I see right through it all. I lay off and just let her have her fun. She deserves it. After all she has been through she deserves more than just a boyfriend.

The last time I spoke to my mom we talked a little about Emmy. She told me she decided to stay in town and go to college online. I was shocked. As far back as I can remember, Emmy always wanted to get away from "Disgusta" as she used to call it. The fact that she hasn't tried to find out where I am and the fact that when she had the opportunity to contact me, she strangely gave it to Daniel, is all unsettling to me. It's weird. My mom obviously thinks so too because she never talks about Emmy, and when I bring her up, she just switches the subject.

The last time I spoke to my mom, she reminded me of the letter Aunt Destine left with her estate lawyer. She said she would be sending it with Joseph, whenever the coast is clear for him to come. Recently, earthquakes have been occurring almost weekly on the coast of Southeast Asia. I realized mom didn't want to talk much about it when she reminded me of how much time we had left on our call. Sucking it up, I switched subject.

Sitting in this hotel all alone, day in and day out, is enough to drive someone mad. The best thing for me to do is to find something to look forward to.

Joseph.

The last time I saw Joseph he was being dragged away by two FBI agents. During the short time I've known Joseph, I have developed strong feelings for him. They are unexplainable and it's so hard being away from him right now. He tells me that things have died down, but I really don't believe him. He's just trying to keep me from worrying—just like my mom. We get to talk every other week, but it just isn't enough. He usually calls when he leaves the office, but the wait is torture. The day doesn't seem to go by fast enough. Our last conversation was three days ago and it was a little over two-minutes. Because of our small mess up, I've been worried for the past three days. Joseph says he always calls me on a secure line, but my reply is always, "if it's secure, why can't we talk longer? He replies with, "we still need to use precautions." He always manages to make me feel safe in the most unlikely circumstances. I trust him. He is the only reason I haven't broke down and snuck back to Georgia. He says he will visit me soon and he has a surprise for me, so I've been busy thinking of what the surprise could be.

———

Fumbling for the alarm button, I stretch wildly across the large, plush bed. I thought that I would never get used to waking up in this strange place, but it has happened so easily without me ever noticing. Waking from a dreamless sleep, I roll over to grab my phone from the small side dresser. I sit up and lean against the backboard, trying to recollect today's date. August 14th clicks into my foggy thoughts as I rub the sleep from my eyes. I look down at my phone and see that I'm right, the date has been staring right back at me the entire time. I begin reading Proverbs chapter 14 just to get my morning started with a dose of wisdom. After reading, I get up to pull back the curtains, welcoming light into the room. I look out over to the park that sits right across the street. My seventh floor view shows me it's already filling with people walking their dogs and runners getting their work-out in early. The trees that surround the landscape make it a cozy place to relax and feel hidden from the rest of the world. I smile at the realization of just how fortunate I am to have a place where I feel safe. The ominous cloud of being alone, hovering over my head, vanishes in an instant. A rejuvenation fills me with excitement, so I decide to get started on my thirty minute pilates video so that I can head straight to the park.

Tired from the exercise, I flop down on the bed right after I shower. The fluffy bathrobe is so comfortable, I could fall right to sleep, but instead I decide to take a look at the list I made. I lean back against the headboard reading the title out loud, Joseph's Surprise Possibilities. Then, I giggle at the absurdity of it all. Boredom has no boundaries, I guess.

Joseph's Surprise Possibilities
A letter from Emmy.
I miss her.
Twizzlers.
The stores near my hotel don't sale them.
A dog.
I am desperate for some company.
A bike.
The market is five blocks away.
A ring.

Just as I am scribbling over the last reason, I hear a light knock on the door. I glance over at the clock—it's 9:17 a.m. *Who could it be?*

Slipping on some shorts and a T-shirt, I tip-toe to the door—trying very hard not to be heard. Joseph knew what he was doing when he picked out this hotel. The maid service comes at the same time every other day. They respect my privacy, and in three months, have never surprised me. I inch a little closer to the door to look through the peep-whole. Slowly, I squint one eye, then another sudden knock comes, jolting me back two steps. I freeze, hoping that whoever it is didn't hear my shuffle. Then, I hear it. I hear the voice, I have been waiting to hear for months.

"It's me, Naomi. It's Joseph."

THREE

Joseph

Waiting for Naomi to open the door is like holding your breath under water—just after running a mile. On the other side of the barrier between us, I can hear her fumbling around. My heart pounds in my chest, the waiting is torturous. What is she doing?

"Naomi," I call out again. "It's me."

I step to the side and press my back against the wall, when I hear her footsteps coming back toward the door. Maybe scaring her isn't such a good idea, but looking at her face to face after all this time is too much for me to imagine right now. I need time to catch my breath. When the door finally creaks open, my chest grows bigger. I hold my position—unmovable against the wall. I hear her whisper, "Joseph." The sound of her voice fills me with an emotion I can't describe.

Giving in to the temptation to reveal myself, I lean forward off the wall ever so slightly in an effort not to scare her. And there she is—my sweet Naomi. Before I can take in all the features that make up the girl I love, she throws her arms around my neck and I hold her close, hoping she will never let go. Still holding her, I walk forward into the room, closing the door behind me. She sobs into my neck.

"Oh, I missed you so much."

"I know. I missed you too. I couldn't wait any longer."

I pull back just a little to see her flushed face. She's even more beautiful when she's crying. I place both hands on her neck and pull her in for a light kiss on her cheek. She closes her eyes, we both exhale.

After several embraces and tears, Naomi orders breakfast and we settle at a small wooden table furnished with two kelly green, cushioned chairs. Taking in the room Naomi has had to live in for the past few months, I accept the fact she is okay, my chest loosen a little. The room is cozy and she seems to be getting along just fine. She hasn't lost any weight which means she's at least eating okay. There's somewhat of a fully equip kitchen just a few feet away from where we are sitting. With two small burners and a tiny oven right below it, I imagine her cooking dinner for one, and this brings back the tightness in my chest. But then, I'm reminded of what I am here to tell her and I feel lighter once again. She even has a refrigerator with a freezer, but only a weeks' worth of food could possible fit in it. I peek around the corner where her bed is and notice the bathroom stocked full of toiletries. Still scanning the room, I notice her eyes fixed on me.

"Oh, I'm sorry. Everything okay?"

She takes me in, smiling that beautiful smile that I've missed so much. "Yeah, I can't help but to wonder if you're okay. You haven't said a word in the last few minutes. You're too busy being nosey."

I grin. "I was just checking the place out. How do you feel? Are you liking this place? I mean, it's as good as we can do right now, but if you are just miserable we can work on finding you somewhere more comfortable. You would tell me if you were miserable, right?"

She laughs. "Joseph, this place is perfect. Other than getting lonely every now and then, I am doing fine."

"Good." I say.

The surprise I have to share with her is holding burning a whole in my chest. *Come on, Joseph. Just hold on just a little longer. This isn't the right time.*

"It's fine. I understand this is what I have to do right now," she says.

Her eyes move to the window and there's deep silence for several minutes.

Finally she asks, "Are you hungry. Want me to order some breakfast?"

"Sure." I smile. "I am starving!"

Naomi shows me around the small hotel room and shares her view from the huge window that almost takes up the entire wall next to her bed. Just this feature alone makes the room feel larger. *I hope .* The park across the street catches my eye.

"We should go for a walk after we eat." I suggest.

Naomi's face lights up and she gushes. "Yes! We should." She claps her hands together.

Great! I will tell her on our walk, I decide.

A light knock comes to the door, followed by a male voice. "ROOM SERVICE!" bellows from the door. Naomi hops up from the table, then peeks through the peek hole. I'm impressed she takes this precaution. Making sure the so called 'ROOM SERVICE' is actually who they say they are. Maybe I'm rubbing off on her.

A young man enters the room. Sizing him up, he seems to be around 19 or 20 years old and stands about a foot taller than me. His ginger hair pulled into a ponytail makes him appear a bit older. He smiles at Naomi like he's been waiting to see her all day.

"Good Morning, Gale." He chirps.

Naomi cuts her eyes at me. I avoid eye contact. Leaning back in my chair, I'm eager to hear her explanation later.

"Good Morning, George. How are you?" she asks.

"Oh, I'm better than well, Gale."

When he lays eyes on me, the color leaves his cheeks. His eyes dart between the cart and me as he unloads our food. He doesn't speak to me and I don't speak to him.

"So did you get a chance to read the book yet?" He asks Naomi as he pours our drinks. "Oh, George, I love it! Thank you for letting me borrow it."

He blushes. "Anytime, Naomi. Let me know if you want to borrow more."

During the exchange he never seems to focus on her, but he is more so focused on me and I on him. Then, it hits me. *He likes her.* I adjust in my chair feeling a tiny bit annoyed George is still here.

"Thank you, George. I will let you know what I think of the next chapters. I am excited to share!" Naomi says with a little to much excitement.

I wonder if the air is on because I suddenly feel very warm.

"Me too. I mean," he clears his throat and looks over at me, "I can't wait to hear what you think."

He walks over to the door then turns around before opening it. "And please, let me know if you need *anything*."

"Oh," she pauses then looks over at me, "I sure will."

When the door finally shuts, it takes everything in me not to begin asking the twenty-one questions firing off in my head. On the inside I am boiling—ranting and raving about all the reasons she shouldn't even entertain this guy, but on the outside I am calm, cool, and collected. One part of my training as an FBI agent is to keep my cool—no matter what. Never let your emotions take control of the situation. I choose my words carefully.

"So, you met a friend. That's nice." I slide the plate of food that looks like what I ordered, closer to me. Unwrapping a roll of silverware, I keep my eyes on her, patiently waiting for a response.

She doesn't look at me. "Yes. I have."

I push a little further.

"Do you order room service often?"

She looks up at me as she begins cutting her waffles and bacon, "I do."

"Oh. Why the name Gale?"

Before she puts a slice of bacon into her mouth she responds, "Because I like it."

I'm holding it together, but my heart is racing.

"Very cute, but this is serious, Naomi. It's not safe getting to know strangers in a strange place. I am glad you gave him an alias and all, but…"

Naomi laughs out loud and my words trying to burst through the air drop like dud fireworks.

"What's so funny?"

She doesn't answer and the laughter continues. After several minutes of me staring, the laughter stops.

"Okay, I'm sorry," she says.

I straighten up in my seat, clearing my throat, I feel a slither of embarrassment making it's way through my body. Maybe I am over reacting.

"Am I overacting?" I ask.

She dips her eyes back down to her plate. "I was sensing a little jealousy, maybe?"

Oh! I guess that's what jealousy feels like. I've felt this before, but that time feels like forever ago. I guess I am a tiny bit jealous, but it's still not safe for her to get too close to anyone here.

"No. I'm not jealous. Just cautious. All I'm asking is for you to be careful. That's all."

"I met, George two weeks ago at the park. He was walking his dog and sometimes I go there to people watch."

"Sounds fun," I say.

"Well, I'm here all alone, so I had to find something to do. I have started writing a short story—people watching helps me develop my characters."

Irritation or jealousy, I'm not sure what's causing my knee to jump, so I change the subject. "It's fine Naomi. How's your breakfast?"

She rolls her eyes and continues with what she was saying, "Anyway, little did I know, George happened to work at the hotel. We got into talking about the story I'm writing and it turns out he writes, too. He gave me a book to read that he thought would help with my writers block."

"I see."

"What do you see?" she asks.

I say it. I finally say it because I can't take it anymore and the reality of it is making me so jealous, it's embarrassing.

"He likes you."

At the sound of this, she drops her fork and leans back in her chair. The flat expression on her face tells me nothing. I look right back at her, interested in her response.

"Really, Joseph?"

"Oh yes! The ways he was sizing me up—there is no doubt in my mind. He likes you, Naomi."

Saying it again makes my jaw clinch. My knee is doing overtime under the table and I'm not sure why this whole thing is making me feel so emotional. I look over at her, still staring at me with those big beautiful eyes. She's my every thought since I met her. There's no wonder I am undone.

Naomi folds her arms across her chest, then exhales and says, "And I *love* you."

FOUR

Joseph

My mom raised me on her own. My dad left before I was even born, but after I graduated from college and went into the academy, they decided to get remarried. When my mom first told me, I was angry. As time went on and as the wedding date approached the thought of them together grew on me. She wouldn't be living so far away by herself anymore and she wouldn't grow old alone. Although, it's strange for me, the two of them living a life together I don't get to be a part of and never had the chance to be a part of as a child. My grandmother told me the story behind their divorce years ago. And true enough, it wasn't entirely his fault that I grew up without a father, but whenever I think of how he never really tried to get to know me, the anger I harbor towards him is triggered.

My dad was a soldier and he wholeheartedly took the vow to support and defend the Constitution of the United States very seriously. Nothing, not even my mother, would stop him from living up to his vows. They met during his first deployment to Germany. At the age of seventeen my mom had traveled a short distance to visit family in Germany, before she would begin college. She was the epitome of what any father and mother would want in a daughter: intelligent, beautiful, respectful, and trustworthy. She graduated at the top of her class, which was something her parents prided themselves in. My mom, or Madi as they called her—short for Madison—loved her home in the UK, but wanted desperately to get out of her parent's house for as much time as they would allow. Being prepped for college all her life was one thing, but the scrutiny she endured as the only child proved to be too much for any teenager to handle. She lived in a cage. A caged animal on display for all to see, as she sometimes described it. She would put on a show for those that came to view her in that cage, saying just the right things, wearing just the right clothes and laughing at just the right time, but when the show was over, she felt just as empty as she did before they came. Being alone was her natural habitat because that is all she knew, but she longed to be free.

My dad was a nineteen-year-old, southern gentleman and had recently completed Advanced Individual Training for the United States Army. He was ready and eager to go on his first deployment oversees, with nothing holding him back. My mom and dad were an unlikely couple because of their cultural backgrounds, and of course, the color of their skin. They met on a ferry ride. My dad was out with some of his "battle buddies" living it up, while my mom was just trying to get back to her hotel after a day of site seeing. They ended up meeting off of a bet. My dad's friends bet him that she wouldn't give him the time of day and being known to never blow off a bet, he went over to talk to her. Her sunny blond hair and exotic blue eyes didn't deter this towering, barrel chested young boy. He walked right up to her, introduced himself and asked her name. She was intrigued by the attention and the fact of meeting someone new, so she said yes when he asked her out after an hour of cordial conversation. It was love at first sight—well— at least that's what I was told. They married within a year.

My mom was a junior in college, majoring in criminal justice, when she found out she was pregnant with me. Two days after finding out, my dad came up on orders to PCS to Arizona. And then, their flawless bubble burst. Although my mom loved my dad more than the freedom she experienced being with him, she refused to give up her dreams. She wanted to stay to finish college first and my dad wasn't having it. He couldn't understand why she wouldn't put her dreams on hold to keep her family together. My dad blamed her decision on her parents. Knowing the prejudice they held toward him for being a black man, he ended the marriage with the belief that she chose an education and her family over him. Early in my teens, I pressured her to tell me about my father. Reluctantly, she told me the truth and because of the dark truth staring me in the face every time I looked at her, I began to resent her for it. We argued everyday about everything. We barely spoke to each other unless we were arguing about me waiting to long to take the garbage out, or me playing basketball too late on a school night. Our relationship became none existent. Then, I decided to reach out to my Grandma Josephine, my dad's mom.

We developed a relationship through letters, video chats and phone calls. Through our long phone calls, I was capable of getting a sense of who my dad was, although, he didn't seem interested in getting to know me. Still, I wanted to be closer to him. Without my mom know, I planned a visit to Grandma Josephine. When Grandma Josephine found out, two months before I as due to come, she wasn't having it, so she reached out to my mom right away. To my surprise, my mom was more than happy to fund my first trip to the States. I flew to Virginia and I met my dad for the very first time. We spent a month together and then, like a vapor, he was on to his next duty station. I was devastated and couldn't imagine going back home. I pleaded with Grandma Josephine to allow me to stay with her. It took the rest of the summer to convince my mom to let me stay with Grandma for the rest of my high school years, but eventually she relented. She was crushed, but I believe somehow she knew this decision was best for our relationship.

Unbeknownst to us all, spending my high school years with Grandma Josephine was a blessing. Although my mom took me to Mass every Sunday, I didn't really develop a closer relationship with God until I moved in with Grandma Josephine. She was so tender and sweet over the phone, but no sooner than I got to Norfolk, Virginia I was sitting in a non-denominational church pew four times a week. There were no exceptions. I grew in my faith and consequently my mom grew as well. Every summer I visited my mom and our relationship healed over time.

Now, my mom is a very successful criminal investigator. She is coming up on retirement, but I doubt she will take it. She is still a workaholic and I can't see her sitting around the house while criminals run rapid on the streets. My dad, on the other hand, retired from the military a year before they remarried and immediately moved to London to be with my mom. I've avoided seeing them since they have reunited, but here I am. Who would have thought I would be sitting right here in London, faced with the most amazing girl and she just told me she loves—*me*.

FIVE

Naomi

The weight of those words coming out makes me feel like I could just float up to the ceiling. Three months ago, when Joseph left me on the Amtrak in Atlanta, the last words he whispered were, "I love you." Then, he was gone, apprehended by his so called partners. Since then, those words have been weighing heavier and heavier on me because holding them back over the past few months has been extremely hard.

Joseph gets up from his chair so fast, I can barely comprehend how he ended up kneeling down in front of me. He clasps both my hands in his and kisses them. My heart flutters.

"Do you know how hard it's been waiting to hear you say that to me?"

I lean over to kiss his forehead, "I wanted to tell you face to face, you know, extend you the same courtesy you extended to me. I mean, George *is* cute, but he doesn't come close to you." I grin.

"Ha. Ha…not funny. You just make sure room service is where that relationship ends," he says with a straight face.

Then, I kiss him before I can second guess myself.

Breathless, I pull away. Embarrassed and scared to even look at him, I fix my eyes on my hands in my lap, then the window. A cool breeze blows the sheer white curtain into the air.

Joseph clears his throat. He continues the conversation from where I interrupted it.

"Uh, um. There's no sense in you getting close to someone when you are definitely not going to be around much longer."

I suck in a big breath of air. My heart stills.

Still kneeling on the floor in front of me, dangerously close, he says, "I'm here to tell you, you are coming back..."

I don't allow him to finish. I throw myself into him, almost sending him backwards onto the floor, but his strength hold us both upright.

He struggles to get the rest out, "...home, but..."

Pulling back, I allow him to regain his balance, I laugh incapable of containing the joy I feel. Then, I acknowledge the 'but.' "But what?"

He smiles back at me, slowly standing to his feet. Then, the smile fades. All the joy is sucked out of the room.

"But what, Joseph?" I demand.

"It's safe enough to come back to the states, but not to Georgia."

My hands fly up to my chest. I exhale in relief. "Oh! I thought it was something worse. I thought you were going to say something...never mind. I don't even want to say it."

Joseph's smile returns. "So you are okay with that?"

"My gosh, yes! As long as I'm closer to my mom. Where am I going?"

"In a few more weeks you will catch a flight to Virginia. My grandma Josephine lives there. She has agreed for you to live with her, until we come up with another plan."

I begin thinking of a thousands things at once and Joseph slows them down with the next thing he tells me.

"I got a transfer to Norfolk, Virginia."

I take in a huge breath, but I hold my reaction because he's still talking.

"But, I have to tie up a something's first. I should be permanently there next year." He looks at me with a smile that could melt anyone's heart. "So, I won't be that far away either."

His smile widens and my cheeks are a blaze.

"Are you happy?" He asks me.

"One thousands times, YES!" I jump into his arms once again.

———

After breakfast, Joseph and I take a stroll to the park. The morning sky is a comfy gray with an overcast. A cool breeze blows ever so often so I am grateful I chose to wear a light sweater and jeans. Joseph dressed in a light jacket as well. He's always thinking ahead. As we walk, I can't help but to feel overwhelming emotions of gratitude. Something new is on the horizon and there's so much to look forward to, especially with Joseph. For the first time, in a long time, I feel *joy*. I glance over at him while he takes in the grassy hills and lush trees. It is amazing how much I love him in such a short period of time. I know with full assurance that if he asked me to marry him today, I would. I brush thought away quickly. What am I thinking. I'm only eighteen.

"So how long do I have you for? You said I don't leave for a couple of weeks, right?"

He hangs his head, "Yeah. I will be here until Monday."

"Oh wow, that's great! I thought you would say until tomorrow."

"I'm glad you think so. I just want us to enjoy each other and I don't want to think about leaving until the time comes. Okay?"

"Okay. Let's not talk about it. I am so excited! I want to show you the bookstore over on Kensington. And oh, there's this amazing art museum that I just ran up on the other day! We can go out to eat tonight, but I don't really know anything about any of the restaurants."

Joseph grins, "Okay…slow down. I know a great place to take you."

"You do? Have you visited London before?"

Still smiling he says, "Yes, I used to live here. I grew up here. That's how I knew what hotel to set you up in, where I knew you would be safe."

I'm dumbfounded. Here I am thinking I know him and this huge fact about his life has seemed to coast by me.

"Oh," is all that escapes my lips.

We finally reach the bench where I usually do my people watching and write. It rests right in front of a pond accompanied by a bulky hazel tree towering over the edge. When we sit down, the silence between us is so loud I can't sit still. It's obvious there's more he wants to tell me, so I brace myself.

"Naomi, there are a lot of things I haven't told you. It's not that I have been hiding them from you, it's just that I haven't found the right time to tell you until now."

My thoughts race and I'm not sure what to think. I rub his hand to assure him that it's okay, "What is it, Joseph? You can tell me anything."

He doesn't look at me which makes the situation even more uncomfortable, but I hold my composure.

"Yes, I have been here before. I grew up here and I have seldomly come back."

For the next several minutes Joseph shares his story with me. The story of his father and his mother. He tells me all about their breakup and the difficult time he had forgiving them both. Then, he shares their serendipitous reunion. His memories of growing up in Grandma Josephine's house reveals how much his loves her. When he is finished, I feel like I know him so much better. He looks at me with eyes that can melt the coldest heart.

"Are you angry with me? You know, for not sharing this with you before?"

I confess, "No, I'm not angry, but I am a little confused as to why you never really spoke of your mom or your Grandmother.

He hangs his head, "It may be hard to understand this, but I was ashamed."

"Of what?" I ask.

He exhales, "I don't come out to see my mom much. Especially since they are back together. It's weird for me. On one hand, I have a dad that never really tried to get to know me and on the other I have a mother that chose her career over having a *complete* family. I love them all very much. It's just hard drudging up my past.

Squeezing his hand, I say, "I understand. I'm glad you told me."

Joseph looks at me again. "I'm surprised you haven't asked about the surprise yet."

My heart skips a beat.

"Oh! I thought the surprise was you! You are here. Then, I thought it was the fact that I get to go home—I mean to the states?"

"Oh no! It's much bigger than that."

My breathing picks up and my heart beats triple. "What is it!" I pant.

He scoots to the edge of the bench and grabs both of my hands. I hold my breath.

He calmly says, "I want you to meet my parents, Naomi."

SIX

Joseph

Being here, the place where I grew up, with the women I love is an experience I can't really process, but lately, I have been feeling like a failure. The ups and downs at work and the idea of being demoted has really worn on my conscious; my ambitions to move up on the ladder diminished. Yet, the moment I laid eyes on Naomi, all of my worries disappeared. I feel rejuvenated and ready to conquer anything.

When she agrees to come with me to my parent's place, it settles the nervous stomach I have had since landing here. Although she seems to be okay with the idea, I can't help but worry how this reunion will go. I still have some unsettling feelings about the whole thing. For one, it's been a while since I've seen my mom and one thing I know about her, she can be a little snooty to people she just meets—especially to girls I'm interested in. My dad on the other hand, I don't know. I really don't know enough about him to introduce someone I love to him, but to show Naomi how serious I am about her, I need her to meet them both. If introducing her to my semi-broken family isn't enough, I don't know what will.

We sit at the park for a couple of hours and Naomi tells me all about the story she has been writing. I joke with her about one of the characters, Benjamin, because he sort of reminds me of *me*. She insists he doesn't, but I'm not buying it. We finally get hungry and decide to head to a restaurant a few blocks from the hotel.

"Nanny's has always been one of my favorites," I tell her. "My mom and I always came here when money was low, or when she was just too tired to cook."

Nanny's sits right on the street with metal white tables lining the side walk. The restaurant is just as I remember it. We chat casually about our lives since the chase. Then, Naomi asks about the inevitable.

"So, how are things in the states, really? There's no need to hide it from me, there are newspapers here. I just want and need your true perspective."

"So, what *do* you know?" I ask.

"Enough to know everything is not 'okay.' I read the other day Hawaii is 70% under water—dormant volcanos are now active. I know the government is doing nothing to evacuate those poor people. I also know that the earthquakes haven't stopped. California is experiencing level four earthquakes on a weekly basis. The economy is bad and is only getting worse."

I touch her hand. "Lower your voice, Naomi. It's not as bad as they are making it seem. The situation is under control."

"Well, why are you keeping these things from me," she whispers.

"I know. Your mom and I decided to only bring up things close to home. You know, things happening in Georgia. I wasn't trying to keep anything from you."

I squeeze her hand a bit tighter, then I lean in, caressing her cheek with my other hand.

"I don't want you to worry about anything. God, has seen

us through a lot in the short time we have known each other. I have no doubt He will see us through this."

A smile tiptoes across Naomi's face and I'm grateful for it's brief presence.

After dinner we head back to the hotel. When we walk through the door I am acutely aware that I have to say a temporary goodbye to her. She lays her jacket down on the bed and I take her in, savoring every moment left of this day. As she sits her bag down on the counter, her dark coily hair drips down into her beautiful eyes. She catches me staring. I stand admiring every aspect of her. Yes, I feel awkward staring at her like this with nothing to say, but I can't take my eyes off of her.

"What is it?"

She walks over to me. Her fragrance is hypnotizing: vanilla ice cream. I'm never sure if it's her hair or her perfume, but whatever it is, it always sends me to a place of euphoria. I wrap my arms around her, taking all of it in. My mind tells me to let go of her now, but the rest of me says no—let's hold on a little longer—so I do.

"Joseph," she whispers. "Are you going to sleep here tonight?"

"Why? Do you want me to?"

She pauses, then shifts in my embrace, "No. I don't think that would be a good idea."

I hold on a bit tighter. "Right. I agree."

I pull back just enough to look down into her piercing brown eyes.

"Can I kiss you?" The words escape before I can overthink the question.

She avoids eye contact, "Do you think that's a good idea right now?"

"Probably not," I admit.

I feel stupid even asking. Why would I ask her that now?

Here we are, alone and in love. Now is definitely not the time, but the danger of it all makes me want to kiss her all the more. I pull away from those thoughts and consider what she just said. She must think I'm trying to get her in bed. Yes, she has to and is probably about to throw me out.

But, she doesn't. She just laughs and holds me a little tighter. I'm relieved. We spend a few more moments like this and finally let go. I walk toward the door and then remember something I was supposed to give her earlier.

"Oh, I almost forgot. I have a letter your mom wanted me to give you. It's in my suitcase."

"Okay. And where's your suitcase?" she asks.

"I didn't anticipate sleeping here—with you, so I got a room down the hall." I gesture toward the door, feeling more awkward around her than ever before. "I will slip it under your door."

A glorious smile spreads across her face and she says, "You are such a gentle-man, Joseph. Thank you for thinking ahead."

"Of course, Naomi. I respect you."

She comes in a bit closer and again her smell sends me into the clouds. I am convinced this must be exactly what Heaven smells like. I put my arms around her waist and stare down at her. Feeling bold, I want to express myself with no filter.

"There is no way I can sleep in the same room as you. I would just be fooling myself. But, there will come a day, here soon, when I will never have to sleep in a room down the hall from you, again."

I kiss her gently on the cheek and leave before she can respond.

SEVEN

Naomi

*W*ow! The door shuts behind him. His words have knocked me out of reality— into a dimension where he and I are married. Then, I drift back down to reality and my pessimistic thoughts undo what he has done.

Maybe he's just caught up in the romanticism that fills the streets of London.

I walk over to the bed in a daze, then I hear a light knock come to the door followed by a white envelope gliding across the floor. I walk over to retrieve the envelope and listen to see if he will knock again. He doesn't. Which is a good thing. With him being here after all these months of not seeing him, the privacy we now both have, and us doing all the things couples do, emotions I didn't think I had have come alive. It's difficult not to want him to stay here with me, but we both know him staying in his own room is for the best.

Sitting down on the bed, I hold the envelope up. It's not mom's handwriting, but it looks familiar. Then, it hits me!

My Dear Johanna,

If you are reading this, you know I am gone on home to be with the Lord. I hope you are not sad for me because you and I both know that my life here on this earth hasn't been the best, but you and Naomi made it worth every second. Johanna, continue to strive. Don't let past failures keep you from reaching for tomorrow. You are beautiful inside and out. Pick yourself up and prepare for your Boaz!

Tell my sweet Baby Girl I love her. Tell her that God has trusted her with a precious gift. Although I have moved on, God has given her the Holy Spirit to help guide her and to help her interpret all that God is saying. He trusts her to seek Him and to reveal the dreams only if and when necessary. Tell her never to forget that.

The money I am leaving for you and Naomi is a result of several stocks I capitalized on over the years. There are also some asset paperwork in the safe deposit box. Use that key I left you to access them. I trust that everything I have left you will be spent wisely and I hope it brings a whole new outlook for you, Johanna. I love you both so much.

See you soon,
Destine

Tears roll down my cheeks on to the letter, smearing the ink. There are a few other smeared words on the page, which probably means mom cried when she read the letter too. Folding the letter back up, I think of the dreams I've had of Aunt Destine since her death. In the dreams she is always alive and thriving. She's all dressed up on her way somewhere, and other times, she is just sitting talking with me. Having these dreams bring me comfort because, in a way, they assure me she is okay.

—————

Once I shower, I decide to pick out what I should wear tomorrow. If I am going to meet Joseph parents for the first time,

I want to look *respectable*, as some of the older woman say here. I decide on wearing a flowing, burgundy skirt that drapes down to my mid-calf and an ivory blouse. Out of the three pairs of shoes I brought to London with me, the shiny black flats will have to do. As I get into bed, thinking of Joseph's final words to me before he left, the fluorescent bright light of my cell phone lights up the ceiling.

"I hope the letter didn't make you sad. Are you okay?"

"Yes, I'm fine."

I smile at the sheer fact he cares. Holding the phone close to my chest, I think of what to say next. There's no use in playing hard to get anymore. He has me already. He has me like the sky has stars.

"You truly made my day today. I can't tell you how excited I am to see you tomorrow."

"As am I. Beautiful."

I gush at his response.

"Sweet dreams, Naomi."

A smile builds in my heart and makes its way to my cheeks, warming every part of me. I close my eyes in an attempt to let everything that has happened and every worry that may try to creep into my mind, fade away.

Falling off to sleep was no easy task. I toss and turn for a while before sleep washes over me. I dream of a couple standing in an empty house. The women looks around at the boxes lining the walls. Then, she begins to walk through the house as though she is looking for something and eventually she finds it. She reaches an empty bedroom occupied by a little boy and a little girl. The little boy drapes one arm over his sister's shoulders as they stare out a huge window. The sun is setting over a vast landscape in the backyard. Suddenly, the two children's faces contort into something that illustrates fear. Then the women walks over to see what they are staring at. She sees it, then I see it—a huge title wave coming straight for the house. In an instant my glides into the women's body. With gentle hands, I touch their tiny shoulders and calmly say, "Come on kids. Let's go to the front room." Just as the words leave my mouth, Joseph walks into the room. He sees the concern on my face and leads the kids to the front room, while I stay back. Seconds later, he is standing next to me watching the fast approaching wave. He awakens me from my daze and I motion for him to come away from the window, but he stalls as the wave closes in. Just as the massive wave smacks into the window with a loud crash, we both jump back, me falling to the floor. The glass then cracks and thin spider webs of cracks appear on the windows surface.

I yell, "Come on, it's going to break!"

We exit the room quickly. As soon as we shut the door, I hear the violent rush of water filling the room. The odd thing is, the water only trickles from underneath the door. Joseph and I make eye contact, amazed the explosion didn't over take the house. We then step right across the hall into the front room where the kids are waiting. This room also has a window. This window faces the front yard. We pull the kids closer to us and we all get down on our knees and begin to pray.

I cry out, "Father, have mercy on us." Then we all begin praying *The Lord's Prayer.*

Our Father, which art in Heaven, hollowed be your name. Your kingdom come. Your will be done…

Once we finish, there's nothing but heart wrenching silence. We wait for several minutes and nothing happens. I come to the conclusion that He is not coming for us. First, sadness and despair set in. Then, it hits me! We are still alive. The wave never reached the front of the house. I look down at the floor to see that the carpet is completely dry. The sound of sirens cause us all to rise from off of our knees and we all rush over to the window. Miraculously, I see small holographic vignettes of different news stations, broadcasting what is happening in the sky. On one station, people are robbing homes and looting, on another, women are fighting in the street for gender equality. Crowds are storming the Whites House with multi-colored flags. Homeless people are lining the street in another image. Men of all ages are jumping to their death from bridges. It is utter chaos. The sound of the broadcasts are deafening. Our kids place their hands over their ears. Joseph and I turn to look at each other and in my ear I hear a voice say, *"There is still much work to be done."*

EIGHT

Naomi

I tug at the long wool skirt as I examine myself in the mirror. One side of me says, *this looks respectable,* while the other side says, *yeah respectably grandma-ish.* The black flats I brought with me look dreadful paired with the skirt. I could go for a middle-aged nanny.

Ugh! I should have bought more clothes by now, but no, Joseph had to show up without a warning and throw this hug surprise on me. Frustrated, I take off the skirt and settle on a pair of jeans and a black blouse. I finally move on to my hair. Living in a foreign country without transportation or without any knowledge of an ethnic hair store being in reasonable distance is definitely not recommended. I wouldn't wish these circumstances on my worst enemy. My hair is a knotted mess. Quickly, I brush it up into my typical bun. I would love for Joseph to see me with a different hair style for a change, but this will have to do today.

A light knock comes from the door, so I grab my jacket. Anticipating Joseph, I open the door without asking who it is.

Standing before me is George, holding a silver salver in his right hand.

"Good Morning, George. What do you have there?"

He smiles gently, "Good Morning, Naomi. I have a post for you."

Which technically means, he has a piece of mail for me. He removes the silver dome then extends his hand. On the salver lies a large yellow envelope addressed to me. I pick it up and analyze the handwriting. My mom and Joseph are the only two people who know I'm in London and staying at this particular hotel, but the handwriting is neither of theirs. I take the envelope and place it under my arm.

"Thank you, George."

"You are very welcome, Naomi." He bows before me, never allowing his eyes to leave mine. "Are you okay?" he asks.

"Yes, I'm fine. Talk to you later?"

"Yes. Sure." He says with crinkled eyebrows.

I close the door immediately. With the envelope still under my arm, I walk over to the chair near my bed. Looking at the handwriting again, I notice there isn't a return address. My palms begin to sweat. I feel around the envelope trying to get an idea of what is in it and suddenly another light knock comes from the door. *Oh Father, I hope this is Joseph.*

This time I ask, "Who is it?"

"It's me."

I breathe out a sigh of relief and open the door. Joseph walks in with no hesitation and embraces me tightly. I allow it for as long as he holds on to me. It's comforting, but I can't help but stare at the bright yellow envelope now lying on my bed. He finally loosens his grip and peers down at me.

With a smirk he says, "Did you sleep well, Beautiful?"

"Yes. I did."

That thing on my bed seems to be getting bigger and brighter. I can't take the suspicion another second. I run over to retrieve the package and hand it to Joseph.

"What's this?" he asks me.

"I just got it in the mail—I mean, from George—I mean George just brought it up for me. I don't know, just open it."

"It's addressed to you, Naomi."

"I know. Isn't that weird. Do you think someone followed you?"

Joseph looks just as confused as I am which makes me all the more uneasy. He walks over to the bed and takes a seat. He runs his fingers over the contents, examining it just as I did.

"Let's not open it." he says.

I join him and have a seat on the bed, "Why not? I don't think I could function all day without knowing what is in it."

"Because, whatever it is, it's going to ruin our day. This is my last full day with you, in the place where I grew up and I want us to pretend like this never happened."

"Okay, but what if it's important? What if someone is coming to arrest me again! What are we going to do!"

He puts one arm around me, "Calm down, Naomi. If the agency knew where you were, they would have come to get you by now. Believe me, they wouldn't send an envelope."

At the realization of this, the beat of my heart slows. I lean into his embrace.

"Okay. You're right. Can we open it tonight?"

"Yes, as soon as we get back we will open it— together."

NINE

Joseph

Worry infiltrates my thoughts as we head to London's tube station, aka, The Tube. Although I am keeping a smile on my face for Naomi, I am anxious to see what is in the envelope, as well. I push those thoughts away when she takes my hand and squeezes it gently.

"No worries, it's probably my hotel bill," she jokes.

"I doubt it," I protest. But, we aren't talking about this, remember?"

Boarding The Tube brings back so many memories from my childhood. The crowded, small space is comforting in its own unique way. There's standing room only which causes my mind to drift back to a time when I was eight standing in almost this exact spot. I look over at Naomi. She's in another world next to me— taking in the locals and easing a bit closer to me.

I lean over her shoulder. "When I was a little boy, maybe eight or so, I remember being on one of these for the first time. My mom took these all the time, but my first tube ride, I will never forget. She wanted to take me sight-seeing, and since there's so much to see in London, I had never really paid much attention to the history of the buildings. My mom wanted me to know them by sight and know their history."

"What like Big Ben, and Tower Bridge? Or, St. Paul's Cathedral and Buckingham Palace!"

Naomi's excitement boomed from her voice.

"Yes! St. Paul's Cathedral, Buckingham Palace and then some! Every Saturday she would teach me the history of a landmark and we would visit the site. One Saturday, after boarding the tube, I remember watching my mom study a map to locate St. Paul's Cathedral. I was so excited to visit this site for the sheer fact cathedral being a part of it's name. It just sounded so grand to me. It was the fifth and final place on our list of places to visit before school started back. Once we got out of the station, mom pulled out the map and began to study it again, making it clear she still wasn't sure where we were."

"So why wouldn't she just ask someone? Is she one of those people who hates to ask for directions?"

"Remember everything I've told you about her?"

"Yes."

"Well, add to that very strong willed."

I laugh at the thought of how stubborn my mom is. I don't like admitting it, so laughing about it makes it easier.

"So how did you find it?" she asks.

"May I continue?"

She grabs my arm and leans in a little closer, "Sure. Go ahead."

"While she studied the map, I became mesmerized by my surroundings and being the inquisitive young man that I was…"

"And still are," she interrupts.

"…all I wanted to do was look and explore the architecture right there in front of me. Before I knew it, I had walked several yards away from the station and didn't see my mom anywhere in sight. Turning in circles, looking down every street, it was as if there were thousands of people in every direction. After, maybe, five minutes of just standing there looking at every face, I began to panic. That's when I began to walk in the direction I thought the station was, shaking.

As I walked, for what seemed like forever, I began to think of every horrible, scary thing that could happen. Then the tears started to roll. I wanted to give up. I tried to recall what she had on and started looking for my mom's coral shirt and her short blonde hair. The tears were flowing now, and I hated myself for being so foolish. I just knew I was as good as kidnapped. Then, I realized that if I wanted to find her, or if I wanted her to find me, I had to change the way I was thinking. That day was the first for many things. This was the first time I really prayed. Any other time was strictly out of habit or because I was told to, but this time was because I truly needed God to listen and come through—fast!

Calm came when I finished praying, I took a deep breath then began to walk in the opposite direction. This time, things started to look familiar and the crowd seemed to thin out. This gave me hope that maybe I was closer to The Tube. Out of nowhere, I heard a faint call of my name. Stopping in my tracks, I turned in the direction of the echo . As soon as I turned, there she was. With a tear soaked face, I had found my mom.

"Well you had some help?"

"Yes. I did. He answered my prayer and lead me right to her."

"Was she mad at you? I would have been so mad at you!"

"Oh no! She hugged me so tight I thought I was going to start crying again."

We both laugh at the memory, but even though I am laughing my heart is heavy. I have been suppressing how much I miss having my mom to talk to everyday. Since her and my dad remarried, I've kept my distance. We have had our rough times and there are still times when I am so mad at her for the decisions she made regarding our family, but we got through a lot together. I was her sidekick during those years and she was mine. Although, it is tough sometimes, I respect her for sticking by me and never voluntarily sending me away. Today, I hope my visit with the girl I love shows her how much I do respect and love her.

For the rest of the ride, I continue sharing stories. I share more about my mom and as much as I could about my dad. Talking about him causes me to become even more nervous. Now that I think about it, I have never seen my parent's *together*, let alone, married. Now, I'm taking Naomi to meet them, for the first time. My stomach sinks. What was I thinking.

When The Tube stops and the intercom announces our destination, I am thrown back into reality. Naomi moves before I do. She looks back at me, and I know from the look in her pretty brown eyes, she sees the resignation in mine. She smiles and my soul lights up.

"Come on," she says, "No worries, there's nothing we can't face together. Right?"

I grab her hand and force my feet to move, "Right."

We exit the crowded station and before I know it, we are right on my parent's door step. Staring at the familiar pale blue door brings back bitter-sweet memories. The small duplex looks exactly the same with the exception of a well kept rose bushes lining the walk to the steps. I take a deep breath and glance over at Naomi, who is smiling from ear to ear. She leans over and steals a kiss from me.

"I love you, Joseph," she says.

"I love you, too."

This is exactly what I need to gain the courage to knock— to open the door I was so quick to close. And just like that, I am face to face with a mirror image of myself—my dad.

TEN

Naomi

Wow. It's as if am staring at Joseph twenty years from now. Yeah, his shoulders are broader, his face a little fuller, and his skin a shade darker, but I could pick him out of a sea of men claiming to be Joseph's father.

He beams with a big smile peering down at us. Joseph says a simple "Hello," pats his dad on the shoulder and walks right pass him. "Hi, Mom!" He says in a big breath. He embraces her so tightly she gives a little exhale when he finally releases her. She wipes some tears away from her stunning blue eyes and notices me still standing in the doorway.

"Well, who is this delightful young lady, Joseph? You didn't tell me you were bringing a guest."

She shoots him a half smile and takes me by the hand leading me pass the entry into what looks a sitting room. Nervous, I check for Joseph over my shoulder, but he is no where to be found. My guess is he hung back to speak with his dad, who seemed a little stunned by Joseph's passive, and quite honestly, shady greeting. Inside, I pray he is at least talking with his dad.

The room Mrs. Peters leads me to is beautifully decorated

with pretty pink floral couches. The leaves blend perfectly with the pale green walls. At first sight, it's shockingly colorful, but the colors bring me a sense of calm. Mrs. Peters is silent as we enter the room and she extends her hand for me to sit. She sits down right beside me. As she fidgets with the silver pendant necklace around her neck, I realize her mind isn't with me, but is still in the entry way with Joseph and his dad. She brushes invisible strands of hair back and releases a sharp breath.

Frustration? No. More like nerves—I hope.

"Would you like some tea?" she asks.

"Oh. Yes, Ma'am, that would be fine."

She cocks her head to one side. "Are you from the south?"

"Yes, Ma'am?" I grin.

She eyes me quizzically. Then, a small laugh escapes her. "Yes, your Southern dialect gave it away immediately. I am pleased, but call me Mrs. Peters. Thank you."

Her smile is wiped away immediately and without a moment of hesitation, she stands, then leaves the room. My guess is she's going to get the tea, but she is also going to eves drop on the two men possibly still standing in the entry way. My first impression is, she's brash, but I kind of like it. She says what she means which is something I definitely need to learn to do.

Since she has left me all alone, I take the liberty of scoping out the room for pictures. The first thing I notice is how immaculate this room is—it almost glows. There isn't one item out of place. The wooden coffee table right in front of me is polished to perfection. I can see my reflection. The crystal vase sitting at the center sparkles from the sun rays shining through the windows. My eyes move to the four level glass fixture right next to the window. *Yes!* I found them. There are pictures on every shelf. I walk over to get a closer look, then I back away. Should I? Snooping around someone's house is definitely not my thing? Minutes pass and I decide.

Snooping it is! Everyone has clearly forgotten about me.

The first photograph that catches my eye is largest frame on the glass fixture. A little boy is kicking a soccer ball through a field of fallen leaves. There's no doubt in my mind who the little boy is as I get closer. My heart warms and I can't help but smile at his sandy brown curls and rosy cheeks. One level lower there are a few pictures of Joseph as a teenager with a girl, who looks about his age. There's another picture of him with the same girl where the both look a little older. On the final level of the fixture there are pictures of him at the academy and some of his graduation from the academy with an older African American woman. I peer a little closer at this photograph, but I am jolted from my thoughts when I hear, "That's Joseph's grandmother, Josephine." I turn around to see Joseph's mom placing the silver tea tray on the coffee table.

"She's so pretty."

She takes a seat on the couch and pats the cushion next to her, gesturing for me to come sit down as well.

"I named Joseph after her."

Watching every move that I make, with what seems to be ridiculing eyes, she waits for me to sit before she begins pouring the tea. Suddenly, I hear voices for the first time. The commotion sounds heated. We both make eye contact and there, in her eyes, I see the tension she has been trying to hide since the moment I walked through the door. My being here is probably making thing even more uncomfortable for her.

Trying to draw my attention back to our conversation and not the now louder commotion coming from the hallway, she asks, "So, tell me your name again and how did you come to be here in London."

For the next several moments I answer all of her questions as honestly as I can. She seems undaunted by any of my answers, and I can tell that she isn't really listening. My story about how I got here requires more explanation than I'm giving her, but she doesn't dig. As each minute passes, I find myself becoming more and more frustrated with Joseph. Not because he is hashing it out with his dad, but because he didn't prepare me for this. He could have discussed an alibi with me or something, but then again, he may not have anticipated his mom whisking me away and leaving him alone with his dad.

When I finish my second cup of tea and the interrogation seems to be coming to a close, Mrs. Peters asks me one more question.

"Has Joseph ever told you about, Nina?" She sits her tea cup down on the tray, then sits back in the couch, crossing one leg over the other.

My stomach lurches. "Um…" I bite my lip, unsure of why she is asking this question.

Whoever Nina is, she must be important. Could she be the girl in the pictures still gracing the pristine glass shelves. I finally answer "No."

Mrs. Peters leans forward and just as she is about to reveal Nina's identity, Joseph walks into the sitting room.

"I'm sorry I left you two alone for so long." He walks over to me and gestures for my hand. Reluctantly, I place my hand in his and he pulls me to my feet into a tight embrace. He whispers in my ear, "I'm sorry, Naomi. I am so sorry."

With the frustration still stirring in my chest, his words extinguish it and I decide to let it all go—for now. He has enough to deal with besides my hurt feelings and my curiosity about Nina. I kiss him on his cheek.

"It's okay, Joseph, I forgive you."

He exhales.

"Thank you."

The aroma coming from the kitchen is breathtaking. I am so hungry, I can't stop looking at the time. My stomach beacons for the call to dinner. When I offered to help with preparing the meal, Joseph's mother insisted I sit and entertain the men. Helping her was my way out of the fiery furnace, but after getting to know her for the past few hours, I have a funny feeling she knew that and wanted me just where I am.

Joseph sits with me, making every effort not to look at or speak to his dad. Although, his dad makes small talk with me which is kind of awkward without Joseph joining in. We talk a little about growing up on the east coast. Then he asks me about my interests and about my family, which isn't much to talk about. I do most of the talking, with each new conversation fizzling out fairly quickly.

"Dinner is ready!"

Mrs. Peters calls from the kitchen and this time her voice sounds like angels calling from heaven. *Hallelujah!* My stomach praises at the sound of those words.

The dinner table is quiet, as we wait for the food to arrive. Every now and then Joseph's dad will ask a question that only requires a yes or not answer. Are you liking it here? Did you get to see any historical sites yet? Did you like what you saw? Did you meet each other here in London. Joseph answers this question.

"No."

And he doesn't elaborate.

"I'm sorry it took so long," Mrs. Peters scurries out of the kitchen placing a large casserole dish in the center of the table, "but I think this roast will redeem me."

She takes in a deep breath then scans all of our faces. We all are still sitting comfortably with the stable silence.

"So—dig in!" she demands.

Although, I am starving I patiently wait for everyone else to serve themselves. "First impressions are vital," my mom always told me, "don't waste them."

Peering up at me from her plate, Mrs. Peters insists, "Please help yourself, Naomi."

And I do as I am told. The roast is tender and covered in a beautiful brown gravy. Butternut squash, brown rice and soft, buttery rolls accompany the hardy roast. The squash and the rice are certainly not something I am used to eating, but I am so grateful for the home-cooked meal. After preparing my plate, I notice everyone has started eating except for Joseph. He looks over at me and curves his lips into a smile. Closing my eyes and bowing my head, I feel his hand close around mine under the table and he begins to pray, so that everyone can hear him. Without opening my eyes, I can hear that both of his parents have stopped eating. Once he is finished, I open my eyes and begin eating.

"So," Mrs. Peters begins, "I tried to listen in on your conversations while I was finishing up dinner, but I failed to get all the details of how you came to be here in London, Naomi."

Before Joseph can attempt to answer that question, I motion for him to allow me. "Well, like I was sharing with you earlier, my mom wants me to have some experiences before I begin college. I have always wanted to visit London, so this was sort of my graduation gift from her."

She doesn't look up, but continues with the questioning, "Wow, your parents must be very established to send you away, alone. How many months did you say you have been here?

Hesitantly, I confess, "Uh, three, ma'am. And it's just my mom and I. My mom and my dad are no longer together."

Pursing her lips, she carries on with her interrogation, "So, when are you planning on going back home? Doesn't the fall semester start sometime this month?"

Joseph drops his fork, causing all of us to look at him. I touch his hand under the table.

"I don't plan on starting college this fall. The idea is to see this beautiful country and enjoy a few months here before I get back to the states. My major is still something I'm trying to decide on, but I am leaning toward majoring in English and minoring in creative writing."

Finally, there's silence, with the exception of Mr. Peters' chewing and the slow steady tapping of Joseph's fork against his plate.

Then, out of nowhere, Joseph asks, "Are you satisfied, Mom? Did you get all the details you wanted?"

She looks up at him with a look I've seen countless time from my own mom.

"Don't you dare take that tone with me. I am still your mother even if you haven't seen me in years! Show some respect!"

At this point Mr. Peters stops eating. He calmly wipes his face with his napkin. He looks over at his wife. "Honey, please, there's no need to get upset."

I agree, "Right, it's fine. I will answer any questions you have Mrs. Peters. I am an open book."

Joseph locks eyes with his mom —searching for an answer to an unasked question. She breaks her stare when she hears my comment.

"Good, because I have several."

ELEVEN

Joseph

My mother is pushing every button I didn't even know I had. Yet, I am trying to maintain my composure and be respectful just as she has taught me. She drilled Naomi about every detail of her life during dinner and now she expects me to sit through evening tea?

My father is just as quiet as ever. He sits right across from me in a love seat with my mother, but it's like he's a thousand miles away. Sipping his tea, legs crossed and gazing out the window, we are all invisible to him.

That's it! I can't take it anymore! I lose all sense of honor and I let them have it.

"Are we boring you dad? I mean, I know mom is only interested in trying to find something humiliating about my girlfriend, but really, you have nothing to say?"

Beside me, I feel Naomi's body tensing up. Making her uncomfortable is not my intention, but this has to happen. It just seems to be inevitable. My dad, places his tea cup on the coffee table, then begins to rub circles on my mom's back. She leans back into his arm.

"Son, I—

"Please don't call me that. You don't deserve to call me that."

"Okay," he glances over at my mom, "Joseph. Your mom and I are sorry if us being back together has caused you any grief," he looks into my mother's eyes, "but we never stopped loving each other."

"Oh really," I ask. "Where did I fit into this love that never stopped."

He sits forward. "I never stopped loving you either."

"Well you have a fine way of showing it, Mr. Peters."

"Listen up, Joseph." His voice lifting an octave higher than normal. " I have listened to you all day. You have been disrespectful to your mother and very disrespectful to me. What you fail to realize, young man, is whether I raised you or not, I am still your father."

Surprised by the sudden change in his tone, I sit silent. I have never seen my father get upset. Better yet, I have never heard him speak so passionately. He sits back again, exhaling.

"Joseph, the three of us have been through a lot. I am truly sorry for my part in making your life difficult. My goal is to make it up to you and your mother," he gazes over at her again. She caresses his cheek. "I don't want to waste another day because I have already wasted so many. I will spend the rest of my life regretting leaving you and your mother, but I won't add another day of regret. This day is going to count for something. Today, I want to ask for your forgiveness, Son. I know it's hard and it may be too much to ask for right now, but I'm willing to wait just as long as you will consider it?"

With tears running down his face, my dad finally says the words I never thought I would hear. For years I contemplated if he would ever apologize and if he did, would I forgive him. With Naomi now gripping my hand so tightly and my mom sobbing in my dad's arms, emotions that haven't resurfaced since I was a teenager, are engulfing me. I can't handle this right now. I stand to my feet and walk out the front door.

I walk until I come upon the small coffee shop, two blocks from my mother's house. When I was a kid I would walk pass this place on my way to school. There would be a few people sitting right out front in small, black wooden chairs reading or conversing about whatever adults talked about back then. This evening, it's as if nothing has changed. As if time has been at a stand still.

I walk up and take a seat at one of the tiny round tables. Then, resentment sets in. It's incredible how my absent father could come back after all these years, and my mother could take him back without any objections—and— he expects me to do the same. The feeling of abandonment is hard to shake, especially when you grow up with no role model to tell you how to be a man. I fume just thinking about all I had to learn without him: riding a bike, changing a tire, shaving, asking a girl out, driving a car. On top of all of that, what about all the mistakes I made precisely because he wasn't there. How come he's let off the hook so easy. What makes him think he deserves for this to be easy? We didn't have it easy. *Who does he think he is!*

Just as the storm begins to build even stronger inside of me, I feel a light touch on my shoulder. I look up only to realize I walked out not only on my parents, but Naomi too.

Coming to my senses, I jump up.

"Oh, Naomi! I am so sorry." I reach for her. "I know I keep saying that—this whole thing has really gotten to me."

I hold her in my arms hoping she can understand. She's been so patient with me today.

"I get it," she finally says. "Remember, my relationship with my father is probably just as bad," she laughs.

I gesture for her to sit. "I don't know about you, but this day hasn't been all that I imagined it to be. I don't know what I was thinking bringing you here. We have so many unresolved issues."

She locks eyes with me and her face is flat.

"What's on your mind?" I smile, to take the edge off.

Settling into her chair, she says, "I am concerned about you, Joseph. I hate to see you this way. Honestly, this is the first time I have ever seen you angry."

My heart drops. This is the last thing I wanted to happen. We haven't seen each other in over three months and I manage to destroy everything we have built. I hang my head in embarrassment. The reality of it makes me sick to my stomach.

"It's not that I don't understand how you feel, or how hard this is. I actually think what has happened today is a good thing, I mean, after watching what just happened, I realized something."

"And what was that?" I ask.

"I realized we have more in common than I thought. You feel like he doesn't deserve your forgiveness. Right?"

"Exactly. Not at all."

I clench my teeth. Naomi's eyes softens as she reaches across the table for my hand.

"Can I share something with you?" she asks me.

"Anything."

TWELVE

Naomi

When I was a little girl, my dad left my mom and I. But, it was years later whenI started to feel abandoned. You see, at first, I was actually relieved and strangely happy about it. Don't get me wrong, my father and I had a pretty good relationship. I was his precious baby girl, but the things he subjected my mom and I to were borderline abusive. I imagined how easy life would be if he wasn't around and here's why.

My father was a heavy drinker. There were nights he didn't make it home and sometimes days. His alibi would be, "I'm drunk. I can't drive tonight." or "I'm going to stay at Tyson's house tonight to sleep it off." They argued almost everyday about the same thing. Eventually my mom got fed up with him not coming home, so they came to a compromise. The agreement was, he would call her to pick him up on the nights he was too wasted. The only problem with that was my mom had driver's anxiety (if that's a thing). She hated driving at night because of it, so she was never calm behind the wheel.

For the next couple of years, my mom woke me up well pass

midnight on Fridays and Saturdays to go with her to pick him up. Most kids waited for the weekend with anticipation, but me, I dreaded it like Monday mornings. It was torture. My mom weaving in and out of lanes, 20 miles across town to pick up my plastered dad. I'd close my eyes tight, praying we would make it home alive, while thinking if I closed them tight enough, God could hear me clearer. I slept lighter on those nights, dreading the call. Oh how I hated to hear my mom's phone ring. I always knew who it was.

One Saturday night, I was pulled from a light sleep by the sound of my mom's phone. "Okay, I will be there in a little bit." I heard her say. Trudging from my bed to slip on my shoes, I wiped the sleep from my eyes. My mom hated when I slept in the car, but sleep beckoned me, no matter how hard I tried to stay awake. Did she want me awake to see our inevitable demise—I don't know—but on this particular night, I was so tired, I fell to sleep. I'm not sure how long I was out, but it was long enough for my mom to hop a median and swerve frantically back on to the road. I screamed in horror as my head hit the passenger door, jolting me out of my sleep. Thank God there were hardly any cars on the road, because when she over adjusted the stirring wheel she sent us powering into another lane.

With the dark silence surrounding us, my mom pulled over to the side of the road to catch her breath. "You okay Naomi?" she asked. Of course I wasn't. Nothing about this situation was okay or normal. After thanking God and gaining our composure, we continued to our destination. There was no point in turning back now. We were almost there. When we reached my dad, we were still a bit shaken up and even with his intoxication, he noticed. He laughed when my mom confessed the near death experience we'd just had. A confession I believe she felt would cause him to think twice about his decisions. Instead, he laughed even louder and took the keys from my mom. She didn't protest.

The sound of my dad slamming the heavy door of my mom's pearl white Cadillac could have just as well been my coffin. To this day, I still question why she let him take those keys.

My heart began to beat faster than normal and I could hear it. From the backseat I pleaded, "Please be careful, Daddy." To this, he didn't respond. As the car accelerated to 65 miles per hour my life began to feel light and weightless. There was nothing I could do. I was helpless and my life was now in his hands. Tears filled my eyes. Each curve and corner brought new heights of fear, and with each swerve of the car, my mom yelled for him to slow down. A "Just let me drive!" then a fit of laughter following each time.

Although he was right there in the car with me, I couldn't have felt more abandoned. Love? What was love if my own father would put his only child and his wife in danger. My tears eventually dried and no longer did I feel sadness. The feeling left at the core of me was wild flames of anger mixed with torrents of fear. A few miles from my house was the part of the drive I always dreaded whether my mom was driving or my dad. It was the darkest area on the drive home because there weren't any street lights. Nothing but tall, dense trees lining the road. On top of that, the road was long and winding with a cliff drop off if you weren't careful. To my dad, this wasn't the time to slow down, but the time to press the gas even harder.

Completely transported to another time, I see my seven year old self, chest pumping, eyes tightly closed sitting in the center of the suede, navy blue backseat.

"Naomi…Naomi!"

I refocus my eyes. Joseph is staring right at me.

"I lost you for a minute. You okay?" He rubs my knee.

I pick at a hang nail I can't quite get rid of. My head is spinning from the memory of it all. Joseph leans in. His face is streaked with something that looks like anger, but I can't tell.

"Did you make it home okay?"

"Yeah, but after that, our relationship was never the same, so I guess I wasn't okay. The part that hurt the most wasn't that we could have died, and he didn't care, but it was the fact that he laughed. He laughed in the mist of the most traumatic event of my childhood. The person who was supposed to protect us—wasn't."

Joseph reaches for my hand.

"I don't tell you this to gain any sympathy. I just wanted you to get an understanding of what my dad was like. Everyday he decided to pick up that bottle was a choice. Every night my mother had to drag me out of bed risking both our lives, was a result of a choice he made. And everyday he cheated on my mother and didn't come home to her was a choice."

"So why are you telling me this?"

I gather the courage and I answer. "Your dad didn't have a choice."

Joseph squints his eyes as if my words just pushed him in the face.

"Now, that's not fair, Naomi. You can't compare us. Please don't do that." He releases my hand, gently placing it on the table.

"I'm not trying to compare our situations, Joseph, but have you stopped to think how he felt when your mom refused to go with him? She does seem to be a very stronger willed person."

"Yes, and I was very angry with my mother for allowing this to happen. I told you that."

Joseph's whole demeanor changes. He withdraws into his seat, focusing his attention on a couple and their little girl, seated adjacent to us. The little girl, wearing a pale blue dress, flits around their table like a butterfly. Joseph watches intently. I know he's frustrated with his father, but now he is frustrated with me. It's hard seeing him this way, but this is just a part of getting to know him. I love him even with his folded arms, furrowed brow, and slightly jutted bottom lip. He is everything I never knew I needed. Joseph has turned his life upside down for me, the least I could do is help him with this.

I scoot my chair just a little closer to his. "You have to let him go, Joseph. If you want to move past this— if you want to move on in your life, you have to forgive him."

"It's not that simple, Naomi." He looks at me and then back at the little girl, who is now blowing bubbles in her lemonade.

"Can I tell you another story?"

Joseph looks at me, then shrugs his shoulders.

"I guess that's a yes. Well, right before my Aunt Destine passed away we had one of our long talks. She noticed how I constantly brought up my dad in the most awkward circumstances. Like one time my mom got a flat tire after he had gone out for milk…"

I pause—waiting for a reaction to my joke. He doesn't as much as smile, so I continue.

We had to call her to come help us. I blamed it on him because he should have taken care of my mom's car better. It didn't matter what it was, I blamed everything on him. So, Aunt Destine was fed up with my attitude. She brought it up.

"Jesus had to suffer," she said, "yet in the midst of His suffering, He forgave those who had done him wrong and asked God to forgive them."

That was it. I had never compared my situation to Jesus' situation, but when I did, it shook me to my core.

After everything they did to him, he still chose to forgive them?

Seeing it that way, changed my perspective entirely. From that day forward, I vowed to speak well of him or not to speak of him at all. I decided, for myself, to forgive him. Although he wasn't around for me to tell him to his face, everyday, if I happened to think of him, I said out loud, *I forgive you, Dad*. And each day it got easier. Until one day I realized I had *truly* forgiven him. I no longer felt the need to tear down his character whenever someone spoke of him. I actually began to feel sorry for him. Now, if I had the opportunity to be in his presence, I would tell him to his face, *I forgive you, Dad*.

Joseph's eyes are empty.

Still looking in the direction of the little girl, he says, "I hear you, Naomi."

"You do?"

He looks at me.

"I do. But not today. I don't want to spend the rest of my time here ironing things out with him." Then he stands, pulling me up with him. "Did we just have our first argument?"

"No, it was just a disagreement."

He grins, then holds on to me and I know that maybe his trip here will end on a good note.

THIRTEEN

Naomi

Joseph and I walk the two blocks back hand in hand. The sun is setting, emitting a soft lavender and periwinkle color. A light breeze chills the air. Joseph drapes his firm arm over my shoulders warming me from the inside out. We walk without saying a word, savoring the time we have left together.

When we finally reach the doorstep of his house, Joseph lets out a slow breath.

"It's okay," I say. "Remember, you said you weren't going to try ironing things out. Just let it happen naturally.

"You're right."

He takes another deep breath, rolls his shoulders back, then rings the bell. In no time the door flies open. Mr. Peters is on the other side of it with an expression I can't make out. Is he happy to see us or is he upset we both left unannounced?

"Joseph?" he say.

Joseph doesn't hesitate, he walks right up to him and looks him straight in the eye. "Dad," he says, places a hand on his shoulder and walks right by.

I don't know, this time, there's something different about

Joseph's greeting and I guess Mr. Peters notices too because he is still standing there, looking directly at me, with the brightest smile on his face.

We all have small talk for the next couple of hours. The reassurance that Joseph has let his guard down with his dad comes when they continue talking after Mrs. Peters and I head to the kitchen for more crisps, as she calls them. When it's time to say our goodbyes it is bitter sweet. I'm happy it's time to get from under Mrs. Peters critical eye, but I'm sad Joseph and his dad didn't have more time. They both promise to visit soon as we head toward the door.

Joseph throws his arms around his mother. "I'm going to miss you Mom."

She holds on to him long after his arms loosen from around her. When she releases him he hesitates before he walks over to his father. Mr. Peters reaches for him, then pulls him in close.

"I love you, Son," Mr. Peters says, with his hands still on Joseph shoulders.

Joseph nods in response, then walks back over to me. Mrs. Peters holds out her arms towards me. Surprised, I walk over to her.

"I know I was hard on you," she says releasing me to look into my eyes, "but you must know, this young man standing next to you," she nods in Joseph's direction, "He means the world to me. No one is going to come into his life that I haven't thoroughly questioned," she chuckles.

Even with the laugh, I know she's serious. Joseph's eyes scale mine and I wonder if this Nina person, she brought up earlier, was questioned thoroughly. I make a mental note to ask later.

We leave just a little past 8pm. Under a full moon Joseph and I walk hand in hand on the same route back to the hotel. We board The Tube which, at this time of night, isn't as crowded so there's sitting room. Squeezing in right under Joseph's arm, I lean into his chest. The ride is peaceful and we chose to sit in it. My tranquil thoughts are then interrupted with the realization he's leaving in the morning.

I turn to him. "I don't think I can do it, Joseph. I miss my mom and home so much."

"You'll be fine. In just a few more weeks I'll be coming back to get you."

He pulls me in even closer, holding on to me even tighter as tears roll down my cheeks.

We get off the tube and begin our two-mile trek to the hotel. The path we take to get back to the hotel is almost clear of people with the exception of a few here and there. Each step we take is just one step closer to Joseph leaving and one step closer to me being alone—in a foreign country—again. My thoughts get heavier and more warped by the minute. I look over at Joseph who seems so far away.

"Hey. What's the matter."

"Just act normal. Okay?" he says.

His pace quickens.

Trying to keep up, I ask, "Why? What's wrong?"

"There's a guy following us."

As we turn the corner of Kingsington Lane, I notice a man in jeans and a green bomber jacket walking on the opposite side of the street.

"Is that him?" I ask.

"Yeah, that's him."

Joseph stops abruptly and kneels down, pretending to tie his shoe. The man across the street stops as well. He looks to his left, then to his right, I guess pretending to be lost.

Joseph looks over his shoulder at him, then back at me.

"Okay, when I get up we are going to sprint for the hotel."

"Okay." My heart picks up.

"Don't look back. Just run."

"Wait." I slide out of my flats, picking them up in a quick sweep. "Okay."

"Ready?" he asks.

I nod.

"One…Two…Three!"

Joseph shoots up from the ground and we both sprint like our lives depend on it. I hike my knees in cadence with pumping my arms, just as I was taught in during my days on the track team. From the looks of how I am keeping up with Joseph, the method is full proof. I run with what little energy I have left from this emotion day and all I can think about is the story of Lot from the Bible. I never understood why his wife would do something so stupid and look back when she was specifically told not to. Now, I realize how hard it must have been for her. The suspense of not knowing if this strange guy is right on our heels is too much. I want to look back. I want to look back so much, but I don't. I keep my eyes focused in front of me and I *run*.

When we reach the hotel we don't slow down. Joseph pants, "Keep going." We past the receptionist desk and the night clerk, Claudia, waves in confusion. Instead of taking the elevator, Joseph heads for the stairwell. My legs burn as I pump them up and down beckoning for the third floor to appear sooner than later. Feeling like I might just pass out, I focus my attention on the sounds echoing in the stairwell and realize the only steps I hear are ours. I listen even closer, realizing the only labored breathes I hear are ours. There's no one behind us.

When we reach the last flight of stairs, I stop to catch my breath. Hunched over, I pant, "there—is—no—one—behind—us."

Miraculously, Joseph hears me and he stops at the top of the stairs. With his hands on his hips and sweat dripping from his face, he turns around to see if what I am saying is true.

Taking in a deep breath, he sits down on the top stair.

"We have to get you out of here."

FOURTEEN

Joseph

Within the hour, all of Naomi's things are packed. Still looking around, checking to see if we missed anything, she goes into the bathroom for the third time. Meanwhile, I look up redeye flights to Virginia and find one leaving at 11am. In the bathroom, I hear nothing, movement has stopped. I walk over to see if everything is okay to find Naomi sitting on the edge of the tub.

"You okay?" I ask, easing down beside her.

"Yeah, I'm okay.".

She doesn't have to say a word because I know what she is thinking. Life as she knew it is over. The realization of that fact must be hard.

"I'm sorry," is all I can think to say.

She lifts her red strained eyes to mine.

"Don't be," she says. "My time in London has come to an end. I just didn't think I would be on the run again when it happened."

"Yeah. Me either."

"Who do you think that was?" she asks.

"It wasn't an FBI agent, that's for sure."

"How do you know?"

"An FBI agent wouldn't sneak around if they already have you identified. When we found out where you are, we find you and we come to get you. I think it was someone trying to scare you."

"Oh, they were successful," she grins.

Without warning, she jumps to her feet and runs out of the bathroom. When she returns, she is holding the yellow envelope that was delivered this morning.

My mouth drops. "I completely forgot about that," I admit.

"Me, too. I was so busy trying to exonerate myself during your mom's interrogation, I didn't think about it at all."

Even though I know she is trying to lighten the moment, the shame of how my mom treated her returns and lingers in my chest.

She hands it to me. "Open it."

I pinch the two brass clips together and pull out a letter typed on ivory card-stock. Naomi looks at me and I at her. She nods and I know she wants me to read it.

Hello, Naomi,

You probably didn't expect to hear from me all the way in LONDON. It's amazing how easy your FBI counterpart made it for us to locate you. The situation you find yourself in is a very sensitive one. You know something that the world doesn't. If you haven't noticed, the world is in a pre-apocalyptic state. All we ask of you is make us aware of what comes next. You have done such an excellent job of revealing the first stages why not share the remainder. Think of all the people you will save if they know how to prepare. Millions are purchasing the magazine simply because they await your next dream. You have no idea how happy this has made me. Remember, there's nowhere you can go that I won't find you. Send me what you know, or prepare to spend the rest of your life running.

P.S. The FBI doesn't have to know where you are if you simply come forward with the information I need. Send it to 1666 Broad Way, Augusta, GA 30906 and we will gladly allow you to live your life free of distractions.

Sweet Dreams,
Damian Draegon

Founder and CEO
The Spark Chronicles

Sliding the letter back inside the envelope, I notice there's something else inside. I turn it upside down and a magazine falls on to the floor. Naomi picks it up. It's a current addition of *The Spark*. The front cover features a huge photo of the New York stock exchange building. The headline reads, "WHAT DO WE DO WHEN MONEY DOESN'T MATTER ANYMORE?" At the very bottom of the front page a side headline features a picture of a red journal. It looks very similar to Naomi's. I read the caption out loud, ANONYMOUS PROPHET SOON TO REVEAL WHATS NEXT. When the last word leaves my mouth, Naomi rips the magazine from my hands and begins tearing it up, page by page. Once the magazine is in a pile on the floor, she grabs the envelope containing the letter, puts it in her small book bag, then slips on a familiar blue baseball cap. She turns around to face me.

"Let's go."

Boarding the red eye flight is nerve wrecking to say the least.

Naomi refuses to believe she is not a fugitive on the "no fly list." My explanation of her case not actually being a case *at all* isn't holding up with her. During our drive and our walk through airport security I attempted to reassure her, several times, her case is simply one of suspicion not criminal activity. Damian Draegon enjoys exploiting her case, but it's only for his personal gain. The FBI just wants to question her and determine what she knows, but I hindered them from doing that so a promotion may not be in my future any time soon. Hopefully, once we are in the states again, we can figure out how to give them what they want without Damian getting the credit.

The first three hours of the flight are awkwardly silent. I can feel Naomi's angst. Not knowing what else to say to ease her mind, eventually I fall off to sleep. In the darkness I dream of Naomi running. She's so tired, but she just continues to run and run and run, until she arrives at a door.

I shudder out of my sleep. Trying to recollect what caused my frightened awareness, I look down at my watch to see how long I was out.

"You were out for about an hour," a whispered voice says.

I look over at Naomi, who is gazing out of the window.

"Did you sleep at all?" I ask.

"No," she whispers.

I grin, "I had a strange dream."

She looks at me, now intrigued, "Oh yeah. What about?"

I grin a little wider, "I don't know. It was strange. My dreams never make sense."

We both laugh. Then, her laugh turns into a smile, but it quickly fades. She turns back to the window. She speaks without looking at me.

"You know, I haven't dreamed much in the last three months, but the one dream I do remember won't stop replaying over and over again in my mind."

"Can you tell me about it or is it one of those dreams you have to let marinate?"

She looks at me with those big brown eyes. Her lips curve into a smile again and I breath a little easier.

"It's a little private, but…" she pauses.

"But what?" I smile back.

She blushes and my hand involuntarily makes it's way to her cheek.

Her eyes meet mine. "I know I have to tell someone."

Naomi has a hard time looking at someone when she's blushing, scared, or not sure about something, so I know when her eyes dart back to the window, then back at me, she's questioning whether she should tell me.

I peer down at my watch and rub her hand. "All we have is time. Approximately two hours and fifteen minutes."

She tells me a dream about a women, a husband, two children and a flood. Once she finishes, she exhales, leaning back into her chair.

"That's a relief," she confesses. I've been waiting months to share that one.

"Is that it?" I ask.

"Yes."

We sit for several minutes as I replay the dream in my head, seeing it come into full vibrant color right before my eyes.

"The couple in the dream—who do you think they were?" I ask.

Her cheeks flush.

"I think they were us."

I nod in agreement and lean in closer to her. I can't help but to lean in closer to her. The way I feel about her is something I can't hide and I don't want to. Her dreams are nothing short of a reality that is soon to come and out of all of the realities she has shared with me, this one brings a sensation I have never felt. Pressing my face closer to hers, the only words sufficient for this particular moment come out so effortlessly.

"I love you so much, Naomi."

She opens her eyes to look at me, then presses her soft lips against mine.

"I love you more," she says.

Noses touching, we stay close for a few moments.

"So what do you think it means?" I ask.

"I think this was a warning dream. Another dream about what is coming. I think the wave not over taking the house is symbolic to how everyone will see the destruction coming, but it won't harm us. Maybe it's encouragement to keep fighting because whatever I have to face back home will not beat me. When I read the letter from Damian, it set off a fire inside of me. I can't allow him to scare me anymore. I have a plan."

Eager to hear it, I lean in just a little closer.

FIFTEEN

Naomi

While Joseph slept, I thought about the stories Aunt Destine used to tell me from the Bible. Recalling the stories of Elisha, Daniel, Jeremiah, Ezekiel, and Joseph gaves me hope. Out of all the stories I remember, Jeremiah's story stands out. He, like myself, was afraid to share what he knew to be true—afraid of what people might think—afraid of how people would react. Eventually Jeremiah couldn't hold the truth in any longer. He had to tell the people what he knew and no matter how unqualified he felt, he told them anyway.

"I have to go public."

Joseph gives me an unexpected smile. "Okay."

"That's it? Just 'okay?'"

He runs his palm over my cheek. "I trust your decision. So, what's the plan?"

"That's the plan. Go public and make sure Damian has nothing to do with it."

Joseph nods slowly as if there's more coming, but there isn't. That's all I got.

"Okay. Got it." I says slowly.

"I don't know how, but I believe it will come to us," I tell him.

"You're right," he says. "I believe that too." He faces the seat in front of him. "Naomi,…"

"Yes."

"Keep in mind and be prepared if some people don't like what you have to say."

"I will. I am not afraid anymore."

And I mean it. The fear of it all is somewhere roaming the streets of London.

By the time we arrive at Norfolk International Airport, the tension in my shoulders has vanished. We retrieve our bags, then pick up the rental car without incident. There's an overcast. The thick gray clouds creep across the sky and withholding the rain until we are safe in the SUV. When we get on the interstate the rain begins to fall. The SUV is roomy, so I recline in my seat grateful for the drive and time to get my thoughts together before I meet Joseph's grandmother.

"So, have you told your grandmother anything about the mess I'm in?"

"First, be sure to call her Grandma Josephine. She will not except it any other way. I called her when we landed, so she is expecting you. She knows enough. Don't worry Naomi. My grandma is the coolest grandma you will ever meet. Just be yourself. "And," he cuts his eye at me, "loose the 'grandmother.'"

The rest of the drive, my thoughts are consumed with how I am going to tell the entire world what is coming. First, I think about making a social media post, but it dawns on me how much I discredit social media posts. You can't believe everything you read. Then, I consider going to a news station and asking them for some air time.

Now that's a stretch.

I banish the thought as soon as it comes. Frustrated, I focus on the mile markers counting down until Joseph gets off on exit 9.

About five miles down the road he says, "We are here."

Taking in as much air into my lungs as I can hold, I focus on the narrow road ahead of me. The sun has yet to make it's appearance. There's a light fog hovering over the graveled road, making giving the atmosphere a ominous appearance.

"Is there a lake near by?" I ask Joseph.

He smiles, but continues looking at the road. "Yeah, there is. It's a nice quiet spot, west of the house. I spent a lot of time there as a teenager. I will take you to see it once you get settled."

A Lake! I've always wanted to live near a lake or any body of water for that matter. Although this day has been pretty gray, this adds some color.

Now, just a bit further up the road, I see a quaint brick house manifesting. A rickety white fence tells me the house has been standing for some time, but the sky blue shutters give the house life. With matching blue shutters, right behind the house is an even house which doesn't look as old.

As soon as we pull into the heavily gravel driveway, a figure appears behind a screened door. Joseph hops out of the car and quickly runs over to open my door.

"Well, hello there," the figure in the door calls out.

Throwing my book bag over one shoulder and grabbing my hand, Joseph responds, "Hi, Grandma Josephine," his smile almost reaching his ears.

He almost runs to her, this boyish energy radiating from him is foreign to me. We climb three wooden steps before the screen in door creaks open. I almost loose my footing at the site of the women standing at the door. My heart drops to my stomach.

"Well, come on in you two. I have been expecting you."

I stare directing into her eyes unwilling to move. Joseph gently pushes the small of my back, urging me forward.

"Naomi?" he whispers.

I don't move. My feet are planted.

"Is everything okay?" Joseph asks, still gently touching my back. "What is it?"

I whisper, "It's her."

"Who?" he asks.

"I mean, she looks exactly like her."

"Like who?" he whispers.

"My Aunt Destine."

SIXTEEN

Naomi

I was sixteen when my Aunt Destine passed away. It was a day I will never forget.

Daniel and I had recently started dating. His aunt had dropped us off at the theatre to see a scary movie, called *The Deceased*. It was a movie about three teenagers who decided to raise their father from the dead. I was determined not to go, but because of my need for attention and affection, I caved and agreed to go. My mom had allowed me to have a cell phone so she could contact me when I was away. She texted or called me every hour on the hour, so when a call came through during the movie, I intentionally ignored it and silenced my phone. Once the movie was over, we stood out in front of the theatre to wait for our ride. Daniel was ecstatic about how the film ended. I, on the other hand, had no idea what was so exciting because I barely paid any attention. After a few minutes of listening to him rant, I remembered to call my mom back. When I pulled my phone out of my purse, I noticed I had eleven missed calls, all from my mom. I couldn't dial her number back fast enough, dropping my phone twice before my shaking hands obeyed.

"Hello, Mom? Is everything alright!?"

"No, Baby Girl," she pauses. "Your Aunt Destine just had a heart attack. She is in the ICU."

With fear, and regret bubbling up inside of me, I asked, "Where! What hospital?"

"We are at Medical University Hospital."

I hung up the phone immediately walking over to a cab parked near the curb. I could hear Daniel still talking about the movie to himself as I rushed into the cab.

"Daniel, I have to go. My Aunt Destine just had a heart attack."

Dumbfounded he walks over to the cab. "But, my aunt is coming she should be here in fifteen minutes."

"I don't have time to wait. Please apologize for me." Pulling the door closed, I set my attention on the driver.

When I reached the bedside side of Aunt Destine, I was grateful she was awake. With tubes trailing done her throat and up her nose the joy of seeing her awake fades. My mom is asleep in a nearby chair, but I don't wake her. Aunt Destine reaches out her hand for mine and with tears in my eyes, she tries to speak. I pat her hand and tell her it's okay. She looks at me with those deep, wisdom filled eyes as she always did and some how, deep down, although I didn't want to, I knew exactly what she wanted to say.

I'm tired.

Breaking down into tears, I knew what that meant. She squeezed my hand gently reassuring me that everything will be okay. I knew this was her way of telling me to be strong. Two days later, she was gone. It took everything in me to attend the funeral. I didn't want to go. I was angry—confused. Confused as to why such a beautiful person would be taken so soon. After days of refusing to accept her passing and refusing to even prepare for her funeral, my mom convinced me to go. She said, the funeral wasn't really for me, but for others who needed closure, so I went.

The night after the funeral, I dreamed of Aunt Destine. In the dream she was sitting in her living room watching her favorite soap opera. She called for me to go get her some water.

"I'm thirsty, Naomi—I'm so thirsty," she said.

Right away, I went to the kitchen to get her a glass of water and she drank it quickly. Again she spoke, "I'm so tired, baby girl. Oh so tired," said in between labored breathes.

Sitting down next to her and she hugged me tightly, repeating those same words, over and over, again.

"I'm so tired—oh so tired."

Waking up the next morning, a sweet peace filled my heart. I finally had assurance that what I saw in her eyes that day in the hospital was true. She *was* tired. Tired of depending on machines to breath for her. Tired of all of the doctors probing her. I was assured that the three days she lay there, in the hospital, hooked up to every life preserving machine known to man, God gave her a glimpse of heaven. Who could turn down eternity in paradise for a life of pain? Aunt Destine's decision was simple: continue to here and deal with all of her medical issues, or go home with the Father.

Aunt Destine lived a beautiful life, spreading her wisdom to whomever was smart enough to listen. Sometimes things were tough, but she always found a reason to laugh. I know she is somewhere in heaven, right now, drinking coffee and laughing with Jesus.

SEVENTEEN

Naomi

Grandma Josephine looks at Joseph for answers.

"Everything okay?"

"Yeah, Grandma. She's just been going through a lot lately. Let me just get her in the house."

I finally force my feet into moving cross the threshold. Joseph guides me to a room with a cozy red couch and a television. A leather, brown recliner sits in the corner and at the foot of it is a small, wooden coffee table. I notice a wicker coaster with a steamy cup of coffee atop it. The striking resemblance of this woman and my late Aunt Destine is enough to make me dizzy. Staring down at the coffee, I coach myself: *Stop acting crazy, Naomi. Get it together!*

"What's up with you, Naomi," Joseph whispers, "You are acting really strange."

Grandma Josephine trails in behind us, "You all want some coffee? I just made a fresh pot."

"Sure, Grandma. Naomi will take some, too."

She scurries back out. I scan her entire frame marveling at the identical features. Joseph turns back to face me, with a tightened jaw, he continues, "So tell me, what's up? My grandma can smell something from miles away, so it's best to come clean before she points it out."

My conscience says to just brush it off and keep it to myself, but heart has something else in mind.

"She looks just like my Aunt Destine."

He leans down to whisper a little softer, "I know. You said that just a few moments ago."

I put one hand on his shoulder, "No, you don't get it. She looks identical to her. She even speaks like her. I'm losing it, Joseph."

Joseph stands a littler taller. "O…okay."

"Yeah. It's really messing with my head."

"Really, Naomi? I'm sorry. I thought this would be just what you needed."

The charged excitement once radiating from him has vanished at the thought of me possibly not wanting to stay. Even though I'm thrown off balance, there's no way I'm diverting from the plan.

I cup his face, staring into his eyes. "No. No. I'm staying." Then I laugh, "besides, there's no way I'm going back to London. I would rather stay here than anywhere else."

His lips curve into a smile, "Are you sure?"

"One hundred percent."

"You two must be tired. Go on and have a seat," she demands as she strolls back in carrying two cups of coffee. "Joseph, go on in the kitchen there and grab that cream and sugar. I didn't add any cause' I don't know how Miss Naomi here likes hers." She peeks up at me from her glasses.

I gently take both cups from her, "Thank you," I say, trying not to meet her eyes. She plops down in the recliner just as Joseph is returning. He hands me a small canteen of creamer and a bowl of sugar. As I prepare my coffee with three spoons of sugar and enough cream to make the dark coffee turn a caramel brown, Joseph and Grandma Josephine catch up.

Sipping my coffee I quietly listen as they talk about Mr. Peters and the trip.

"Does he plan on visiting soon?" she asks.

Joseph dodges the question, then begins to tell her about how Mrs. Peters treated me.

She looks over at me. "Oh girl, don't go following up that women. She's always been a priss…pre-madonna, or whatever you want to call it. Don't pay her no-never-mind."

I laugh out loud at her take on Mrs. Peters.

"The young lady Joseph wanted to marry had to deal with far worse."

My breath catches, all of the air leaves my lungs. I glare over at Joseph. His face is flat. Grandma Josephine looks at me, then at Joseph.

"Well, what's the matter? You know that she was horrible to that girl."

Silence. Dead silence.

Joseph finally takes a slow sip from his coffee and sets it down on the table. The room is off balance. I have to remind myself to breath. I look at Joseph for some kind of grounding. Why hasn't he ever spoken of his past relationships especially someone he intended to marry. I guess from our silence and Joseph's inability to look at either of us, Grandma Josephine has a realization.

"Oh my, Lord! Joseph, you didn't tell her about Nina. Lord, if I would have known that I would have minded my manners!"

Joseph smiles, "It's okay, Grandma. We just haven't had the opportunity to talk about *a lot* of things."

I chime in, "Yes, it is fine. It would silly of me to think I'm the only girl Joseph has ever…been with… I mean dated." I smile through that statement. The bitter taste of it coming out makes me squint.

To be honest, the thought of Joseph with another girl had never crossed my mind until I saw the picture of him and Nina on his mother's shelf. Since then, finding the right time to bring it up continues to escape me.

Grandma Josephine leans over the arm of the recliner looking at me just how Aunt Destine used to when she wanted to crack a joke.

She whispers to me, "You can ask him *all* about that latter."

She winks at me and I nod. Joseph sips his coffee.

We spend the next hour chatting about the news. Then Grandma Josephine asks about my mother. She even asks about how everything is going with the FBI and *The Spark*. It's awkward talking about all of this, but it would be expecting a lot of her to let me stay here without a decent explanation. Plus, the thought of Joseph sitting down telling her everything there is to know about me, kind of makes me blush.

"No one ever comes all the way out here, Naomi. Nobody but the postman and Joseph. You'll be safe," she says. "I take that old truck, out back, to town maybe twice a week. You welcome to drive it if you get bored."

Her voice and kindness melts my heart. I sit hand in hand with Joseph as they continue to catch up. Eventually, Grandma Josephine begins to falls asleep in her cozy recliner. When she's finally out, Joseph stands up and grabs my hand.

He looks down at me with a bright smile running across his face, "Come on, let me show you around."

He first walks me through Grandma Josephines kitchen. It's small but tidy, each cabinet worn dark wood. Nothing seems to be out of place. Everything has it's spot right down to a big, yellow sponge sitting a top a white plate near the sink. Joseph walks over to a big ceramic strawberry on the counter, near the coffee maker. He picks up the green stem and sticks his hand inside. Only when he pulls his hand out do I realize it's a cookie jar.

"Want one?" He asks, then takes a bite of his chocolate chip cookie.

"I'm fine."

As he leads me down a short hall, I finally recognize the smell I've been trying to identify since we arrived, ginger and citrus. Walking into a fully furnished room, I take a deep breath in, savoring the aroma.

"This is my old room," Joseph says.

The walls are a cloudy gray. A full size bed is pushed against the furthest wall and there's a small desk in one corner with various medals and trophies lining the wall above it.

I walk over to pick up one of the medals, "What are all of these for?"

"Some are for soccer, but most of them are for track and field. I was a 100m state champ in high school."

"You never told me you were a runner."

He smiles, "You never asked," he says, dusting off one of his trophies. "There's a lot I haven't told you."

I cut my eyes at him, "Don't I know it."

He ignores me and walks back out into the hallway. I follow. He opens another door down the hall. When I reach the room aromas of peppermint and marshmallows fill the space. My eyes are drawn to a large window with sheer white curtains draping down each side. A powder blue cushioned bench sits right beneath it. I walk over to the bench, surprised at the gorgeous view overlooking the lake. This might be my favorite part of Grandma Josephine's house by far.

I take a seat on the bench and realize Joseph is watching me, intently. Then I notice the large bed and a small dresser with a mirror.

"This is the perfect spot for reading," I say.

"Do you like it?" Joseph asks.

"Do I! I love it!"

"I'm glad. This is going to be your room while you are here."

My mouth drops. "Really?"

"Really." Joseph laughs.

"This is such a large room. Probably the biggest in the house?" I question.

"It is," he says.

"No. I am not taking Grandma Josephine's room."

Joseph pulls me up from the bench. He holds my hands. "You're not. She moved out of this room when my Grandfather passed away. She never could sleep in here without him."

I turn to take in another view of the lake, "Wow. This is amazing."

"There's more to see." He pulls me out the room and to the back door of the house.

Joseph leads me outside to the smaller house just behind the main house. He puts his hand on the door knob to open the door, but he pauses.

"This place is very special to Grandma Josephine. She spends a lot of time here, if you are ever wondering where she is. So, if you want to come in here just knock, or ask first, okay?"

"Okay."

He opens the door revealing a single room with thick tan carpet and endless shelves of pictures and ceramic figurines. In the far corner of the room is a white, wooden rocking chair engraved with the word PRAY. Behind the shelving is a large window stretching from one side of the room to the next. The room glitters from the light bouncing off of the crystal figurines and glass picture frames. It's almost difficult to look at, but you can't help but marvel at the magnificent glow of the room.

"This room takes my breath away," I confess.

Joseph grins as he takes in the sparkling shards of light casting in every direction. "I guess it's safe to say Grandma Josephine likes things that shine?"

"It is!"

"This is where she comes to spend time with God," Joseph explains. He begins to look at the photographs. "She says the pictures help her to remember who to pray for and the prayers that have been answered."

"I think it's beautiful, Joseph. I would never want to leave."

I begin scanning the photographs on the shelf. Then, at the center of the shelf, I come upon a glass frame. It shine is hands down the brightest and is definitely pause worthy, yet it does not justice for the gorgeous picture it holds. It's a photo of Joseph standing in a field of yellow flowers, hand and hand with her—Nina. I feel Joseph's presence behind me as I stare. My eyes are glued to the photo and all I want to do is release everything in my stomach on to Grandma Josephine's clean tan carpet.

I suck in a breath and manage to speak. "We have to talk."

EIGHTEEN

Joseph

Not wanting to ruin our day, I tried to hold off telling Naomi about Nina. Now she's standing here staring at our old engagement photo. Two years ago my entire life evolved around this one girl. Now I have to explain to the girl I can't imagine life without who the girl in the photos was to me. I thought I could just forget about her and move on with my life, but for some reason, my past keeps finding it's way into my present. Trying to keep the memory of Nina hidden has only brought her to the forefront of our relationship and thinking that door was officially closed years ago was obviously a mistake. My mom and Grandma Josephine still having pictures up of that season of my life is evidence that door is still wide open.

Naomi follows me down to the lake. The walk is brutal. Every step we take, my heart beats faster and faster. Drudging up a part of life I have tried so hard to forget isn't something I anticipated today, but since I met Naomi I have had to expected the unexpected.

The cool Autumn breeze is fresh and crisp. The crutch of the leaves that have already fallen conjure up memories of my childhood days, playing flag football in this exact spot with my friends. The leaves slowly losing their color, reminds me of how quickly seasons change, yet they are a sign of how in time everything comes to an end and change is inevitable. I had hoped our first walk down to this area would be different. The wooden bench my grandfather built, years before I ever came, is still here. The last time I sat on it was about two years ago. When the memory begins to take form in my head, I hesitate and stop in my tracks. Naomi notices.

"What's wrong? Why did you stop?"

With something that feels like guilt taking resident in my chest, I explain, "Let's go sit under that pine tree over there instead." I point to my right.

Being the strong welled and skeptic person she is, Naomi rolls her eyes and walks over to the bench anyway. When she reaches it she examines it, then her head falls back. She turns to look at me, then she walks back towards me with an expression I can't read.

"I am starting to get a little annoyed, Joseph." She kicks at some leaves. "How come you haven't told me about this girl? She must been pretty amazing and very important to you. I mean—everywhere you take me, there she is!"

"Naomi, you know better than me that we haven't really had quality time. I mean we pretty much stop seeing each other, then it was your graduation, then the FBI, I…"

My head is spinning. How do I even begin to tell her.

I roll the tension out of my shoulders. "The only time I can remember that I could have told you was right before you graduated. Before *you* said we needed some time apart. Besides, this…she isn't important to me, whatsoever, *anymore*. That chapter of my life is over, but I do realize I owe you some kind of explanation since two of the most important women in my life still have photos of her."

"Uh. I would think so."

She is annoyed. I've never seen her so annoyed. Taking her hand, I guide her over to the pine tree. A cool breeze pushes through the pine needles. Naomi shivers. I take off my jacket and wrap it around her, a peace offering before I start. My hands shake and I'm not sure if it's because of how cool it has become or my nerves. I clasp them together, intent on getting this over with whether I'm nervous or not.

"Nina Silva. We met in eighth grade. On the very first day of school she walked into class about three minutes after the bell. There was no ignoring her entrance because she commanded everyone's attention just by her presence. She was the most beautiful I had even seen."

Naomi doesn't flinch at my candor, so I continue.

"Because I have never been shy, I told her as soon as I got the opportunity. She laughed at my boldness, but it sparked a conversation and from there we became friends. Everyone in school wanted us to date, but we both respected our friendship so much we didn't want to blur the lines. Well, you know how friends can be sometimes, they never stopped trying to get us together. But, we weren't having it, at least, she wasn't. I had fallen in love with her, but I valued her friendship too much to tell her. She didn't hide that I was her best friend, but I was tormented each day I didn't tell her how I truly felt.

We did everything together. We studied together, laughed together, went to dances together—we even got in trouble together. Then, the summer before ninth-grade, my best friend Richard decided he was going to ask her out. Because he knew there was no way I was this close to her and didn't want more than just a friendship, he asked me if it was okay. Inside, I was furious with him, but I told him to go for it. So, he did and she said yes.

"Wait." Naomi stops me. "So this dude was your best friend and he really thought you didn't care?"

"There was nothing I could do. He was set on asking her out whether I agreed to it or not, that's how he was. Our friendship, at this point, didn't matter to him anymore. He was in love with Nina too, or so he said. Needless to say, I was heartbroken. When our ninth grade year started, Nina saw less and less of me. Although we remained friends, I had to distance myself from her and make new friends. Eventually, I started dating. Dating other girls kept my attention off of Nina and Richard's budding relationship, but deep down I couldn't wait for them to break up. It was a long wait, but right before our tenth grade year ended Nina broke up with Richard. Richard's dad received orders to Japan and Nina didn't want to date long distance. That day, I felt like I could literally fly. After he left, Nina and I started hanging out more and more. It was like old times. We were inseparable.

When her sixth-teeth birthday was closely approaching, she asked me if I would be her escort to her Debutante Ball. Of course I said yes. That day, she made a vow before her family and friends to remain pure until marriage. What she didn't know is right along with her, I vowed to wait with her and for *her*."

Naomi's eyes leave me for a moment. Maybe this is too much for her, but I continue anyway. If I am going to tell her about Nina, I have to tell all of it.

"We took a photo together that night and that was the picture you saw at my mother's house. That summer we grew even closer. I could tell she missed Richard, but I kept her company to ease her mind because being there for her was helping me as well. I needed her too. Pretending that all I wanted from her was her friendship lasted for sometime, but the summer before twelfth grade, I had a long talk with Grandma Josephine. I poured my heart out to the only person I could at the time. She advised me to tell her. She said, "You have nothing to lose. What's God has for you is for you." So, since I had saved a few bucks from my summer job, and Grandma agreed to let me hold the truck, I planned a nice evening with Nina. Most of my money went to a promise ring. If she accepted what I had to say and shared the same feelings, I would present the ring to her, if not, I kept the receipt."

I laugh, peering over at Naomi, trying to thin out the thick air between us.

"The night was beautiful. Everything went exactly how I had planned it. We went to dinner at her favorite place, Menchies, then to the movies to see this cheesy chick flick she wanted to see. Afterwards, I brought her back here. We sat down on that bench right over there and I told her everything. From the time I first saw her, to the day Richard asked me if he could ask her out, to the painful days I spent waiting for them to break up. Then, I told her about the night I made the same promise she had made. When I finished there was dead silence, with the exception of the hundreds of frogs croaking in the woods. Man, I wanted to kill those frogs for ruining the mood. She sat there with her head down, stoic, for what seemed like a century, until I finally saw tears dripping down into her lap. She finally looked up at me and confessed she felt the same way, but never wanted to ruin our friendship. I couldn't get the ring out fast enough. That night we promised ourselves to each other and then we carved our names in that bench over there.

I lowered my head feeling like maybe I should stop. The memory of it all is a lot for me. I can't imagine what Naomi is feeling right now.

"Are you okay, Naomi,… you know, hearing all of this."

"Yeah," she says, still staring out at the lake. "I know this can't be easy for you."

She rubs my back and looks at me. "It's okay." She bumps my shoulder with hers. "This story still leads you to me."

I smile then I continue.

"After that night it felt like my life had finally started. We were the perfect match and everything in the universe was singing our praises. Once we reached our final year of high school we started thinking about our future together. Nina was interested in journalism and I had always wanted to major in criminal justice. When got accepted to the University I wanted to attend, I leaped at the opportunity not really considering how far away it would take me. Nina decided to stay close to home and go to the University of Virginia. She accepted the distance my pursuits would bring between us and so we both began walking out our dreams. We planned how we would accomplish our goals and simultaneously keep our relationship strong.

Three weeks before leaving for college I planned to propose to her. I was sure this would solidify how serious I was about her. As you know, she said yes. Before leaving, her parents arranged for us to have engagement pictures taken which became the picture you saw in Grandma Josephine's prayer room. It doesn't surprise me that she would pray for us. She knew better than anyone how in love I was with Nina, so it's also not a surprise that she would continue to pray for my broken heart—hence the picture still being front and center.

We planned to have a wedding when we both finished our sophomore years. Every six months I would visit her or she would visit me, but our schedules were becoming so busy that the constant visits only lasted for a year. We both agreed to wait a little longer before we began planning for the wedding. Everything seemed to be fine, until one-day Grandma Josephine called and asked me a very strange question. She asked if I knew Richard Sands had moved back into town and was now attending the University of Virginia. I didn't even have to guess what she was thinking. It was crystal clear to me, but what bothered me is what

I know about Grandma. She never asks questions she obviously knows the answer to. She knew I didn't know and this was her way of telling me. After hanging up with her, I immediately called Nina. We talked for a good thirty minutes and she never made mention of Richard. So, I bluntly asked if she knew he was there or had ran into him. She said no, but I knew her better than she gave me credit for. She was lying to me.

My visit came a bit early that year and I didn't tell a soul I was coming. When I reached Nina's parents house and saw an unfamiliar car in the driveway, the sky starting to spin. With my heart pounding in my chest, I banged on her parents door. The rage inside of me knocking me off balance. Another knock later, Nina's mom answers the door. And just as she opens it, I see Richard and Nina walking toward the door as well. I came undone. All I remember is pushing past Mrs. Silva and landing on top of Richard. Before I could pound his face in, Mr. Silva came to his rescue. I haven't seen either of them since."

"I'm so sorry, Joseph," Naomi whispers.

Looking at her now, I say, "Don't be. I'm not. If I didn't find out then what kind of person she was, I would have probably married her. I thank God I found out."

"You're right," she says, then leans into me. "You are amazing, you know that?"

"Oh is it because I was a sucker and my best friend stole my girl twice?" I laugh.

"Oh no! Because when you love, you love completely. You promised yourself to her."

Gazing off to the now setting sun, I realize how much I have overcome in the past two years. Leaving that relationship was just about the hardest thing I ever had to do, but God in is amazing grace saw me through it.

"You know what, Naomi? I did give my all to Nina. There's

no doubt in my mind that she gave her all to me at one point too. She got caught up in old feelings and allowed herself to succumb to them. If she hadn't done what she did, I would have never moved on. I was actually thinking about giving up FBI academy for her. But, if I would have never joined, I would have never found you. You needed me, and I needed you. I am a firm believer that God works all things out for our good."

Naomi eyes sparkle when she looks at me and I lean in. Our foreheads touch before our lips meet for the second time today. My mind goes blank and all of my faculties are taken over by all things Naomi. Then, without warning I am jolted back to reality. The space between us goes cold. I open my eyes. Naomi is standing.

"What is it?" I ask.

Her face is serious. "So, you made that promise to her."

"Yeah."

"So, you never got married?"

She paces.

"Right…I—I'm confused," I admit.

She stops and then looks at me. "So, did you keep your promise? You know, even though you didn't marry *her*?"

Now, I know where this is going. I get up from the ground and I walk over to her. I've never spoken to anyone about this, but today is a good a time as ever.

Grabbing her chin, I whisper, "Yes, Naomi. I kept my promise to myself."

She closes the space between us and I am afloat—weightless.

For the first time, in years, I feel proud of the promise I made to myself and God. I am happy I waited and even happier I waited for the right person.

NINETEEN

Naomi

Tomorrow morning Joseph leaves to go back to Georgia. It's unnerving to know I will be without him again, but I am appeased by the thought he will be back soon. After a few hours of sleep, Joseph texts me dinner is ready. I head to the bathroom to wash up. As I splash water on my face flashbacks of Joseph and Nina's love story invade my thoughts. I tried to stay calm during the whole chronicle, but it was hard to listen to how much he loved her. They had something so pure and so strong. *How can I live up to that?*

I stare at my self in the mirror.

She is gorgeous and probably has a great career. I just got out of high school. Who knows when I will have a clear head to start college.

I wonder if she stayed with the Richard guy.

I wonder if she ever reached out to Joseph.

I wonder if she is still in love with Joseph.

The thoughts won't stop coming.

A light knock comes to the door. I slip my furry pink house

shoes on and open the door. It's Joseph. We have had a long two days, traveling through the night with maybe only five hours, of sleep, if that. Joseph looks as good as ever, but I can see the sleeplessness in his eyes.

"You ready beautiful?"

"I'm starving!"

The aroma permeating the house is amazing. I can't really put my finger on what exactly it is, but it smells savory and sweet all mixed in together.

"Grandma Josephine is an amazing cook. You will not be disappointed." Joseph shares.

I smile, excited that I will be staying with someone who can probably cook just as good as my mom. My heart quakes at the thought of my mom. *I miss her so much.*

"Come on, sit down," Grandma Josephine demands, "I was expecting you, so I made Joseph's favorite. I hope you like pepper steak, Naomi?"

"Oh, yes ma'am! I am grateful for whatever you have prepared!"

"Well, sit down before it gets cold."

Her smile is so grand it warms me from the inside out. The pepper steak is cut into small tender stripes soaked in a rich gravy along with small cuts of bell peppers and onions. Grandma Josephine pours the saucy concoction over a bed of white rice.

While they hold their own conversation, I savor every bite. It's fine by me, and I make no attempt to join in. Grandma Josephine and I will have ample time to get to know each other later.

Soon, after we finish dinner, Grandma Josephine brings out a pint of vanilla ice cream. When she does I notice a buttery brown bunt cake on the counter that I didn't notice before. She walks over with three plates accompanied with three slices of cake for us. My mouth waters. You would think I hadn't eaten in months. In actuality, I haven't, not a home cooked meal anyway. Joseph nudges me as Grandma Josephine serves us both one scoop of ice cream.

"I told you she could cook."

I lick my lips. "You were so right."

We both grin and just like that, his face goes blank. He clears his throat which I notice he does when he needs to say something that makes him uncomfortable.

"So, tomorrow I leave for Augusta," he says.

The spark inside of me goes dull.

"Yeah, I know."

I look over at him and everything fades into the background—even the pound cake—and he is all I see.

I guess Grandma Josephine takes that as her cue to leave because she excuses herself and begins clearing the table.

"I think you are going to like it here, Naomi. I mean, at least you are not alone and you are back in the states, right?"

"That's true," I admit.

"Okay, there are a few things I want to discuss with you," Joseph pulls a cell phone from his pocket. He tells me, "This is going to be your only source of communication until we decide how you are going to go public. Don't call anyone from Grandma's phone and *do not* email anyone. Do you understand?"

I put my right hand up to the corner of my forehand. "Yes, Sir!"

He gives me the eye, "I am serious, Naomi."

"I know, I know. I had to lighten the mood a little."

He continues, "Let's see, it's September now, so I should be able to get some time off in November. I will let you know the exact day once I find out how many days of leave I have. If you decid to go into town be sure to use an alias. Try not to make friends with anyone." He rubs his head.

"Is that all," I ask.

"Yeah, I think that's it. You should be safe here. I don't think the FBI is looking for you anymore or else they would have found you by now."

"Thanks for that. It's one thing to know Damian Draegon is following you, but the FBI tailing me is so much worse for some reason."

"I can't imagine, but lay low just in case they are." Joseph's eyes light up, "Oh yeah! Now I remember. Don't give your number out to anyone. I wouldn't suggest that you try contacting anyone, but your mom."

"Okay."

I guess contacting Emmy is out of the question. I get up from the table taking an empty glass Grandma Josephine has forgotten.

"Do you need any help, Grandma Josephine?"

"No, I'm fine sweetie. Go on and take a load off. You two spend some time together. It's going to be a while before you see each other again."

I give her a gentle hug. "Thank you." I whisper.

Joseph and I head to the living room. He grabs the remote and turns on the small television. When it clicks on, the first scene we see is a man standing in the middle of a street in front of a bank. There are literally hundreds of people flocking into the bank, police are trying to create a barricade to keep people from being trampled. A man in a navy blue suit and red tie gestures toward the bank:

Today, banks across the country sent out an alarm to its customers that their doors would be closing temporarily. In concern and fear, customers rushed to the banks to withdraw funds in hopes they still could.

Joseph and I meet eyes.

I spoke with this particular bank's manager today, and he has no idea when their doors will reopen or when customers banks cards will be usable. We seem to be heading toward more turbulent times, more turbulent than we have ever seen before.

Joseph turns off the television. He leans back in the couch. Putting one arm around me he says, "Make sure you call your mom tomorrow. I will stop by to check on her as soon as I get a chance."

Saying goodbye to Joseph this time is harder than it was the first time. I shed several tears even though Joseph tries to be nonchalant about it.

"I will see you in two months. It's no big deal," he says. Then, he hugs me one last time, then he gets into the rental car and he's gone.

After his car disappears down the road, Grandma Josephine tries to make me feel right at home by making me a big breakfast: pancakes, sausages, cheesy grits, and scrabbled eggs. How does she know I like my sausages practically burned, and my grits cheesy? I don't know, but I'm grateful for her and it does make me feel at home. She refuses my help cleaning up the kitchen, but requests I stay and chat as she works.

"Sit down right here, Naomi. I want to talk to you for a bit before I take my morning nap."

"Okay, Grandma." I pause. "Is it okay if I call you that?"

"Oh my. You don't have to ask me that! Of course it's okay."

She loads the dish washer, wipes off the counters, then sits down at the small wooden table with me. When she places her coffee down, I notice her hands for the first time. Even her hands reminded me of Aunt Destine's.

"So, Joseph thinks I don't know what's happening in the world, but I do. The news stations, and all, may fabricate stuff, but I got a news channel that's way greater…one that informs me of everything I need to know."

I sit quietly, smiling in recognition of her reference to God.

"Joseph told me how the good Lord speaks to you. He also told me some horrible people are looking for you to write it up for their magazine. I tell you one thing, they better not come on my door step looking for you. One thing about my late husband, he made sure I knew how to protect myself whenever he was away." She nods her head. "Um, hmm." Then takes a sip of her coffee.

I take her in. Enjoying every familiar mannerism.

Leaning forward in her chair she whispers, as if Joseph is around the corner, "Did he tell you about that Nina, yet."

"Yes ma'am, he did."

Twisting her lip and now talking out the side of her mouth, "She's a harlot. I'm not one to gossip and the Lord knows I am not a slanderer, but that girl did a number on my grandson. Don't let what they had discourage you from giving my grandson you whole heart. He loved her, but there's no going back for him. She hurt him deeply. The only reason I kept that awful picture of her in my prayer room is so that I would remember to pray for him to forget her." She pauses for a bit, taking another sip. "She slept with someone else while she was still engaged to him! Did he tell you that?"

"No ma'am, he didn't."

I understand why. This situation is difficult. Since she's sharing, I take the liberty to ask a question I have been wondering about.

"So, did she marry Richard?"

"She sure did! They were married just a little over a year ago."

Doing the math in my head, I realize she married Richard pretty quickly.

Grandma Josephine rises from the table, "Well, thinking about that no good gal has made me tired. Please help yourself to whatever you need, Naomi." She walks over to the counter to put her coffee in the microwave, just as my Aunt Destine used to do, in hopes of keeping it fresh.

She turns to me before she exits and says, "Don't be afraid, Naomi, the good Lord will guide you through this. I know he will."

Feeling a little tired myself, I make my way to my room and flop down on the bed. I pull out the cell phone Joseph gave me. My first instinct is to call my mom, but for some reason, the urge to call Emmy is more tempting. The last time I spoke to my mom she told me she hadn't heard from her. This isn't like her. She always checks in with my mom when she can't get in contact with me. I dial her number instead of my mom's, disobeying Joseph's instructions completely. The phone rings three times before she finally picks up.

"Hello."

It's not her voice.

"Hello."

It's a male voice. *It sounds so familiar.*

"Hello," the voice says again. "Who is this?" the voice asks.

I drop the phone to the ground. "It's him!"

It's Daniel.

Emmy's voice echo's out through the receiver. "Who is it?"

"I don't know," Daniel says, maybe one of those robocallers."

I reach down, grabbing the phone in one quick swoop and press the red button.

TWENTY

Naomi

I run to the bathroom and dry heave over the toilet. Nothing comes out. The sound of their voices replay in my mind and then I release everything Grandma Josephine just served me for breakfast. I catch my breath, then rinse my mouth out and sit on the tub.

My best friend?

I'm finding it hard to swallow. My heart has not slowed down since I heard the first 'hello.'

How could she?

How did this happen?

Was there something going on before and I just didn't notice?

The questions keep coming, until I decide there's no use in thinking about it. I don't love him. But, *she's my best friend. Doesn't she know how he hurt me.*

The pain cuts through my chest, and I succumb to it. The tears won't stop, so I gather the strength to get up and walk back to my room. Burying my face into the pillow, I cry until I fall asleep.

I sleep until the next morning. When I wake up from a dreamless slumber, I stretch my aching body all the way to the bathroom. Once I brush the bitter taste out of my mouth, I trudge back to the room and flop down on the bed, grabbing my cell phone. The battery at the top flashes red. I look at the time and realize how late in the afternoon it is. I try to recollect yesterday, but nothing comes into a clear picture, just fuzzy reflections of Joseph leaving and part of the conversation I had with Grandma Josephine.

Ah! Grandma Josephine. I almost forgot I was here with her. I can hear her rummaging around the kitchen. I wipe the sleep from eyes still trying to gain awareness. A slight hint of pain strikes through my temple. My head spins and I hold on to it to keep me steady. Now, the memory of yesterday morning comes flooding back.

Emmy.

Daniel.

Pain.

Then anger rises inside of me and all I want to do is call her back, so I do—no matter the consequences or who picks up this time.

The phone only rings once this time.

"Hello?"

I don't speak.

"Hello! Who is this!"

"Hello," I say, "It's, Naomi."

"Hi…Naomi! How are you? I—I've been worried about you."

"If you were so worried you would have thought to stop by to see my mom."

"Uh, well. I really have been pretty busy with college and stuff."

"Uh, well, I guess you have been busy. Like getting with my ex-boyfriend the moment I left the country!"

She doesn't say anything to deny it which makes me even madder.

"Why would you do something so trifling, Emmy? All this time I thought you were my friend, no—my *best friend*. How did this even happen? You have always hated him.

"Naomi, I really don't know. It all started when I saw him one day after school. He looked so bad: skinny, and pale. I walked over to speak to him and he looked brighter or like he had came back to life. From there, I just decided to at least talk to him because he looked like he needed a friend. At first, I just served as a reporter to him as to how you were doing. After the day of the party and the earthquake, and you being in the hospital and all, he asked me to get a letter to you. You had disappeared and no one knew where you were. I paid a visit to your mom and she told me you were okay. She said I could write to you and she would get you the letter. I didn't know what to say to you, so I decided to allow Daniel to write you instead. Weeks later, neither us had heard from you. We started spending more time together just to pass the time and…"

"It just happened." I cut her off. "You have no idea why I had to be taken to the hospital do you, Emmy? I mean really, I thought you would have been smarter than this. You are beautiful and probably could have any boy you want, but you decide to choose someone like Daniel? Do you know he tried to rape me that day? Did he tell you that when you were trying to be his friend? You were supposed to be *my* friend! My sister!"

She whispers, "With everything that's going on lately, Naomi, I'm not sure who or what I am anymore."

"Well, you can know this *for sure*, we are done! Goodbye, Emmy."

Those words leave a bitter taste in my mouth, yet, I feel ten times lighter. I sit catching my breath and replaying it all in my head. When I feel a little calmer, I finally decide to call my mom. Rolling the tension out of my shoulders, I try to sit a little taller and hopefully my voice sounds normal.

"Hello?"

She sounds so happy.

"Hi Mom!"

"Oh my goodness, hi Baby Girl, how are you?"

I lie, "I'm fine. How are you?"

"Oh, I am doing just fine! Joseph called me yesterday and let me know everything that has happened."

I feel horrible for not calling her sooner. I stand and walk over to the window. The morning fog has just about disappeared from the surface of the lake.

"I'm sorry mom, I meant to call you yesterday, but I was so tired I fell asleep."

I gaze out at the lake until my sense of awareness is clouded with the FBI, The Spark, Emmy and Daniel.

"Hello? You still there?"

I snap back to reality. "Yeah. I'm here."

"You sure you are doing okay? How is everything there? You and Grandma Josephine getting along alright? You don't seem yourself."

It doesn't matter how hard I try to hide things from her, she never fails to notice when things are off with me.

"Oh yes, ma'am. Everything's okay. I'm just trying to get used to my new environment and living without you. Grandma Josephine is great and an amazing cook. She reminds me so much of Aunt Destine. She evens looks just like her!"

"That's all great, Baby Girl. I can't wait to meet her. Please let her know how much I appreciate her letting you stay with her until all of this dies down."

"I will."

I walk back over to the bench and sit under the window,

allowing the cool morning breeze to chill my skin. "So, how is everything with your finances, Mom. I saw the news the other night. Banks are closing and people aren't capable of using their bank cards. Are you making it okay?"

"Oh yeah. We are doing just fine. I started putting money away, in a safe, months ago."

I laugh.

"What's so funny?"

"You just said 'we,' Mom?"

She exhales. "Did I really just say that?"

"Yes you did." I laugh again.

"Do you remember your doctor, Dr. Ward? The one you said was cute?"

Sitting on the edge of the bench, my cheeks burn with excitement. "Yes."

"Well we have been spending time together that's all. I like him. His company keeps me from being worried sick about you."

From a few hundred miles away, I jump up and down. I don't want to jump too far ahead of the friendship and think marriage, but I do, with thought only.

"Thanks cool, Mom." And I leave the topic alone.

"Have you heard from Emmy yet?" she asks.

"Yeah."

I really don't want to talk about this right now.

"And how was that."

"Different," I say.

"Oh. I guess you don't want to talk about it."

"Right."

"Okay. Let's talk about something else. It's nice talking to you without being on a timer."

I look down at my hands, then I start to bite my nails.

"Yeah. It is." I pause for a few moments, contemplating if I should tell her what I've been thinking about.

"You there?" She says.

"I want to go public, Mom, but I want it to be on my terms."

"Okay. If you are talking about what I think you are talking about, please know, that will not be easy. Everyone is not going to like what you have to say."

"I know.. I've thought about that. Joseph said the exact same thing."

There's a pause and finally she says, "Well, I believe you should share it, too. How do you plan on doing this. Please tell me you didn't give in and decide to publish it in that magazine."

"Oh NO! I'm just waiting to see what direction I need to take."

My mom takes a deep exhale. "I'm behind whatever decision you make, Naomi."

———

Just as I am getting off the phone with Mom, there's a knock at the door.

"Naomi? Are you okay in there?" Grandma Josephine calls out.

"Yes, ma'am. I was just talking to my mom."

"Oh. Okay. Breakfast is on the stove if you want any."

Just then my phone vibrates. It's a number I don't recognize.

"You must be starved."

I don't answer it.

"Thank you, Grandma Josephine. I will be out soon."

Then a text message comes through from the same number.

"Okay, you don't have to rush, Sweetie."

I hear Grandma Josephine's bedroom shoes sliding down the hallway. I look down at the phone, thumb just inches from the notification box. I look up to the ceiling, then back down at the message. Throwing caution to the wind, I press it.

I am so sorry you had to find out about Emmy and me this way. You have to know that we never meant for this to happen. It just, kinda did. I meant everything I said in the letter. I love you and I always will, but Emmy has my heart now. I am in love with her. Please find it in you heart to forgive her, if not both of us. She is all broken up about this.

I'm glad you are okay. Where have you been? Call me if you feel up to it. Emmy doesn't know I found your number in her phone. Unlike you, she doesn't have a security code to keep me out of her business. She told me that you were the person who called and hung up.. Where are you? That area code was weird. Anyway. I hope to hear from you soon.

Daniel

I throw the phone to the floor, more angry than I was after I spoke to Emmy. Who does he think he is? I couldn't careless that he has moved on. It's my ex-best friend I'm worried about. He's always been so cocky—too self absorbed to care about what anyone else is going through.

I roll off the bed on to the floor to retrieve my phone, praying I didn't break it. Gratefulness fills me and I dial Joseph's number hoping to find some sort of solace. He doesn't answer.

TWENTY-ONE

Naomi

SEVEN WEEKS LATER

With only one week until Thanksgiving, I am optimistic about life getting back to normal. Life as I knew it has definitely changed, but at least I have something to look forward to. I am ecstatic to see Joseph. My mom isn't capable of coming because Joseph still believes she's being watched. Every day is an obstacle, knowing she's so close, but yet so far away. Although I try to focus on the positives, she will definitely be here for Christmas—no matter the consequence.

There hasn't been much happening around here, but its peaceful. I spend most of my days writing and reading by the lake. It has become my safe haven when my thoughts become suffocating. I didn't tell Joseph about my phone calls to Emmy or the text from Daniel. I figured, what he doesn't know, won't get me in trouble. I've learned my lesson anyway. Now, the only calls I'm making are to my mom or Joseph.

Over the past several weeks, I've learned a lot about

Grandma Josephine. One thing that makes me laugh is how many naps she takes before bedtime, but when she's awake we spend all of our time together. A few weeks ago, she invited me into her prayer room and we prayed together. My eyes were drawn to a specific spot on one of the glass shelves. The space where Joseph and Nina's picture was is now taken up with with a crystal angel. That made me smile.

Joseph and I spend countless hours on FaceTime. We never run out of things to talk about, but if by chance one of us just falls off to sleep, we text goodnight and resume our conversation the next day. My love for him has definitely grown during our time apart. I guess the age old saying about absence making the heart grow founder is true. I miss him like crazy.

My mom and Dr. Ward have decided to get married this upcoming year. It's huge turn of events since September. I had a feeling they were more than "just friends." Although I haven't gotten to know him as much as I would like, I feel like I have known him all my life. When my mom and I talk, he's all she seems to want to talk about. They are always together when I call, so he and I talk a lot too—mostly about my recovery and gifts he wants to buy my mom.

Since some of the major banks announced their closing, not much has transpired. Four weeks ago, they opened back up for business. I saw something in the news about a stock market spike, but I have no clue what that means. Joseph says it's a good thing, but only time will tell. The country and the nation seems to be bouncing back from the chaos and everything does seem to be getting back to normal. But, where does that leave me. *What about my dreams?* What about letting them all know there's more to come? The pressure of it all is so daunting which is why I have to get out of these four walls.

Last week, I got this crazy idea to go into town. Grandma

Josephine said I could borrow the truck this week after it was serviced and filled with gas. Thankfully, Joseph was cool with the idea, but not before he emphasized how important it was for me to give out my alias and to keep conversations surface level. I assured him I would follow all of his instructions, then and only then did he agree.

"So, what are you going to do today? There's a $2 matinee every Monday at the theatre over on Greene Street." Grandma tells me.

Placing a slice of banana bread on to a napkin, I answer, "Well, I want to possibly get something new to wear for Thanksgiving dinner and then I will check it out."

The feeling I have inside is indescribable. I can't even remember the last time I've been to a movie.

"Alright, have some fun. No worries about being back anytime soon. Just make sure to start back by night fall. These back road get pretty dark past six."

"Understood, Grandma. I will be back before five. How's that?"

"Sounds good."

She walks over to me and kisses me on the cheek. I hug her.

"See Grandma."

I grab the keys off of the counter and walk out into the bright fall day. It's chilly, but the sun seems to be shining brighter today. Grandma Josephine's cherry red pickup truck looks like it just rolled off a used car lo. Never has it looks so clean. When I open the door, a sweet fragrance hits me right in the face. I climb in and notice a note on the dashboard.

Have some fun on me.

Paper clipped to the note is a $20 bill. I smile knowing that Grandma Josephine had everything to do with how clean the truck is and the delicious aroma inside.

I drive for a while with only the roar of the heat blowing through the vents, then I realize this old thing has a radio. Keeping my eyes on the road, I turn the little black nob until the radio clicks on. A voice booms from the radio, making my heart leap in my chest. I turn down the volume.

You are listening to 104.7 Praise, the number one Christian radio station in the south. I am your solo hostess for today Nina Sands…

My eyes dart to the radio like I can possibly see the person who's speaking and I swerve off road to the rivets on the edge. Adjusting the truck, I reach over to turn up the volume.

Yes, Saints, Richard is in Orlando today hosting a praise rally. Keep him in your prayers and hang in there with me today. I am blasting old school gospel all day! Send in your requests!

Then, the music starts and I am perplexed for a moment. Is this a dream or did I just hear Joseph's Nina on the radio? I shake my head and reverse that thought. Is this a dream or did I just hear Nina on the radio? My mind goes blank. I don't know what to think right now. The song playing is one I know and it catches my attention.

Trust and obey, for there's no other way
To be happy in Jesus, but to trust and obey.

I begin to sing along and suddenly it hits me! The answer I have been looking for since I arrived in Virginia.

———

Thankfully, I find the clothing store I am looking for pretty quickly. The streets are busy, but I find parking pretty close to my destination. If I want to be taken seriously, I must do something with my appearance first. The two story boutique is just what I needed. Nice and affordable casual wear and business wear. Within minutes I find a few things I like, but definitely need to try on. I locate a women hanging clothes on a rack.

"Excuse me? Can I try these on?"

"Sure!" she says with a smile.

With a voice that could wake up a sloth, she flags down another sales associate.

"Mindy!"

Out of nowhere a girl, who looks about my age, shuffles from the back of the store. "Please see this young lady to one of our dressing rooms."

"Yes, Momma," she responds.

She doesn't make any eye contact with me, but Mindy gestures for me to follow her. She unlocks a dressing room door.

"Let me know if you need anything, Ma'am."

"Okay, I'm…," I hesitate trying to think of the alias I used in London, but decide to use something else, "Leslie."

"Okay, Ms. Leslie."

"No. It's just Leslie," I smile and close the door.

Then I realize Mindy's feet haven't moved from in front of my door. I peek my head out the door. "Mindy, you can leave now. It's going to be a few minutes."

Her chubby pink cheeks break into a smile, "I'm okay waiting for you," she begins to whisper, "If I don't look busy, my momma's gonna make me do something stupid like count the hangers or refold all of the jeans. I'd rather stay here and help you with what ya need. If that's okay with you?"

"Oh. Oh sure," I whisper back.

Closing the door, I giggled to myself.

The first outfit I try on is the one I've picked out to wear today—a royal blue blazer paired with a white kami, and a black pencil skirt. I walk out looking for the floor length mirror I saw earlier.

"Oo, I love it!" I hear Mindy say from behind me.

She's sitting in a chair next to my dressing room.

"I wish I had a shape like that!" she exclaims.

"Thank you, Mindy."

I turn to look in the mirror and to my surprise, everything fits perfectly.

Mindy pipes up, "So what shoes did you pick out?"

"Let me show you."

I run back into the dressing room to retrieve the new black flats I picked out. When I come back, I see Mindy peeking over her shoulder and I guess she is looking for her mom. I put the flats on.

"See, Mindy? What do you think?"

"N to the O! No! Those look like your grandma's auntie's shoes! Where you think you going looking like perfection with a pair of, " she points dramatically, "THOSE on?"

"Well, I don't really wear anything else other than sneakers. Besides, they are comfortable."

"Where are you headed?"

I hear Joseph's voice on replay in my head. *Keep conversations surface level.*

As usual, I disobey him. "I have a meeting with Nina Sands."

I hear her gasp, and before I can focus in on her face she is in my face, her big blue eyes pulsing.

"You mean to tell me you have a meeting with *the* Nina Sands.

I don't tell her that I am hoping for a meeting. I just say, "Yes."

"And you want to go meet *the* Nina Sands in flats?"

"Yes?" I look my self over in the mirror again and suddenly feel like a little girl.

My hair is in a half frizzy, half fluffy afro. My bare face looks back at me in the mirror and I am overcome with nerves. Nina must be some type of celebrity and here I am, eighteen going on nineteen showing up like she is just going to agree to spontaneously let me on her show. Mindy stares at me, then breaks out in a smile.

"I will be right back."

Mindy shuffles away. In seconds she returns with a shiny pair of black pumps.

"Here. Try these one," she says.

Hesitantly, I do as I am told. When I stand up, I am four inches taller. I walk over to the mirror once again and it's obvious, the look is complete. I turn around to face Mindy and her cheeks turn into two ripe cherries.

"You like them, don't you?"

I smile back, "Yes, I really do!"

Mindy eases back down into the chair, looking over her shoulder again as she does.

"It's amazing what a pair of pumps can do for a girl. My momma always says turtles can't hear what giraffes are saying, so be a giraffe."

I do a double take. "Huh?"

"Never mind," she flags her hand.

Keeping track of the time, I head back into the dressing room. From the inside I hear, "Mindy get up off your fourth point of contact and find something to do!"

I grin and continue to gather my things.

"See," I hear Mindy whisper from outside the door. "I never get a break. That's what you get for working for your momma."

When I come back out, I look for Mindy who is doing just what she said she didn't want to do—refolding jeans.

"Thank you, Mindy."

"No problem, Leslie. You look just as stunning as Ms. Nina, so go in there with your head held high."

My confidence needed a boost and Mindy's words do the

job. I pay for my things, and before I leave I search the store for Mindy. I give her a big hug.

"Aww, go knocks 'em dead, Sister!" She says.

Then, I strut out of there with the confidence to rule the world.

I have one more stop to make before heading to the radio station—the beauty salon. My GPS pulls up two salons in the vicinity. My first choice is a small salon filled with waiting customers, who look like me. I decided not to take the chance of going in because, from experience of getting my hair pressed, it could take me literally all day. My second choice is a much larger salon with little to no customers. This makes me skeptical, but I am in a hurry. A tall and slender man in black, leather pants grabs my attention.

"Hi, Gorgeous! What can we do for you this morning."

I'm too busy fan-girling over his blue Mohawk, he has to repeat his question.

"I'm—I'm sorry?"

"How can I help?"

I refocus my attention. "Oh, I would like to get my hair shampooed and pressed. Do you all do that kind of thing," playfully, pointing to my mess of curls and tangles.

"If you mean do we straighten hair—yes, of course. I will have you looking like a movie star in the matter of a couple of hours."

He grabs me by the arm and whisks me away to his station. And true to his word, Frank, the name I noticed on his badge, is finished with my hair just shy of two hours. When he spins the chair around I almost don't recognize myself. My hair has grown so much in the past few months and now it falls like silk down my back, free and loose from all the coils.

Frank manipulates a few hairs, framing my face with strands of soft curls.

"Would you like our make-up artist to finish the look?"

Thinking of the few hundred dollars I have left, I ask, "Uh, how much would that be?"

Frank whispers, "Don't worry about it. It's on me. You were my first customer today and you trusted me with one of your most important assets. It's the least I could do."

Feeling blessed and oh so adventurous, I agree to the makeover.

When I arrive to the radio station I park, maybe, a block from the building. Why? Because I over think it. Considering I'm in Grandma Josephine's truck, I don't want anyone thinking it's Joseph, or someone meddling, and Grandma or Joseph finding out I was here.

I check my lip gloss in the rear-view mirror. My make-up is flawless. I have cheekbones I didn't know existed.

If only Joseph could see me today.

Staring in the mirror I see a reflection that resembles a young version of my mom. With the memory of my mom reverberating in my heart, walking down the busy sidewalk, I feel confident and ready to come face to face with the women I can't seem to avoid even if I tried. Maybe it is all coming full circle today. Maybe Nina is apart of my path.

Once I reach the address, I realize the radio station isn't the only business in this massive building. I peer up at the skyscraper towering over me, trying with all of it's might to intimidate me, but I forge ahead anyway. When I enter the building, I look around for some direction. To the right of me are the elevators and right next to it is a marble wall with a list of several business in the building. At the top of the list is 104.7 Praise. It is listed on the 20th floor.

"...The reason I'm here really has nothing to do with him, but I really need your help with something. All I need is about fifteen minutes of your time."

Nina looks back over at Anita as if I've said nothing.

"Anita please have that document ready by three."

"Yes, Ma'am. Right away," Anita chirps.

Then Nina looks back at me. "Follow me."

My heart sinks. She doesn't wait for a response, but I quickly obey, following her back through the hidden door down a long hall way. We pass a studio filled equipment and the sound of music. I assume that's where she was before she walked out into the lobby.

"I have the music on autopilot, so we are gonna have to make this quick," she says over her shoulder."

She leads me into a large conference room and takes a seat at the head of a massive oval table.

"Your fifteen minutes starts now."

When I turn on to the graveled road to Grandma Josephine's house, I feel lighter. The weight of the the past several months seem to have lifted off of my shoulders. On the radio, I hear Nina signing off for the day and I smile knowing everything is left up to her now. I squint at the house up ahead trying to make out what I am seeing. As I get closer, I notice a large, black SUV in the driveway. My heart stops. *Who could this be. Grandma Josephine never get visitors.* I climb out of the truck, confused and afraid. I tip toe through the gravel trying not to ruin my newly worn pumps. Before I climb the wooden steps, the door flies open. I can't believe my eyes.

"Mom!" I scream.

She runs down the steps to me and I grab her, "Oh my goodness, Naomi! You look amazing!" she sighs.

"You do too!" I say.

She pulls me in and I hold on to her like she is my air. Her familiar scent fills me with joy. Tears of relief fall from my eyes.

"Mom, I missed you so much!"

We hold on to each other for what seems like forever. Two voices are coming from the doorway so I open my eyes to see two sets of boots standing on the porch. I left my head hearing just a hint of that familiar voice.

"Joseph!" I yell out.

Giggling, my mom releases me and Joseph hesitates with his mouth agape. He looks just as surprised to see me.

"You look amazing, Naomi," he says as he scoops me up from the ground burying his face in my neck.

Then I get it. I had forgotten all about my little makeover.

To say I've missed him would be a huge understatement. Looking at him, hugging him, smelling him all puts me in a place of euphoria. For a few minutes I think I'm dreaming, then I am distracted by another face. I look at mom, her smile spreading to her eyes. Then I look back at the man staring at me with an infectious smile. He carefully walks over towards me and extends his hand. I push it away.

"We give hugs around here, Dr. Ward."

He laughs then I give him a tight squeeze.

"Well, I will take it," he says and squeezes me back.

<hr>

We all head into the house after I take all of the surprises in. Grandma Josephine is just as surprise as I am. She buzzes around the kitchen trying to make more tuna casserole to feed our three extra guests.

"You are a few days early," I say to Joseph.

"Yeah, I wanted to surprise you both. That's why I haven't

called in a couple of days. I've been so busy trying to get all of my files done before I took leave."

I turn to my mom, "And you! You kept this from me even though we've talked everyday?"

Mom looks like I've never seen her look—at peace.

"Yes, and now you know that I can keep a secret. So, Hah!"

Joseph turns to me. He looks me directly in my eyes, as though he will miss something there if he blinks. "So, how have you been?"

"I have been fine. Grandma Josephine and I find lots to do around here, don't we Grandma?"

She laughs from the kitchen, "We sure do."

Joseph grins, then his eyes scan my entire frame. "So why are you all dressed up? Where were you coming from?"

"Oh. I went shopping."

"In *those* clothes?"

"Do I sense some jealousy here, Joseph." I joke.

"No, no, no. Just concern."

He looks around the table at everyone. Dr. Ward widens his eyes and looks at me. Mom looks down at her casserole and Grandma Josephine continues setting glasses on the table.

Joseph puts one hand up to his head. "Well, maybe sixty percent jealousy and forty percent concern."

Mom drops her fork and everyone breaks out into laughter, even Grandma Josephine cracks up from the kitchen.

After that, Joseph doesn't press me for an answer anymore and I am grateful. I would rather talk to him alone about what I did today. Grandma Josephine finally joins us at the table, bringing a large bowl of fruit salad.

"This tuna casserole is delicious, Grandma Josephine. It almost tastes like my recipe," my mom says.

We all dig in. Mom asks me to pass the sweet tea and when

she reaches for the pitcher, I notice the rock on her hand.

"Wow!" I blurt out.

She traces my eyes to the ring and leans over toward Dr. Ward. "I know. He is such a gift giver. It took me a while to give in to wearing it, though."

Scooping up another big spoon of casserole, Joseph asks, "Why?"

Dr. Ward laughs. Mom responds, "I was afraid I would get robbed!"

We all burst out laughing, again.

The laughs keep coming throughout the rest of the day. We have meaningful conversations and Dr. Ward's presence becomes more and more comfortable with each passing hour. After hanging with us well over her scheduled nap time, Grandma Josephine decides to go and take a late nap.

Joseph keys Dr. Ward in about the lake and the scenery, so he decides to take my mom out for an afternoon scroll. As they walk out the back door, her giggles float into the air and I am in awe of how everything has turned around in our lives so quickly. Today couldn't be more perfect. *Thank you Jesus.*

Joseph and I decide to sit on the front porch in the two wooden rocking chairs. Although they are a constant fixture on the porch, Grandma Josephine never uses them. I have always figured it's for the same reason she moved out of the master bedroom. When we sit down, Joseph reaches for my hand.

"Have I told you how beautiful you are today."

"Yes, but it doesn't hurt to hear it again."

We smile at each other and rock for a long while listening to the sounds of the night.

Then, the inevitable happens.

Joseph asks, "So, tell me, where did you go today?"

I stop rocking and stare out into the woods ahead of me.

Joseph agreed to my decision of going public, but he may not be too happy with how I have decided to do it. If he disagrees, how will I convince him.

I look at him. "Joseph, you know we have been discussing ways for me to go public with my dream for months now."

"Right."

"And how I wanted to do it on my terms?"

"Yes. Have you figured it out?"

"Yes. I have." I look back out into the darkness. "That's where I was today."

Joseph stops rocking. "Naomi, you did this without me, and you didn't tell me?"

"No. I set the stage for it. I am waiting for a response on whether I can use a certain platform to share what I have to say."

"Oh," Joseph exhales, "You scared me for a minute there. So, tell me more. What platform are you trying to use?"

My palms are sweating. I rub the perspiration on legs.I clear my throat.

"I want to go on live radio."

"Okay. Well, what's wrong with that? Why the hesitation?"

"Okay. You have to promise to hear me out. Don't say anything until you hear all of what I have to say."

Joseph eyebrows crash into one another.

"Alright, I promise."

I stand up and walk to the edge of the porch. "Today, I got up with a feeling something extraordinary was going to happen."

I fill Joseph in on everything from the moment I noticed Grandma Josephine cleaned up the car for me, to the trust and obey song playing on the radio, to the moment Nina Sands granted me my fifteen minutes. When I am finished I don't turn around to look at him. The night air is suffocating, until I hear his footsteps coming towards me.

I hear him whisper, "Did you see him today?"

"No."

"Did you mention me at all?"

"No. I told her I am a friend of yours. I believe that is the only reason she agree to hear me out. I told her about the FBI, The Spark, and the dream of course. She seemed pretty taken a back, but she said she would discuss it with Richard and they would have to talk it over with someone else—I can't remember his name, but she said they would give me a call to let me know their decision." I take a deep breath, "I feel like I'm rambling. Are you okay?"

I turn to look at him now. He's standing right next to me peering in the darkness like he's searching for something. Maybe he's mad. Frustrated. I don't know. When he does speak again he voice is low and calm.

"No. I'm not okay."

Stepping down on the step to face him.

"Why?"

He looks at me. "Naomi, if you have to ask me that, I really don't think you know me at all."

"Joseph, do you truly believe I would intentionally seek out your *ex-fiancé* and ask her for a favor after all she has put you through? Didn't you listen to all of the signs I had today, leading me straight to her?

He kicks at a pebble on the porch. "Naomi, I promise you I am completely over her. I just want to move on with my life," he looks down at me, "with you."

He holds on to me. "I am sick of her popping her head up in our relationship."

I lie my head on his chest.

"Maybe this is a door you haven't fully closed and this is not only an opportunity for me, but one for you as well."

His heart picks up and his arms drop from around me. I pull back and look up at him.

"What?"

"You know, you never stop pushing the limits do you?"

He walks down the steps and then into the darkness without another word.

I yell to him, "Joseph, please come back."

He doesn't.

TWENTY-THREE

Joseph

Pride is a hardest demon to kill. It's what you hold on to when you don't have anything else. It's your best friend when you are hurting and gives you confidence when you feel like you are nothing. Pride is what helped me to get over Nina. Because I never faced her and because I never confronted Richard, I was capable of letting it all go without having to look back. It was the same with my dad. Life is funny that way sometimes. You know what is right, but pride will not allow you to do what is right. Richard and Nina have moved on with their lives and here I am trying to move on with mine, but deep down, as long as I insist on acting like they don't exist or what they did didn't happen, I am only stalling my progress with Naomi. Yeah, I know she's right, but my pride makes it hard for me to accept the truth sometimes. Naomi has helped me to see that. My love for her runs so much deeper than any love I ever felt for Nina. She's my universe.

Two months ago, I went out and bought a ring. Going out to get the ring was my way of silencing the alarm going off in my head every time I had a quiet moment. This was the only way my soul found peace. Trying to keep it from her has been tough. It's like keeping a secret from your best friend. You never wanted to keep it from them, and because you have, you feel guilty.

I called my dad the other day. We had a really good talk. I told him I wanted to ask for Naomi's hand in marriage. He was happy for me, but mom wasn't so accepting of my decision. She said she had some reservations. Dad assured me she always would, no matter who I chose. I agreed. He told me if I wanted to do it right, I needed to find her father. So, that's what I did. Being an agent cut the time it took to find him down to a matter of minutes.

We talked for hours about everything. He now lives in Florida with an entirely new family: a wife and a son. I told him how amazing Naomi was and how she fully forgives him for leaving and not being around. Then, I asked why. Why did he leave. Why didn't he ever come back or even check on her. He didn't have a clear answer, so I just let it go. In the end, he gave me his blessing and I gave him Naomi's number. It was definitely awkward because in my mind he didn't know me and he definitely didn't know the young women I love so much.

When I told Ms. Peterson what I had done, she didn't seem to like my decision. She gave me the business for not asking her first, then she graciously gave me her blessing as well. My plan was to ask her this week. I didn't expect to have to deal with Nina or even the thought of her. It was not supposed to be this way. But, if I go to the station, my vouching for Naomi's story, could possibly give her more credibility. I have to do what I can to help even in the face of killing my pride. It won't feel good at all, but I would do anything for Naomi.

I walk and pray until I am sure of my decision. When I get back to the house, I find Ms. Peterson and Dr. Ward watching the news. Just as I am walking past them I get an ear full about the storm coming for the coast of California. I bypass the living room trying hard to avoid bad news. My mood has finally been lifted to a place I would like it to stay, so I keep walking to where I know she will be.

Knocking on Naomi's door, I hope she isn't asleep already. Thankfully, after my knock, I hear her bed squeak and then the creak of the floor boards.

When she opens the door rubbing her eyes, she ask, "Joseph, are you okay?"

I walk past her and into the room.

"Yes. I am actually." I smile. "I'm sorry I walked away from you tonight. I really needed to go clear my head."

"Yeah," she leaves the door cracked and walks towards me, "I know it was a lot to take in."

"You were right. This is an opportunity to end that chapter of my life. I can't go on avoiding them forever, right?"

"Right."

Naomi sits on the bed. I do the same.

"So, I have an idea of my own."

"And what is that," she yawns.

"We can go over there tomorrow."

Naomi's eyes turn into ping pong balls. "TOMORROW!"

"Yes, I think I should go with you."

The next morning, I feel energized because in just a few days, I will ask the girl I love to spend the rest of her life with me. And, today, I get to close the door of my past. Grandma Josephine insists we eat something before we leave for the station, but I refuse. Eating on days like this only distracts me. I will spend so much time trying to calm my nervous stomach, I'll forget to focus on the task. Naomi, on the other hand, doesn't want to be rude and nibbles at the bacon and cheddar quiche Grandma Josephine puts on her plate . Every bite forced.

When we finally get into the SUV, it takes everything in me not to just drown Naomi with kisses and hugs. She looks so good. Her hair looks the same as it did yesterday. This new look is so her. Watching her today, I've notice how she has changed since the first time we met. I don't know. Something has shifted with her and I am hypnotized by it. My thoughts wonder to that day—the day she will walk down the aisle to me. My heart races and I can feel the sweat beading up on my forehead.

"Are you okay?" she asks me.

I wipe the sweat from my head, "Yeah, this is long overdue."

Then I try to bring my thoughts back into focus.

When we arrive, it's no surprise the receptionist is an old classmate from high school. She used to be smaller—way smaller. She yells my name before I can even reach her desk. Her face is familiar, but her name isn't coming to me. I play it safe.

"Hey! How are you?"

She gets up from her seat, and scurries from around the desk. Before I know it, she kisses both my cheeks and holds me in a very awkward embrace. I scan the lobby, hoping no one has noticed this uncomfortable scene. All I notice is Naomi standing idly by getting a good laugh out of my awkward situation. I motion for her to come closer, maybe to interrupt *this*, but she doesn't. The woman then releases me, sort of, because she holds on to my hands. Facing me she begins to whisper.

"I'm so sorry about how Nina did you. She knew that wasn't right, heck everybody knew. You are a good man, Joseph." Her hand traces up my arm. "You know I liked you in school. Heck, I liked you in middle school." She looks me in my eyes. "So, what are you up to these days? Are you seeing anybody?"

This is my cue. I motion for Naomi to come to my side and she does—still giggling.

"Uh, um, this is my, fiancé, Naomi!"

The woman clears her throat. "Fiancé?" She drops my hands, pulling at her blazer.

Her eyes dart over to Naomi, who is giving me a puzzled look. She holds out her hand.

"Hi," Naomi says with a wide smile. "We met yesterday."

She looks at Naomi, then at me. "Oh. Yes. I remember."

In my peripheral vision a familiar silhouette approaches us accompanied with the sound of click clacking heels. I don't turn to look, but Naomi does. The facial expression of the receptionist goes from smug to that adoration in the matter of seconds.

"Good Morning, Mrs. Sands! I was just greeting Joseph and his *fiancé*!"

I turn, laying eyes on Mrs. Nina Sands for the first time in years. She's wearing an all gold business suit. Flashy. It's hard to not look at her.

"Hi, Nina."

She doesn't falter.

"Hi Joseph."

She locks eyes with Naomi. I wrap my arm around Naomi's waist, "I wanted to confirm, the story my fiancé shared with you yesterday."

"Oh. Okay!" She looks back and forth between us. "Come right this way."

Naomi and I follow Nina down a long hallway. I keep my eyes trained on the floor, which is polished to perfection. I'm not gonna lie, Nina looks good, but she pales in comparison to the woman walking next to me. It's odd being here especially with her acting as if she nothing happened between us.

At the end of the hallway is a large, black glass door with the names Richard and Nina Sands etched in a gold plate. She opens the door for us, watching meticulously.

"Please have a seat," she offers.

She walks over to what I think is her desk and presses a button on the telephone. The receptionist's voice rings through.

"Yes, Mrs. Sands?"

"Please page Richard and let him know that I need him in the conference room."

"Yes, Mrs. Sands."

My palms begin to sweat. Naomi obviously notices because she rubs my knee. When I look up, I catch Nina watching us. She takes a seat. Everything is quiet as she sits there exchanging glances with both Naomi and I. Finally, she releases her business posture and leans forward.

"It's good to see you, Joseph."

The comment seems sincere, but why did it take so long?

She continues, "I…I have thought about you very much in the past few days. Then your," she gestures over at Naomi, " fiancé showed up out of the blue and now you are here," she looks down at the table, almost confused, "right in front of me, right now."

She pauses. I don't respond. Nothing in my heart, or my mind is telling me to speak, so I don't. I just listen.

Nina's forehead creases. She places her hand on her forehead, as if she is trying to hide what she knows I have already noticed. Shame.

She whispers without looking at me, "Joseph, I am so sorry."

Tears fall on to the flawless table. *Should I console her*. Just as the thought comes Naomi squeezes my hand, giving me the answer I need. I don't move.

Nina continues, she looks up at me. "You know, a couple of weeks ago, I asked him to help me…" her chest heaves and she forces the words out, trying to catch her breath, "to help me…," Naomi gets up from her chair and grabs a box of tissues from a small table. She walks it over to Nina. "Thank you," Nina whispers. "to help me love my husband. People see us and think we have it good because we have money and status, but the love we thought we had has ran cold. So, I asked God," she inhales, "I asked him what was holding us back and today, He has answered my prayer."

Nina gets up from her seat and walks over to me. I look at Naomi, then stand to face her.

With tears still falling, she asks, "Can you forgive, Joseph. Can you please find it in your heart to forgive me?"

I grab her hands and I look into her eyes. Every moment, from the first time I saw her, flashes through my mind—every moment from the past leading up to this one—the final one.

"Yes, Nina. I forgive you."

Just as the words come out, the glass door opens. Nina doesn't move. I look up to see Richard. His face is cold.

"Nina," he questions.

She looks up at him. Hers cheeks covered with black streaks of make-up. She releases me and I her. Richard walks over to face me.

"Hi, Joseph," he says.

Not sure if he is going to hit me for still holding a piece of his wife's heart, I stand a little taller, ready to defend myself if need be. He extends his hand. I look down at his hand, and then back at him. I grab his arm and pull him in.

"Hi Richard."

I hold on to him in hopes this gesture is enough to let him know I forgive him. Looking up, I catch eyes with Naomi. She smiles at me and I know this day is the beginning of the rest of my life. I mouth, *I love you.*

After we talk and share where our lives have taken us over, Nina and Richard call a meeting with the station producers.

Eventually, they all agree to give Naomi some airtime on the station. Because of the Christian platform of the station, they are honored to be a part of what is going to take place. The only thing is the timing. The holidays are coming up and their calendar is booked for the rest of year, so they decide to have her on in January. By the end of the meeting, January 29th is the air date.

On our way back to Grandma Josephine's, I decide to take a detour. Now that my past is really behind me, I feel—free. I feel free enough to finally ask Naomi what I have been thinking about since I saw her for the second time in that bookstore. Yes, I don't know what tomorrow holds, but that's all the more reason to ask her—now. I want to protect and be there for her through everything. I want to face everything with her by my side.

We park the truck and walk down a bit closer to the river. Naomi turns to me.

"This place reminds me of our first date."

I smile. "Yeah. It does."

Tall lights illuminate the walk way paved with cobblestones. The river runs nice and calm, creating a soothing sound of waves hitting the rocks. The area isn't as crowded as it usually is which makes it that much more special. Naomi walks quietly beside me taking everything in. I know she loves any body of water, so I allow her to enjoy it for just a while longer. We walk past a bench with an older couple holding hands. The sight breakes her silence.

"This is beautiful, Joseph."

"Just like you."

The words come out before I can stop them and I squint in embarrassment. That was so corny. Naomi just giggles to herself and doesn't call me on it.

"So," she says. "Why did you tell everyone I was your fiancé."

I choke on air. "Oh. Um, I was trying to get that receptionist to stop touching me. Remember?"

She laughs out loud. "Oh, yeah!"

"You know, you are really ruining this moment right now, right?"

"Okay…okay," she swallows her giggles, "I'm sorry."

I smile, still trying to find the perfect spot to ask the most important question of my life. My heart pounds in my chest, contemplating every word and rehearsing how I should say them. Walking a little further, we come upon an area where the trees are over-arching one lone bench close to the river. A small metal fence separates us from the quiet river. I gesture for her to sit. As we people watch my thoughts are all over the place and I don't know how to start, so I just let it come naturally.

She lays her head down on my shoulder, "So, what's on your mind? You've been so quiet since we left the radio station."

"A lot," I admit.

"Do you want to talk about it?"

I exhale, then slide to the edge of the bench to face her. "More than anything."

Adrenalin gushing through my veins, she looks at me just as she has so many times before and I am lost in her eyes.

"Naomi, for the past seven months, you have changed the course of my life. My heart aches when I have to leave you even if it's just for a little while, like while you sleep or even when you are getting dressed," I grin in embarrassment. "Time spent away from you is meaningless to me. I want to be the constant in your life and I don't want to miss one moment of it. I want to kiss you awake every morning. I want to hold you as you dream at night. I want to be your partner, protector, and your provider. I want to do life with you and only you until eternity."

Naomi sits up a little straighter as tears fill her eyes. I kneel down on one knee, taking the ring from my pants pocket.

"I'm not a liar and I don't want the day to end with me having said you are my fiancé without making it being a reality. So, Naomi Peterson, will you do me the tremendous honor of being my wife?"

"I...,"

She looks at the ring then back at me. Her hands fly up to her mouth and nothing comes out. I wait. Then, her hands come back down and she places them on each side of my face.

"Yes! I want that so much!"

She falls into my arms and I am pretty sure I am dreaming.

TWENTY-FOUR

Naomi

"Grandma Josephine, can you come here for a sec?" I've always been awful at wrapping gifts and I want Joseph's Christmas gift to be perfect.

"Girl, you betta want sumin important because you are interrupting my soap operas." She slides into my room realizing I indeed need something important. When I wrapped her gifts for her last week she immediately unwrapped them without an ounce of remorse.

"Oh! Sure," she laughs out loud, "We don't want this disaster under our nice Christmas tree, do we?"

She gently unwraps the sweater I bought for Joseph and then slowly rewraps it, guiding me through every fold.

Joseph should get in on Christmas Eve and I can hardly wait. My stomach is already doing summersaults, as if he is coming today. I stretch out my arm to look at the engagement ring he gave me weeks ago. The diamond sparkles as I turn my hand ever so slightly. We decided to have a small wedding in February. He wanted to do it sooner, but I argued we should wait until after I go live. After my mom and Grandma Josephine urged him to do the same, he gave in.

Grandma Josephine, Momma, and Dr. Ward are all know how stressful it is for the both of us to be apart. Mom is making all the arrangements and had a cool idea for us to have our wedding on the river where Joseph proposed. She calls almost every day asking questions about flowers, food, and decor. Joseph's mom hasn't called at all, but his dad assures us they have purchased their tickets and can't wait to see us. I'm a little scared of the version of Mrs. Peters I will have to face now that I am marrying her one and only son, but I understand. This is all happening so quickly.

Lately, I have been dreaming *a lot*, but I can't remember any of them. It's frustrating. A part of me knows my busy mind is the problem. All I can think about is the wedding, Mrs. Peters' silence, my living arrangements with Joseph after the wedding, college, Christmas, and last, but certainly not least, Damian Draegon. In that order. There's no wonder I can't remember my dreams. I have to get focused.

"Naomi, do you mind putting up some lights around the front door for me? Joseph usually does it, but our timing was off this year."

"Sure, I don't mind. This is something I am truly good at."

"Lord, I sure hope so," she jokes.

After putting up a few lights, I head to my room. I flop down on the bed and notice a notification on my phone . There's no use in keeping a phone with me when no one is going to call unexpectedly. Joseph and my mom always call Grandma Josephine when they can't get a hold of me, so I'm nervous looking down at the strange number. I dial it back. And a man answers the phone.

"Hello, did you call," I hesitant to say my name, "Naomi?"

I hear the man on the other side clear his voice.

"Ahem, Um. Yes. Yes, I did I."

Then, I recognize the voice.

"Dad?"

"Yeah. It's me."

There's a pause. I almost drop the phone, confused at how he has this number.

"How are you," he asks.

"I—I'm fine. How are you?"

"I'm just fine."

More silence. I don't know what to say which I is okay. He called me.

"Well, I just wanted to hear your voice and to tell you…"

I can't take it anymore. After all of this time, he finally makes contact with me and he doesn't know what to say to me.

"Dad! Just say it. Please."

Tears begin to burn the edges of my eyes.

"I love you. I always have. My cowardice has always been my downfall and I'm sorry for that. I'm sorry for a lot of things, Naomi."

I exhale into the receiver. "Dad, I have spent years waiting to tell you something and I am so glad that you called me. I forgive you."

Before his speaks again, from the other side I hear several sniffs and groans.

Finally, he says, "Thank you."

Our phone call pretty much ends after that. There's really nothing else I have to say and he seems to be broken from the sheer fact that I didn't reject him. We hang up without making any promises which I am happy about. I lay down on my back. Relieved to finally have told him and to have that gray cloud move on from the back of my mind. While I'm at it, I may as well clear up another storm. I call Emmy.

"Hello! Is this Naomi?"

"Hi, it's me."

"Hey!"

"Hey. How are you?" I ask, genuinely.

"I'm okay, but could be better."

Her voice sounds different. Flat. Lifeless.

"Oh."

I don't know what to say to that.

She speaks again saving me, "Naomi, I miss you. I miss you so much. I was stupid for what I did and I just wanted to say…,"

"You're sorry. I know, Emmy, and I forgive you."

"You do," she interrupts, "I know things will never be the same between us again, but I just want to be able to call you. You know—when I need someone to talk to. You've always been there for me."

"You're right. Things will never be the same. A lot has changed in our lives. All we can do is move on, so yes you can call me whenever you need. How does that sound?"

"That sounds great!"

"Good. How is everything in Augusta?"

"Fine. Most of the roads have been rebuilt and there a new businesses popping up all the time."

"Good."

I wait to see if she will say or ask anything. When she doesn't, I continue.

"How's it going between you and uh, what's his name?"

I hear take in a big breath. "I never thought you would ask me about him." There's a brief pause before she says, "It didn't really work out. It took a while for me to realize my mistake, but I am so glad I did. I deserve better."

"I agree. I one hundred percent agree."

A strong friendship is hard to break, but it does retain cracks and sometimes those cracks will remain visible even though the structure remains. I want Emmy to be happy and I am willing to swallow my pride and let her in, just a little bit. Sharing everything that is going on in my life (the engagement and my upcoming broadcast) was my first step. She seemed to be wholeheartedly excited and I felt it to be sincere. Before we hung up we agreed to check up on each other from time to time and then said our goodbyes.

Christmas Eve seemed like it would never come, but I am finally where I need to be in this timeline—with Joseph safe and sound. Grandma Josephine cooked a hearty pot roast with macaroni and cheese, cabbage, and sweet cornbread. Joseph and I convinced her to let us clean up and to our surprise she took us up on it.

"You dry. I will wash," Joseph says.

"Deal. Drying is easier."

"Well, I guess I know who will be washing the dishes in our house."

We both laugh at the realization we will be living together soon. Joseph starts the dish water and I look for Grandma Josephine's drying towel.

"It's in that drawer to your left," Grandma Josephine calls from the dining room, throwing a fresh new tablecloth over the table.

Then an unexpected knock comes to the door.

Joseph looks over at me then Grandma Josephine, "Are you expecting anyone?"

"No," she replies. Dr. Ward and Ms. Peterson won't be here until tomorrow.

Joseph walks over to the window, drawing back the curtain. Then, he goes to the door and opens it. Peeking around the door, I see there's no one there. He bends down to retrieve something from the porch. He comes back in with a large gold envelope handing it to me. My stomach sinks. Joseph steps back out on to the porch to look around the yard. After a few minutes, he comes back in.

"Who was it?" Grandma Josephine asks.

"No one, Grandma."

Grandma Josephine gets up from her chair and before she heads to her bedroom, she stops in the middle of the hallway.

She turns around to say, "You best reveal your dream as soon as possible, Naomi. Looks like that demon has found out where you are." Then she heads down the hallway into her room, shutting the door behind her.

The handwriting on the envelope reads, Merry Christmas, in the center. No return address, no name. Joseph opens the envelope and pulls out a magazine. It's an edition of *The Spark*. The headline reads, TIME is Running Out. The backdrop is a huge broken clock toppling over a bridge. Joseph flips through the pages looking for what we expect, a letter. We find it and it's addressed to me. Joseph hands me the letter and I read it out loud.

Naomi,

It's been a while. This time it was a little more difficult finding you, but like I told you before, I will always find you. Unfortunately, The Spark will be closing its doors in January. Because of the unrest in our economy we are incapable of providing our readers with the most riveting prophecies we have so graciously provided for them for many years. Our last publication will hit the stands mid-January and I am prepared to offer you a substantial payout for your cooperation. If not, well, I will just check on you whenever my business is up and running again.

I hope this letter finds you well, Miss Peterson. Give Joseph my best.

Damian Draegon`

Joseph and I both look at each other at the same time. I want to scream out loud, but shock won't allow me. Joseph pumps a triumphant fist into the air and wraps the other arm around me.

"What do you think about going on the air a little earlier?" he asks.

"Like how early?"

"Like as soon as possible?"

My stomach turns into knots. "Do you think that's possible?"

"Well, it won't hurt to try. We have had so many doors open for us, why not? I trust this door will open just as easily."

"True."

I think about what he just said.

"Sure. Why not."

Just as Joseph predicted, the door did open for me to go on the air sooner than January 29th. It turns out one of Nina's guest, a prophet who was going to prophecy what to expect with the upcoming year, got sick with the flu and was unable to make it. So, here I am, shaking from the inside out. Filled with the knowledge of what is in store for the entire world. The only thing that's keeping my nerves together is the assurance this must be done and the man standing next to me.

My eyes dart over at Joseph on the phone in another room. He told me he would let Agent Castro know my whereabouts as soon as I arrived at the station. I can't imagine she is happy with him because his expression and his voice booming through the door tell me otherwise. He hangs up abruptly then enters the waiting room I am sitting.

"Is everything okay," I ask, wiping my sweaty palms on my jeans.

"Yeah. She's just upset she wasn't informed sooner. Now she

is calling her superiors to have them tune in to listen." He adjusts his tie. "It's going to be okay, Babe," he kisses my hand, "This all ends today—right here, right now. No more running."

I take in a deep breath and let it out slowly. Nina opens the studio door, smiling.

"You ready, Naomi?

I look over at Joseph. "Can he come in with me?"

"Sure," she waves him up from his seat.

"Okay, listeners, today we have a very special guest, Naomi Peterson. You may remember back in April, a prophecy was released about three category four earthquakes that would strike three states in the US. Well, that prophecy was obtained illegally from Naomi's journal. You see, Naomi has been dreaming since she was a little girl. She discovered at a very young age that her dreams really do come true. She reached out to me a couple of months ago with great concern to share more about the dream that was leaked back in April. Up until, now Naomi has remained silent. Naomi, can you tell the audience why you never came forward before and why you are here today?"

"Hello, everyone. I just want to say thank you for tuning in today. And thank you Nina and Richard for giving me this opportunity."

I look over at Joseph and all of the nervous rumbling in my stomach subside.

"Last April was a tough time in my life. I was betrayed by a close friend who decided to still my journal and possibly sold my prophecy for money. Although this person's intentions may have been pure, his actions were not acceptable. I chose not to reveal my name because the dream wasn't his to share. The portion of the prophecy he stole was incomplete and that is why I to go on the air today. Almost a year ago, God gave me a dream about the end of the world. Since then, I have had several other dreams about what is to come. I don't want to share those dreams specifically, but I do want to warn you all just as the book of Revelation has for centuries.

Hard times are coming. It is time to get your house in order. No man knows the day or the hour, but that day is even closer than it was yesterday. Before my return their will be several events that will take place. The world's economy will suffer tremendously. We will face a detrimental depression that will wipe out a large portion of the world's population. Because of the famine, and the lack of natural resources, violence will plague every country. Suicide rates will rise to an overwhelming high. Children will go missing and the streets will be unsafe. This is not to scare you, but to warn you so that you can prepare. To me a thousand years is just one hour, so don't try to figure out when, just begin to get your house prepared. I do not want anyone to be lost. My heart aches for what is going to come to this earth, so I want to save as many of My people as I can.

Nina's voice transports me back to reality.

"So, Naomi, has God shared with you how we can prepare?"

"To start, if you don't know Jesus Christ as your Lord and Savior, ask Him into your heart today. Make Him the Lord of your life. If you don't these desperate times will be the hardest for you. Secondly, keep some cash on you or in a safe. It isn't safe to keep all of your money in banks or tied up in stocks. We saw what happened a few months ago with the bank crisis. Study the book of Revelation. Study the book of Mathew, chapter 24 specifically. Read Ezekiel and the book of Daniel. God gave us the map and the time table long ago and its time to start paying attention."

Richard's voice, breaks through short silence, "Naomi, I have been hearing that our monetary system will soon fall apart. Has God spoken to you about that at all?"

"The original means of exchange will be crucial in those days. Gold and silver to be clear."

"Gold and silver?" Richard repeats.

"Yes."

"That's good stuff, Naomi. Our regular listeners know exactly why I say that. You are not the first—or even the second guest who has said that God has spoken to them about acquiring gold and silver. The bible says, 'out of the mouths...'" Nina comes in and completes his statement with him, "of two to three witnesses, His words are established."

I feel the need to say something else, so I go for it. "And please remember, God loves you. He does not want us to be afraid, but to be prepared."

Richard continues, "Amen! No fear. Well, you guys, Naomi's time is up but we will be reposting this prophecy on our website and every social media site we can get this information to you. Thank you, Naomi for being so brave to share something so important."

"It is my honor, Richard. And everyone please remember, With Him there is nothing to fear. With Him, all things are possible. God bless you all."

TWENTY-FIVE

Naomi

Ironically, I find myself running down this long corridor in my wedding gown. Enveloped in gold and ivory, my heels click as I run full speed to the man waiting for me with open arms. I finally reach him and he sweeps me off my feet with his strong arms and it's as if my world begins to spin. Everyone is invisible to me, until our first dance when the music begins to play. I lean back to take in the splendor that is called Joseph. He grins down at me.

"Hello Mrs. Peters."

SEVEN YEARS LATER

I toss and turn until I am jolted from my sleep. The sun shines brightly through the sheer drapes. Throwing my arm over to the other side of the bed, I come up short. The space Joseph occupies is empty. I groan when I realize he is not there. Laughs and small voices fill my ears. Joseph has beat me awake again. Joseph Jr. laughs hysterically from the living room and Josie declares, "I gonna get you, Joe!" I laugh to myself willing my feet to touch the ground, but I settle on just reaching over to my night stand to retrieve my journal.

Two years ago I had a few hundred pages added to this old thing. I run my figures over the ruby red cover that has gained some creases over the years. I just can't bring myself to get a new one. This one has definitely stood the test of time.

Trying to remember the dream that jolted me awake, I close my eyes to pray. Then the lights are clicked on. From my bed, I see Josie's pigtails flash across my footboard. The weight of her little body flops down on to my legs. She climbs up to my face and gives me a juicy kiss on my cheek.

"Hey, Mommy!"

"Good Morning, my sweet baby girl."

Just then Joseph walks in with Joe under his arm trying to wrestle his way out of his dad's grip. Joseph gets a glimpse of me and looks down at what I hold in my hands.

He walks over and kisses me on the forehead, "Come on, guys. Let's give Mommy a few more minutes."

"Okay!" They both yell and run out of the room giggling and attacking their dad.

As soon as I put pen to paper the dream comes back to me. People are yelling, "You're not a prophet. You are a FRAUD! A FRAUD!" And just as the first stone hits my head, I wake up.

Joseph comes back into the room as I rub my temple where the rock hit me.

"Joseph, Am I a fraud?"

"What? What are you talking about?"

"Well, when I think about the prophecy God gave me to share so many years ago, I realize none of it has come true up to this point.

Joseph comes and sits down on the edge of the bed to face me.

"No. Honey. You are not a fraud. Noah told the people

about the flood for many, many, years before it actually started to rain. They thought he was a fraud, so they didn't prepare."

"You're right."

I think for a moment. *The flood!*

"Do you remember the dream I had about a flood?"

I flip back in my journal to the dream, titled *The Flood*. I reread the dream about Joseph and I in an empty house with two children. At the very bottom of the dream I wrote, *There's so much more to be done*. I read it out loud.

Joseph looks at me. "Honey, there are prophesies in the Bible that have yet to happen. Just be grateful God chose you to share His words and He will take care of the rest."

"Yes. You're right. There's still so much to be done and so many people that haven't heard the gospel."

"Right," Joseph says. "There's so much to be done.

My heart is calmed. I record last night's dream and Joseph and I say a prayer together.

Father, guide us. Show us what you would like us to accomplish today. Like you said, there is so much more to be done, before you come, so show us what to do and we will do it. Your will be done. Amen.

When I walk into the kitchen where my family is waiting, so much joy fills the air it's hard not to smile. When Joseph Junior sees me, he jumps into my arms, wrapping his tiny limbs around me, giving me the sweetest, tightest hug.

Then he leans back to look at me with those big brown eyes.

He says, "Mommy, I had a dream."

ACKNOWLEDGEMENTS

First, I want to thank my Daddy, my Father, my God for helping me through this once again. I can't do anything without You and I am so glad to know You.

There's only a few who know just how much I went through to get a newly edited version of this story into the world: My husband, my two children, and a handful of family and friends. A huge thank you to my husband, John, for being patient with me through it all. Thank you also to my children, John and Johanna, for your encouragement and understanding. You both just don't know how much I appreciate you. I love you all so very much.

And finally a big thank you to Hampton at T95studios for making an eight year dream, of having a better cover for this book, a reality. You are amazing at what you do. Thank you.

9 798218 242206